PHOENIX OF THE SEA

MADALYN·RAE

ALSO BY MADALYN RAE

Birth of the Phoenix-Adria's Origin Story

Phoenix of the Sea-Elementals Book 1

Guardian of the Sea-Murphy's Origin Story

Spring 2023

Ashes of the Wind-Elementals Book 2

Summer 2023

Embers of the Flame-Keegan's Origin Story

Fall 2023

Fire of the Sky-Elementals Book 3

Winter 2023

For Mom,

* * *

My ride or die reader, who devours all my stories and thinks everything I write is good... even when it's not.

Books are a uniquely portable magic.

Stephen King

CONTENTS

CHAPTER 1

The smell of rot and death hits me as soon as the door opens. It's a smell I'll never get used to. No matter the amount of training I've done in this building, or the number of recruits I've followed inside, it's the smell that hits the hardest.

"What are we supposed to do?" my newest recruit asks as the door closes behind us.

I don't remember his name. Bill, Will... it doesn't matter. Even if he survives training, he won't make it another six months. They rarely do. He'll be another casualty of whatever the hell it is we're fighting.

My entire body runs into his back. I shove him forward. "Never stop. Keep moving no matter what you hear or see." My tone is monotone and flat. He continues moving through the dark hall.

"Why do I have to lead?" His voice sounds shaky. "Shouldn't you be in front?"

"I won't always be there to lead you. You have to do

this on your own. This is one of the final steps to complete your training. You've got to get us out of here, alive." I follow him through the wide hallway.

"What's in here?" He keeps moving, but his voice is low and quivers more than before.

"You'll find out." I keep watch behind us. Bill or Will, keeps his weapon facing forward. I fight the urge to roll my eyes at his lack of common sense. "Danger doesn't always come from the front," I hiss, turning my back toward his, and guarding the rear as we creep through the darkness.

"We're just about there," I whisper, a weak attempt to reassure him.

"Where?" His question is so soft, I have to strain to hear.

"Just don't stop. If you stop, she can get you." He keeps moving until a loud scream explodes through the darkness. I push hard into his back, forcing him forward. "I said, don't ever stop!" We enter the large room where she spends most of her time.

A scream pierces the stillness once again. "What the *hell* is that?"

"*She's* a lesser fire elemental." The energy emanating from him is toxic. His fear will be his downfall. "You can't let her know you're scared. The only way to survive is by not showing fear." He continues moving.

"A lesser? Aren't they the mean ones?"

"They're all pretty mean in my books, but the lessers do the dirty work so they have the worst reputation. Shine your light to the bottom right of the room." She'll be in her favorite spot.

"Shit," he whispers.

"Pretty, isn't she?" I fight to keep the smile from sounding through my words. "Listen carefully. It's about to go down. She's going to try everything she can to touch you. No matter what, you can't let that happen."

"What the hell?"

"Just keep moving. Maybe we'll be lucky, and she'll be in a good mood." I shine my light around the expanse of the room that was built to mimic a sixteenth-century castle. I don't know what it was used for before, but the intricacy in the surprisingly clean woodwork tells me it was meant to be more than a prison for a fire elemental.

The twenty-foot ceiling is the only thing not covered in soot. Windows nearly touch the ceiling and line each side of the room, reminding me of a once magical ball-room. Now it's something from a nightmare. The boarded windows are protected from the outside and covered with ice and constantly flowing water to prevent her escape. What were once curtains, are nothing more than hanging shreds of fibers, evidence of being repeatedly burned through the years. Ornate furniture rests in piles of ashes, placed sporadically throughout the room. The only intact item, an old piano, sits in the back, right corner, the place I knew she'd be. It's where she always is.

Bill, Will... whoever's breathing is shallow and uneven. He's about to lose his shit. "Listen to the sound of my voice," I whisper. "Just because she can hurt you, doesn't mean she will. I've been through this building more times than I can count." My light catches on what looks like charred skin hanging from a chandelier and I fight the urge to cringe.

"Why?"

"It's how I train you to go out and save the world from elementals like her." I pull my light away from the skin.

"No, why has she allowed you to live?" His breathing has evened out slightly.

I don't answer. Instead, I push his back even harder to get us through the room. Truth is, I don't know why she's allowed me to live while others die. I've wondered the same myself. This room is full of decomposing recruits and trainers who weren't as lucky. I've only lost one person to her, a year ago. I block the memory from surfacing. Instead, I focus on getting the latest one to safety. "Keep moving."

My light reflects on something shiny. I fight the sadness at its recognition. My hand slides to an identical object affixed to my uniform. A small dolphin pin reflects my light. Without question, I know it belonged to Hannah. The overwhelming urge to leave my recruit to fend for himself and retrieve it is difficult to fight.

Long brown hair appears in my light beam separating me from the dolphin. The elemental's angelic face is covered in dried blood and the white gown she wears has turned brown with stain. "Adria, how good to see you again."

"Don't come near us," I warn.

The smile on her beautiful face is replaced with a vicious snarl. "I wouldn't dare risk coming near *you* dear. It's him I want."

My recruit stops moving. "Dammit, keep walking!

Get to the other side of the room. She's fast, don't let her get in front of you."

A dark, raspy laugh echoes my words as she disappears from the light. "Go!" I yell, turning toward the exit, we run at full speed toward where I know the door will be waiting.

"I'm in need of sustenance." An evil laugh follows her words.

"Like hell you are." Thankfully, the recruit stays by my side as we sprint through the building. I'm not sure if the elemental is chasing or toying with us, but I'm not taking any chances.

"There." I point toward a small crack in the wall. "That's the door. Slide your card and get out now!" I turn, ready to protect my recruit. The door behind me cracks, flooding the large room with light. He follows orders leaving me inside, alone.

"Ah, that's what I want!" The elemental screams as she moves toward the door. "Freedom."

Not two feet in front of me stands the beautiful woman from before. "Please, Adria, let me out." Her voice is calm, oozing with sticky sweetness.

"Why would I release something like you back into the world?" I refuse to move.

"Release me into the world?" Her words mock my tone. "Girl, my kind has been here since the *beginning* of the world. Since *before* the beginning of the world. You can't hold me here forever. Time is nothing to me. I will escape, and when I do, I will take my revenge for this hell you've imprisoned me in."

"Doesn't look that way from where I'm standing." I

slowly back my way to the door that's now slammed shut. The door is protected the same way as the windows. She can't get out without assistance.

An evil grin replaces the beautiful face. "On second thought, I don't care whose blood you carry, I will kill you." The elemental flies toward me in a rage of flames.

If she touches me, I'll instantly be a pile of ash or worse, dinner. A rumble low in my stomach forces its way through my body and skin, forming a visible bubble of water that surrounds me. I'm dry, but water completely encases me. The elemental responds instantly and flies away in a burst of fire, screaming.

My breath is rough and fast as I try to figure out what just happened. The door behind me flies open, flooding the room with light as Bill or Will wraps his arm around my waist and pulls me out of the building to safety.

CHAPTER 2

"*H*eard your recruit saved your life." Hadley sits on the empty chair across from mine. His mousy brown hair is short in the front and long in the back, making his looks and personality match.

I ignore his attempt to get a rise from me and continue eating my sandwich. Hadley's a trainer like me, but unlike me, he's only been here a few months. He continues to ramble on, and I continue to ignore him. It takes several minutes of being ignored before he gets up to leave. "Bitch," he mumbles under his breath.

I wait for him to throw his food away and leave the café before following suit. Instead of taking the elevator, I choose to take the stairs all the way to the twelfth floor. I don't want to ride or talk with anyone. Making friends only leads to heartache and death. I just want to be alone.

My room is small, but it's home. The cinder block walls are far from comforting, but after painting them my favorite shade of blue, they've lost the hospital vibe. A full-size bed sits on the far wall and beside it a small dresser that holds all three of my outfits. A mirror is propped behind the door and a small chair sits in front of it. Everything in this room, with the exception of my clothes, belonged to other women. There used to be six of us on this floor. Now it's just me.

A loud sigh leaves my lips as I unhook the heavy vest all trainers and recruits wear. It's supposed to protect us, but truthfully an elemental can't be stopped by anything. In a true fight, it wouldn't be of any use. It's more of a thirty-pound security blanket.

I stare in the mirror as I release the butterfly clip that's been holding my hair in place. Long blonde curls flow to my waist and tired blue eyes stare back at me. Even though no blood was shed today, my uniform is filthy. I strip down to my underwear and bra, grab a towel and essentials, and head to the shared bathroom. Being the only surviving girl means it's all mine.

The water feels amazing. I envision it clearing me of negativity from the day. No fire elementals, no Hadleys, and no charred flesh.

As a child, I would take any opportunity I could to get in the water. Lakes, ponds, pools, bathtubs, it didn't matter. I wasn't picky. What I wouldn't give to jump in a pool right now.

Loud banging on my door startles me to reality. "What?"

"Chief needs to see you." I recognize Hadley's voice and don't answer. Several minutes pass, "Adria, did you hear me?"

"I'll be there in a minute." Turning the water off feels

like leaving home.

"Need any help in there?" His words are laced with innuendo and make me nauseous at the thought.

"Not from you."

Like before, "bitch," mumbles from his lips.

"Yea, that's the way to win me over," I yell as the door to the staircase slams shut. Back in my room, I slide on a pair of gray sweatpants and a baggy t-shirt, one of my three outfits. I'd take Hannah's clothes, but they're all too small. Being six feet tall makes it hard to share clothes with regular-sized women.

Running a brush through my tangled hair feels almost as good as the shower. A few quick twists and it's back in its usual place, on top of my head. Truth be told, I'm taking more time than I should. The chief wanting to see me will have everything to do with my recruit pulling me from the building today and me not being the one in charge. It's a weakness, and I'm not in the mood to get yelled at.

I slip on the one item of Hannah's I'm able to wear without looking like a clown. A hooded sweatshirt with an alien in a spaceship. Unprofessional? Yes. Do I care? No.

The training compound was built on top of an old fort and sits in a square, with a large, grassy area in the middle. The dorm building sits opposite the offices, with classrooms on one side and the building housing the fire elemental on the other. The ocean's not far below the seawall and the breeze lifts the smells straight to the compound, relaxing the tension I didn't realize I was carrying.

I take my time walking through the square. White marble statues line the walkway, each symbolizing a conquering hero who was lost in the endless war against elementals. It's a war that's gone on for centuries with no foreseeable end. The fire elemental was right. They were here before there was a *here*.

My hands rub along the base of each statue. I know them from memory, having read their descriptions countless times. "Hello Atticus," I whisper, passing the largest of them all. His epitaph is the longest. Fighting in this war and living past the age of forty is unheard of. Atticus lived to be sixty-four. He fought and stayed alive longer than anyone has before or since.

I touch the last statue before the administrative offices. The face of the only female stops me in my tracks. For years, I've revered this woman. Margaret Fitzgerald was her name. She didn't live as long as Atticus but fought just as valiantly. "Wish me luck, Marge. I have a feeling I'm going to need it."

A statue of two large phoenixes greets me as I climb the concrete stairs into the building. The full glass front doors seem to spy on me as I take my time. Taking a deep breath, I move through one of them and sit in the empty waiting room. "Hello, Adria. Do you have an appointment?" the older, white-haired woman asks, flipping through a notebook.

"Hello, Ms. Betty. No, I don't. I was told the chief wanted to see me." I hide my hands in the front pocket of the hoodie.

Betty's eyebrows raise in response. "Let me go ask and I'll be right back."

I do as instructed, picking up an old magazine to flip through. It's full of pictures of the four types of elementals and the horrors they've inflicted on the world. I flip through the pages of information on earth, air, fire, and water elementals, trying not to laugh at the ignorance contained within.

"Adria, Director Scott can see you now." She smiles weakly in my direction.

I return the smile and move toward the office I know very well. "Come in, Adria," his voice rings out before I have the chance to knock.

The knob turns slowly, and I take a deep breath preparing for what's to come. "You wanted to see me..." My words are cut short. Director Scott is standing at his desk, motioning toward a man I've never seen before.

"This is Adria Kane, the one I told you about." The man stands and at full height is nearly a head taller than me.

"It's a pleasure to meet you, Adria. Director Scott has told me much about you. I'm Murphy McKenzie, and it looks like we might be working together for a while." The man reaches a hand toward me to shake.

What the ever-living hell? I ignore his hand and turn toward the chief. "What's he talking about?"

"Adria, Murphy is a Phoenix from the UK division. He's here to learn how we train our recruits in America and why we're able to have such a high survival rate." His eyes grow large with his words. If their survival rate is lower than ours, it must be close to zero. "You're going to work with him, train him the way you would train any recruit, teach him our ways."

"Bill's my recruit. I don't need another life to worry about." My words sound harsher than intended.

"*Phil* will be finishing his training with Hadley. He requested the change earlier this evening." Phil? At least I was close.

The chief sits at his desk. I know from experience, there's no room for discussion. I sigh deeply and glare at the tall man standing in front of me. His hand still hangs in mid-air, waiting for me to shake it. I cross my arms in front of my chest.

Murphy clears his throat and lowers his hand. "Well then, when shall we start?" He looks between the chief and me, no doubt able to read the tension in the room.

Director Scott clears his throat loudly. "Tomorrow morning will be good. Eight o'clock sound good to you, Adria?"

I force a smile. "Yes, eight o'clock will be fine." I turn to the chief. "Am I free to go?"

"Yes." I turn toward the door feeling the heat of his stare on my back. "I do hope you'll show our guest the best of our training while he's here." Literal translation, *behave*.

I fight the urge to do a one-finger salute. Instead mumbling, "Yes sir," as I exit, leaving the two men alone in the room.

Just what I need, another liability. Training a recruit is different. They're clueless, easy to mold, and wet behind the ears. Training someone who looks the same age as me and should already be trained is a different story. Why the hell did the chief choose me?

"Adria!" a voice calls as I approach Atticus on the

walk. I turn to see Murphy jogging toward me. Dammit, I don't want to stop, but that would be extremely rude, even for me. I fight the urge to run and wait for him to catch up.

"I'm sorry this was thrown on you. Director Scott assured me you were the one I needed to work with. I can tell you don't exactly agree." His red curls glisten in the setting sun.

I wait before answering. "It's not that I don't want to work with you, it's that I don't know what I can help you learn. If your survival rate is lower than ours, that's not saying much." Murphy looks down at my words. "Out of the last ten recruits I've trained and graduated, only five are still alive."

"I know how that feels. It's not easy losing someone you work so hard to teach. I've had it happen to me more times than I care to say. I'm not here to be a burden on you. I'm here to work with you. Learn your ways, learn your skills." He pauses, taking a deep breath. "At least you've had five live. That's five more than me." He swallows slowly with his last words.

His eyes mirror mine in their color and intensity. His large frame dwarfs mine, making me feel small, something I'm not used to.

I look down in defeat. "Meet me here at six."

He smiles, melting some of the frustration away. "What happened to eight?"

"You're already getting on my nerves." I run back toward the dorm.

CHAPTER 3

 *W*alking out of the dorm, a large shadow is sitting at the bottom of the stairs. He's early, that's a plus. I sneak behind him. Pulling the short knife from my training belt, I have it pointed at the back of his neck, and against his spinal cord before he knows I'm there.

"Good morning to you too," he says, not moving his head. "At least I'm hoping this is going to be a good morning."

I sheath the knife before moving in front of him. "Lesson number one, never turn your back without something solid behind you. Always put your back against a wall, a stone or brick wall is the best. Elementals can't get through anything that's been altered." I reach toward him, extending a hand to help him up.

"Believe it or not, I know that." He takes my hand and stands at least six and a half feet tall. I'm not used to being shorter than anyone. Most of our male recruits are the same height or shorter than me. I have to look up to make eye contact with him, which unnerves me slightly. "I let my guard down. You're right. I should never do that, no matter the environment." He follows as we walk into the center of the square.

"So, Murphy?" He nods. "What exactly do you want to work on?" I'm not sure how to start this quest.

"I guess, just train me like you would any recruit. From the beginning." He smiles, helping me relax slightly.

"What kind of accent is that?" I prop both hands on my hips.

"That's a complicated answer," he laughs. "I'm from a small island off the coast of Ireland and Scotland, so I guess it's a mixture of the two, with a little British thrown in."

The fact that he drops letters off the end of words seems strange to my American ear, causing me to concentrate on his words more than usual. I shrug, not caring. "Ok, let's go." I start running past the statues. It takes him a few minutes to catch up.

"Running? I was hoping your days started with a nice hot breakfast, followed by a swim in the ocean."

"I think I've identified the reason your recruits aren't surviving very long," I smirk. "Twenty trips around the square is five miles. Think you can do that before your hot breakfast and swim?"

"Let's do this." He jogs at my side. We run in silence most of the way. "You do this every day?" he asks, as we pass Atticus for the fourteenth time.

"Nah, some days I do ten miles before breakfast. I figured I'd break you in slowly."

"I guess I owe you a thank you then."

Recruits and trainers have to stay in shape, weakness equals death. Even the best of them get winded running this far. Murphy's not even breaking a sweat. The only other person I know who can run this much without getting winded or sweaty is me. We pass Atticus for the twentieth time, neither of us working hard.

"According to my count, this is lap twenty." We continue to jog until reaching the stairs to the dorm. The sun is rising, and I pause to watch it peek over the horizon and radiate on the water from the ocean. "Beautiful isn't it?" he asks, following my gaze.

"It is. This is my favorite time of day. Most of the compound's eating breakfast or still asleep, hence no one's gotten on my nerves yet." Chills flood me, causing me to rub my arms as the sun comes fully into view.

Murphy moves up the stairs, holding the door open for me. "I'll take that as a compliment. Is it time for breakfast?" he says with a smile.

"Don't get cocky. The morning's still young." I duck under his arm and lead him to the café.

Like a scene from a movie, the room becomes no louder than a whisper as the two of us enter. Do they know something I don't? I look at the familiar faces with question, not finding answers.

I thought I ate a lot. Murphy's plate is full of every breakfast protein available along with toast, a bagel, and a doughnut for dessert.

We sit in a corner, away from the whispers. I can't help but stare at the amount of food on his plate. "What? I'm hungry and I'm a big boy."

I hold back a smile. "If you eat all of that, you're going to throw up during our morning session. That run was just a warm-up."

He shoves a piece of bacon in his mouth. "I'm willing to risk it." He chases the bacon with an entire glass of apple juice.

Even though his plate has more food than mine, he finishes first. I stare across the table at the man I'm supposed to train. His bright red hair is full of tight curls. Intense blue eyes sit above a scattering of freckles. In an Opie Griffith kind of way, he's hot. His jawline is strong, topped with sharp cheekbones. He somehow looks like a kid and a supermodel at the same time.

"Why are you staring at me, lass?"

"Lass? Who the hell says, lass?" I mock.

He sits back in his chair, rubbing his stomach. "I forgot Americans don't use our slang. Would you prefer, chick?"

I fight a laugh that will only bring more whispers and stares from our growing audience. "If those are my two choices, lass it is."

"Why are they all looking at us?" He glances around the room.

"I don't know. Maybe they're trying to figure out who you are."

He stands up, pushing his chair over with his quick movement. "Hello, lads. I'm Murphy McKenzie and I've come from the UK to work with Adria. I couldn't help but notice all of you staring and talking, so I thought I'd answer any questions you might have. I'm a Phoenix and fight along with you, just on a different continent. I'm here to learn from your successes." The crowd is silent, and he awkwardly keeps standing. "Okay, carry on with your breakfast." He motions with his hand and sits back in his chair.

You could have heard crickets chirping if there were any in the room. I fight the urge to bury my head in secondhand embarrassment. "I think that helped."

"You think?" I laugh. "I think it's time for more training."

"Yeah, looks like you're right. This is a tough crowd." He follows me to the trash cans and through the door.

We complete a circuit of exercises throughout the morning. Murphy doesn't throw up or even look tired. I, on the other hand, begin sweating like a stuffed hog as the sun rises high in the sky. Our conversation is light and simple, and to my surprise, I find myself letting my guard down periodically. I learned after Hannah not to let people in, and not to get close to anyone. I slide my barriers quickly back in place.

"You're sweating a bit there, lass," he smirks. "Why don't we take a break?"

"I don't usually eat lunch." I continue practicing defensive moves with one of the ballistic dummies.

"This is going to be a shock, but me neither. I was talking about taking a real break." He points to the ocean, visible below the wall of the fort. "I could use a swim and from the looks of it, so could you."

"Asshole."

"I'm not being an arse. I'm serious. That water's been calling my name all morning. It's torture to know it's so close while we're sweating up here. What do you say?"

I look in the direction he's nudging with his head. He has a point. "What happened to learning how to keep recruits alive?"

"Surely a short swim won't keep me from learning anything valuable." His boyish grin wins me over and I agree.

We approach the seawall, slowly descending the narrow stairs to the beach. "These stairs weren't meant for boots this big." He stumbles his way to the sand.

The smell of salt instantly calms the tension I constantly carry with me. Boots aren't made for walking through sand either. I stumble over myself a few times trying to get to the water. "You're right. This is just what I needed." I remove my uniform one piece at a time. I don't have a suit to swim in, but don't care. Murphy's down to his boxers while I'm still untying my second boot. The man standing in front of me is the epitome of the perfect male specimen. His muscles are covered in muscles. His long, lean abdomen, which shows no signs of eating enough breakfast to feed half the compound, is the host of at least an eight-pack of muscles. His arms are the size of small tree trunks.

I strip down to my bra and panties, thankful I chose a matching set this morning with no holes. I don't make eye contact but feel him staring my way. Instead, I listen to the silent call resonating through my bones and walk toward the water. The instant my feet touch the wet sand, a sense of relief flows through me, and my eyes close in response. A deep sigh next to me draws me from my bliss.

"If this isn't heaven, I don't know what is." Murphy's standing next to me enjoying the water as much as I am. "I couldn't be this close to the water all day and get anything done."

The two of us walk until the water is chest high. "Didn't you tell me you lived on an island? I wasn't the smartest kid in school, but I learned enough to know islands are usually surrounded by water." My words are laced with sarcasm.

Murphy wades out deeper. "Aye, it is. But it's not exactly swimmable." He dives below, completely disappearing from the surface. I relax, bringing my feet up and floating on my back. The mixture of sun, water, and sand is just what I needed.

Five minutes pass before I realize Murphy hasn't surfaced. No one can hold their breath that long. Shit, he's only been my recruit for half a day, and I let him drown?

I dive under looking for the large man. As big as he is he'll be hard to miss. The water is crystal clear, allowing me to see at least twenty feet around me. Murphy's nowhere. What the hell? I've always been able to hold my breath longer than anyone, but if he's still under here, he's out of air. I push deeper into the water looking for any signs of movement or worse, non-movement. Still nothing.

A deeper fear strikes me. Did a water elemental get him? One hasn't been spotted here for years, but it's still a possibility. I go into defense mode. No weapons, no protection, I'm a floating bobber of meat for anything that might be hungry.

I break the surface and begin swimming toward the beach. If an elemental is responsible, I have to get to my weapons. Halfway there, something the size of a whale swims under me, moving twice as fast as I am. In my search for Murphy, I let myself get too far out. The beach is further than I realized as I push harder for the safety of the sand.

The large creature swims past me again, sweeping underneath and around. It's toying with me, playing with its food. No doubt, it already ate Murphy, and now it wants me. My toes bump into something solid... sand. I push myself to run while swimming to move faster. In an instant, a large wave pushes ahead of me and raises out of the water, blocking me from the safety of the beach. The lesser elemental stands at least ten feet high.

Although it's made of water, a head, arms, and torso are visible. We face each other. Where its mouth should be opens, revealing razor-sharp teeth intertwined with seaweed. I've never felt so helpless in my life. Any means of protection I have are on the beach and I'm a sitting duck. I refuse to die without a fight.

"Adria Kane," the elemental whispers.

"How... how do you know my name?"

The wicked teeth form into what looks to be a smile. The large wave bows, bending where a waist would be. "My queen," he says, spewing water as he speaks.

A knife points through the elemental, coming close to my chest. I watch as his face contorts into a strange shape and he disappears into the water. Where the wave once was, Murphy stands, holding a knife.

"Are you okay?" He checks me over from head to toe.

"Yes, I think so." I brush my hands down my front checking for knife holes. "I've been swimming in this ocean for years. There's never been a water elemental before. Why did one suddenly appear now?" Ironically, Murphy shows up and boom, a water elemental pops out of nowhere. I stare at the soldier standing in front of me.

Seemingly reading my mind, he puts both hands in front of him. "I can assure you, I had nothing to do with this." He throws the knife he's holding toward the sand and away from me.

I run past him and toward my gear. "How am I supposed to trust that?"

"Activity is picking up around the world. If this is the first lesser you've seen, you're truly lucky. They're taking over other compounds."

"What other compounds?"

"One in Asia, one in Australia and Canada." He lowers his hands.

"Canada?"

"Aye. I'm not here to harm you, I'm here to learn from you." His energy seems sincere, and I release the tension I was holding with a deep sigh. "Are you sure you're okay?" He repeats, pulling a large piece of seaweed off his shoulder.

I nod with my answer. "Yes, I'm fine. He didn't hurt me. He didn't even try to hurt me." I remember the words he used. "He called me..." I stop myself.

"He spoke to you?" He wrinkles his forehead.

I wave dismissively. "I heard what sounded like garbled words, but no doubt that was my imagination."

"What did he say?"

"It was just a big wave of sound, nothing specific." Sharing that the lesser called me his queen with a man I barely know isn't the smartest idea. "What happened to you? I thought you were dead." I change the subject quickly as both of us walk to our clothes, brushing loose sand from the garments.

He doesn't push for answers and slowly slides on pants identical to mine. "I was swimming."

"That wasn't any swimming I've seen before. You were underwater longer than possible. I came to look for you." I slide my undershirt over my head.

"Guess I hold my breath longer than most." I stare at him questioningly as he shrugs and finishes putting his uniform on and we trudge our way back up the hillside acting as if nothing happened.

The rest of the afternoon is spent with repeated tactical moves. Neither of us speaks about the water elemental again. In fact, we barely speak at all. I choose to take my dinner to my room and leave him to fight the stares and whispers alone.

Sitting on my bed, eating the meager sandwich I dragged up here with me, I recall the details of the swim and the elemental. How did Murphy get back on the beach and to a weapon without me seeing? Questions and confusion flood my brain until sleep takes over, taking me to a world of escape and dreams.

CHAPTER 4

*M*orning comes earlier than I want. I realize I never told Murphy what time to meet for training as I stomp down the heavy metal stairs. Pushing the large wooden door open, I find him sitting in the same place as yesterday. Did he not learn from the knife point in his spinal cord? I sit next to him. "I see lesson one made a huge impact on you."

"Oh, it did. I just thought I'd disappoint you this morning by not following the rules." His shoulder nudges mine as he speaks. The touch jolts a part of me that's been hidden deep inside since I was a child. A shudder starts deep in my stomach, forcing its way past my barriers and into my mind. I shake off the emotions I'm not prepared to face, stand, and pat him on the shoulder.

"Congratulations, you succeeded. I'm disappointed." Moving to the bottom of the steps, I add, "Ready to run?"

He joins me on the step. "Yes ma'am. Five miles again?"

"I was thinking more like ten." I pull my arm in front of me, stretching the shoulder blade as far as possible.

"You really are disappointed, aren't you?" His words accompany a smirk and it's sexy as hell. I take off running to keep from thinking.

We jog in silence for the first eight miles. Like yesterday, he isn't the least bit winded. "You run often?" I ask the silent giant beside me.

"Not unless someone's chasing me."

I laugh loudly. "In my case, that's often." We continue moving around the square. "For not running very often, you're in good shape."

"Well, thank you, Adria. I believe that's the first nice thing you've said to me." His words make me smile.

"In that case, I'll be taking those words back. Can't risk being nice to anyone." Murphy smirks beside me. We continue running in silence until we've passed Atticus the proper amount of times.

"Oh, thank gods. Is it time for breakfast? I'm starving." He holds the door to the café, waiting for me to enter. My stomach rumbles loudly as I pass. "From the sound of it, so are you."

Like yesterday, every eye in the room turns to stare. "What the hell do they find so fascinating about the two of us?" I sneer at the men in the room. "What?" Most turn their heads as they continue eating in silence.

"In case you haven't noticed, we're two fine-looking specimens. Not to mention, we're taller than everyone in this room. Come to think of it, we probably look like tall, lanky freaks to them." He has a point.

His plate is as full as yesterday. "I don't know how you

can eat that much and not get sick with all the physical activity." I nod toward his plate.

"I was a small kid, didn't eat much. Guess I'm making up for that now." He shoves an entire boiled egg in his mouth.

"I can't imagine you ever being small." As soon as the words leave my mouth, I instantly regret them.

He slowly puts his fork down and flashes a wicked smile. "That's what she said."

I roll my eyes, making sure he sees the motion. "I see a little bit of American culture has seeped its way into your brain." I take a bite out of what's supposed to be scrambled eggs. "How long have you been a Phoenix?"

"Four years. You?"

"Three."

"So that makes you twenty-four?" He continues shoving food into his mouth at a rapid pace.

"Close, twenty-three for a few more months," I answer, chewing gently.

"Damn, you were recruited young."

"I was. That's a story for another day. You?" I'm not prepared to share that part of my life with him.

"Turned twenty-four last May." We sit in awkward silence for a few minutes. "You don't talk much do you?"

He's right, I don't talk much. Most of my time is spent alone or in training. The art of conversation is something I haven't had experience with for a while.

"Look, I get it. In our line of work, if you get too close, you get hurt. I was like you for a long time. Kept to myself, kept everyone at arm's length, until one day I realized I was a miserable arse and making everyone around me miserable arses." Most of the food is gone from his plate. I watch as he uses a biscuit to slop up what remains.

"I see nothing's changed?" I smirk. "I mean, I knew you were an ass the first minute we met, but what gave you this great revelation?"

"Well *lass*," he emphasizes the last part of the word, "the answer is simple. I was lonely." His words hit hard. I'm lonely and have been for a while. Hell, I've been lonely my entire life.

I pick at my remaining food. "I'm not an ass," I answer softly.

Murphy laughs a full, hearty laugh. "Not on the inside, but the side you show everyone around you is an arse. It's a pretty arse, but an arse nonetheless."

I stand, slamming my chair back to its home. "Outside, ten minutes." I don't turn back as I head toward the trash can and my escape.

Thankfully, he doesn't follow me and I make my way to an overlook off the square. The ocean breeze blows my escaped curls, causing them to swirl around my face in a choreographed dance. Staring into the rolling waves in front of me, the memory of the water elemental from yesterday overtakes my anger. Why didn't he try to hurt me, and did I imagine he called me his queen? Questions play through my mind as the surface of the water stills. "Adria, my queen." A whisper floats off of the sea.

I'm quickly jarred back to reality. What the hell? I listen again, straining to hear more words.

"Don't jump. It's not worth it." Murphy startles me.

"You're not worth me jumping," I retort.

He climbs on the wall beside me. "Ouch, that one hurt." He places his hand over his heart, taking a deep breath. "Can we spend the afternoon sitting here and staring? Looking at the vastness of the ocean calms my soul."

I huff a laugh. That's something we have in common. "Me too." Truthfully, there's something about being near Murphy that calms me, but that's information for me alone.

"I'm sorry if I hurt your feelings earlier. You're right, I can be an arse." He nudges my leg with his. Again, the familiarity that comes with the touch catches me off guard. We sit in silence for a while.

"You didn't hurt my feelings. Well, maybe a little, but you're right. I can be a little *extra* at times." He doesn't interrupt, just gives me time to breathe. "The side I show to everyone isn't nice, she isn't lovable and most of all she isn't weak." Emotions well up inside, I fight to keep them at bay and close my eyes. Why the hell did I just tell this man I barely know my deepest secret?

"I'm sorry I pushed you." Kindness sounds through his voice.

I take a deep breath. "Her name was Hannah. She was my friend, my last friend."

"I'm truly sorry."

I take a deep breath before continuing. "Me too." My hand rubs the matching dolphin pins we wore. Mine attached to my vest, hers on the floor of the training building. "She was killed by the fire elemental." I nod toward the building used for training. He follows my gaze.

"Maybe I need to go meet that bitch."

"That doesn't happen until the end of your training. Considering you're my recruit, I'll let you know when it's time."

"Yes ma'am. Probably for the best. I hate the fire ones. They're the worst." He awkwardly scratches his knee. "Almost as bad as the earth ones."

"They're all pretty sucky in my book." I secretly wipe a tear.

"I'm here to learn from you, but maybe we can help each other. You help me keep my recruits alive and I'll be someone you can let those walls you've built around yourself down. I'd rather connect with one person and lose them, than live the rest of my life alone, walled up in my cell of sadness. We're given this life to learn and grow. Let's help each other do just that."

I look away, trying to hide the emotions his words incite. I jump off the wall. "Get off your ass. We have work to do."

He follows orders. "Yes, ma'am." He follows me into the center of the square. Fighting blocks have been permanently marked off by burned areas. He moves to his side without question.

We take all the weapons from our training suits off, leaving us more room to move, fight and not accidentally stab each other.

"I don't want to hurt you," he says, watching me get into a fighting position.

I laugh loudly. "Is that what you think is going to happen?" We dance around each other in a choreographed sequence of steps and jabs. Neither of us making contact with the other. Tired of the game, I land a punch in the center of his chest. He stops and gasps.

"Damn, lass. You *are* strong." He quickly regains composure.

I lunge toward him again. This time he anticipates the move and blocks my punch. He reaches for my arm but misses as I drop to the ground and kick his legs out from underneath him. He hits the grass face-first. I'm on his back before he can regain his footing, grabbing both arms and pinning him to the ground. "Give up?" I pant.

He bucks slightly, trying to bounce me off. Taking advantage of my long legs, I wrap them around his, imitating an octopus capturing its prey. I try not to notice the tightness of his body underneath mine. I bury my face into red curls, preventing him from moving his head. "What about now, recruit? Give up?"

A pulse hums from his body. It starts as a low vibration and turns into a visible pulsation. It pushes against my body, making me loosen my hold. My legs relax enough that he's able to flip his body completely over and we're face to face with my legs straddling his hips. I quickly regain composure, forcing his hands over his head. In any other situation, this would be highly erotic. In this situation, it's confusing.

"What the hell was that?" I ask, pulling my head up high enough to see his face.

"I don't know what you mean, lass." He manages to slide his arms from over his head to shoulder height, with me still holding on. The reality of the situation and what we must look like comes crashing down. I slowly untie my legs from his and sit up, still straddling his hips. The other trainers and recruits have stopped what they're working on and are staring at us.

I roll off of the huge man and sit beside him. He sits up and the two of us break into laughter. "That'll give them something to talk about." He wears a huge smile.

He stands and reaches a hand to me. I refuse any help and stand on my own. "I think we might need a change of scenery for the rest of the day."

"Agreed. Have any ideas?" He slides his weapons back in place.

"Follow me," I copy his actions and lead him toward an older training area not many people remember or are still alive to know about. We bypass the building holding the fire elemental and away from the ocean. The course is hidden deep in the woods and protected by ancient wards. I tug a long vine that's blocking the start of the course before realizing it reaches at least thirty feet high.

"That sucks." I pull, using all my strength. "It's not budging."

Murphy steps around me. "Let me give it a try." He pulls for a few minutes and manages to move it slightly before pulling a large knife from his boot and chopping it above his head.

"I could've done that, cheater." I walk past him.

"Ha." He follows me into the course. Surprisingly, the rest of the course looks like it used to. Almost as if it has been maintained over the past year. "This isn't half bad." He rubs his hands along a large tree branch close to the walkway. "We can train without the constant stares and whispers." His words mimic what's going through my head.

"Exactly what I was thinking. We gave them enough of a show earlier, they'll be busy for a while." He laughs loudly, making me laugh with him. "I don't even want to know what some of them are saying."

He looks around the abandoned course. "How long ago was this in use?"

I shrug. "I'm not sure. Time runs together here. Maybe a year and a half." I rub a dark patch of moss off the first obstacle and onto my pants.

"What's the goal? First one through wins?"

"Pretty much. At least here, nothing's going to kill you *when* you fall behind, except maybe your pride." I smile, knowing I just struck a nerve.

"Challenge accepted." He begins unfastening his heavy vest.

"No. Lesson two is with the added weight of the vest." He looks surprised. "You up for it? Or, should I simplify it and we go without them?"

"I like how you think." He smiles. "Let's do this. I'm glad to hear there's a second lesson. I was beginning to think your training was based around the one."

"You did so well with that one, I thought more prac-tice was in order before we embarked on a new one." He gives me an incredulous look. "Lesson two it is." I take off in a full sprint down the path and through the course.

Several hours pass, allowing the two of us to make our way through the course four times. With each pass, we improve our time and agility, and each time, I stay a foot ahead of him. "Lesson two is easier than one." He says, coming up quickly behind me. I stop running and check our time. "Fifteen minutes, thirty-one seconds, at least for me. You'll have to add a few seconds to that for your time."

"I was being a gentleman. Ladies are always first." He's breathing harder than our morning runs, but still not as hard as the average human.

"Whatever you say." I pat him on the shoulder. "I think you're right, though. This is almost too easy. We need more of a challenge." I remember a small lake behind the back side of the course. "There's a lake not too far from here." He perks up.

"Let's go," he says, excitedly.

"Don't get too excited Murph. It's beyond the wards and supposed to be off limits."

"What was that?" He puts his hand to his ear. "All I heard was lake." He sticks his nose up, smelling the air. "It's this way, I can smell it." He starts walking.

"Okay, that's not weird or anything." I follow as he leads us right to it. "Don't let your guard down. The wards stop at the last obstacle. There could be elementals here."

We both survey the shore surrounding the mile-wide lake. Trees line the banks. Any of them could be an elemental or hiding one. Water elementals don't normally inhabit lakes, but this is the perfect setting for earth or air. "What better challenge is there than fighting a real elemental? Especially one that's not being held against their will."

He's right, but I'm not sure risking my life or his is the best way to end the day. "You first." I slowly remove my uniform and try not to stare as he strips down to his boxers. It's difficult not to count the muscles on his stomach.

"Have you gone swimming here before?" He sticks a toe into the lake.

I stand behind him, enjoying the view. "Once. I didn't run into anything uninvited, but after yesterday, I'm not taking any chances." I strap a dagger to my inner thigh. When I stand up, Murphy turns away from me quickly. I pretend not to notice.

He moves into the lake, being careful of his footing. "There are some huge rocks in the bottom. Be mindful where you step." I follow his steps until the water reaches my waist. We stand side by side. "Race to the other side?"

I relish his challenge. Swimming is my thing. I've been able to outswim everyone since before being able to walk. "This sounds like lesson three, and I'll take that challenge."

"I'm beginning to see a pattern to your lessons." I'm ready to dive in when he interrupts my premature victory dance. "Wait! We need some ground rules."

"What? Why do we need ground rules? Afraid you're going to lose?" I retort.

"I want to make sure *you* have a fair chance." He sounds overly confident.

"Whatever, but I set the rules."

"Deal."

"Whoever swims to the other side and back to this rock the fastest is the winner."

"That's pretty obvious," he answers, sarcastically.

"We must stay underwater until we get to the other side. One breath, and then underwater to here. No cheating or sneaking a breath." Underwater swimming is my superpower.

Murphy smiles, showing two dimples on his cheeks that I haven't noticed until now. "And here I thought you were going to make it difficult."

"One, two, three!" The two of us dive in perfect synchronicity. The water's murky but clear enough to see the shadow of him next to me. We're even, neither a stronger swimmer than the other. Dammit, I can't let him win. We approach the other side of the lake, our turn-around point. Surfacing at the same time, we breathe in tandem and dive back into the lake. Again, we're side by side, making our way back to the starting point. It's now or never. If he wins, I have a strong suspicion he'll never let me live it down. I reach deep inside and push harder than I ever have until I've pulled several feet ahead. I keep pushing until there's almost a body length between us. The spot where we started is feet ahead. I make it to the rock and stand only seconds before he does. I'm more winded than I've been in a while, but I won.

Murphy stands beside me, just as winded. "Damn, lass. No one swims faster than me." He's at a loss and I savor the victory.

I smile, proud of my accomplishment. "You pushed me harder than anyone has before. It was a challenge I enjoyed. But you didn't stand a chance."

He limps his way back to the shore, laying down, trying to catch his breath. I lie beside him, struggling to breathe. The blue sky above is full of fluffy white clouds, forming shapes of animals and letters. Several minutes pass before I'm able to breathe at a normal pace again.

Murphy's breath matches mine and we both stare at the shapes above.

"How'd you end up here?" he asks.

I sigh deeply. "That's a story for another day."

"Understood."

"Don't take it personally. I've only shared my story with one other person, and she's dead. It's just something I don't know if I'm ready to do yet." My hand floats in the air above my face with my arm fully extended, tracing the shape of a horse in the clouds. I watch as the horse jumps over a tree and disappears into nothing. Moving to the shape of a cat, I continue tracing. The cat is moving faster than the surrounding clouds. While they continue changing shapes in the wind, the cat keeps its formation and is moving toward us. What the hell? "Murphy?"

"Hmm?"

"Look at that cloud." I point to the cat shape moving rapidly.

"Shit." He jumps to his feet. I do the same, grabbing my stash of weapons. "Air?"

"Has to be," I answer, wrapping my tactical vest around me. The cat disappears, giving way to what looks like a swirling tornado, heading straight for us.

"Remember when I said I hate fire elementals?"

"Yeah!" I yell.

"Well, I hate these more!" We form a two-man team, ready to do battle with something impossible to kill.

The lesser elemental lands on the beach, twenty feet beside us. "What do we have here?" he hisses as he spins, circling us with his path.

Neither of us responds. We stand back to back, as

we're trained and train others to do. Never let them get the upper hand.

His circle gets closer. "Two little water babies in the same place," whispers from his slimy mouth.

He must have seen us swimming. "You're not welcome here. Leave or we'll make you leave."

He laughs wickedly. "Don't be daft young one." The elemental moves toward us faster than my eyes can track. Murphy's quick and strikes with his blade. "Stupid boy, what good will a knife do? I'm made from wind. Can metal cut the sky?" The elemental grabs Murphy, throwing him to the ground. He's up in an instant.

"Adria, run," he yells in my direction.

I have no intentions of running. I move to the side while throwing rocks and tree limbs at the roaring force of wind. He loses interest in Murphy and turns toward me. "You're a feisty one. I like that." He's on me before I can respond. Sticks, rocks, and wind pummel my body, knocking me to my knees. This is the first time I've fought an air elemental. They're the only element without an obvious weakness. He stands over me, a mass of swirling air with no definite place to strike. Murphy jumps through the vortex, knocking it to its side. Clearly angry, the elemental turns to Murphy, hurling him to the ground. Rocks and limbs strike him on the head, knocking him unconscious.

"Murphy!" I yell toward the duo. A rumble stirs deep in my stomach. Seeing Murphy passed out with the elemental looming over him brings anger to the surface. The rumble forces its way through my skin and into the world. A bubble of water forms around me, surrounding both me and Murphy, protecting us, as it throws the elemental back toward the surrounding trees. He shrinks from a tornado-sized demon to a small windstorm in a matter of seconds.

"Ah, little water baby has some ability and perhaps something else." In an instant, he disappears into the sky.

CHAPTER 5

"*A*dria?" Murphy moans. "Are you okay?" His words are slurred.

I run to his side. Kneeling, I notice black circles already forming underneath his eyes. His face has scratches from the sand, but he looks better than expected. "I'm good. What about you?"

He sits up with a grunt. "I'm sorry."

"For what?" I help him to his feet.

"I left you to fight alone. What happened? Where'd he go?" He brushes sand and dirt off of his body.

How do I explain that I somehow produced a bubble of water that protected us from an elemental? Until a few days ago, I'd never had anything like this happen. When it happened during training, I was in denial and blocked it from my mind. Today, there's no doubt that it came from me. I produced a bubble of water. What does this mean? Instead of sharing my inner turmoil, I answer, "I don't know. He looked around and then took off as fast as he landed."

Murphy stops wiping dirt and stares at me dumbfounded. "I'm not the smartest in the world, but I'd have to be pretty slow to believe that for one minute. You sure there's not more to the story than you're wanting to share?"

"I'm sure." I flash a smile. The wind the elemental produced dried my hair in troll doll style. It feels like it's standing straight up and full of debris. I step back into the water, dunking my head. Dirt, sand, leaves, and who knows what else floats into the water. Murphy joins me, copying my movements.

"I'm sorry, I let my guard down. An elemental has never gotten the upper hand on me before, ever." His words sound angry. "Are you sure he didn't hurt you?"

"He didn't. I'm okay, you're okay and he's gone." I step out of the water and dress quickly. "We need to get closer to the compound. It's not safe out here."

We walk back into the safety of the wards before Murphy pulls me to a stop. "Adria, what happened back there? You and I both know they don't just get bored and leave. I need you to tell me the truth." He shifts from one foot to the other. "You can trust me."

"Murphy, it's not a matter of trust. I'm telling you the truth. You've fought in this war longer than I have and know elementals don't have any rhyme or reason for their attacks or when they get bored with their games. Our job is to protect humans while they go on living in complete ignorance of the hidden world around them. We're the ones who keep them safe, keep them from discovering the truth." I turn back toward the compound. "What would I gain by lying?" I concentrate on keeping my face void of any emotion and continue walking. *And the Oscar goes to...*

We continue past the fire elemental building and into the square. "Care to join me for dinner?"

He pauses. It's obvious he doesn't believe me but doesn't pursue a more truthful answer. He sighs before replying. "I'd like that." The whispers begin as soon as we enter.

The gruff man behind the counter looks especially pissy tonight. "Steak or chicken?" he asks with a blank stare on his face.

"Chicken, please." I watch as he finds the slimiest piece in the pan and places it on a plate for me.

"Next. Steak or chicken?"

"Both." The man glares at Murphy. "All this training has given me a beast of an appetite." The man adds a small steak and matching chicken on a plate. "Why are they so stingy at suppertime?" he whispers toward me, taking his plate.

"Maybe he's not as impressed with your charms as the ladies that serve breakfast." I shrug.

"Guess I need to step up my game for the evening meal." He gathers every other edible item on the bar and places it on his tray. Looking around for a table, it's even more obvious the crowd is staring.

"Let's take this to my room," I say loud enough for the entire room to hear. Might as well give them more fuel for their fire.

"Sounds like a plan. I'm tired of the stares." He follows me out of the door and into the elevator. After the swim and fight, I'm too tired to climb the stairs. Murphy doesn't question and follows me into the small box.

We ride silently to the twelfth floor. The door opens, revealing the dimly lit hallway. All the dorm rooms are open, except one, mine. I unlock it, ushering him in first.

There isn't much room to put our trays. Murphy chooses the small dresser and I sit on the bed, holding mine in my lap. "Do you have the entire floor to yourself?" he wrinkles his forehead.

"Yeah. One of the perks of being the only surviving female." I laugh awkwardly.

"I'm having to share a room with a recruit named Brian. All he does is stare at me and gets nervous when I talk to him." He laughs gently. "May I?" He motions to the bed, which is the only place to sit.

Scooting to one side, "Of course. Don't make it weird."

"Wouldn't dream of it." He smirks and leans against the small, metal headboard. "The company's better up here, but it's too quiet. You don't have a television or a computer?"

I reach under my bed, pulling out my antique laptop. The top hangs off on one side when I open it, the victim of too many falls. I open my Spotify playlists. "What would you like?"

"I'm a fan of music from the '70s and '80s. It just made more sense than that mess they play today." He's eaten his entire steak and is working on the chicken. "I just made myself sound old, didn't I?"

I huff a laugh. "Yes, you did, but I'm right there with

you." I click on my '70s playlist, *Immigrant Song* begins blaring through the one working speaker.

"Yes, ma'am! That's what I'm talking about." He bobs his head to the beat while finishing the chicken. "Do you ever wonder if some of them know about the world of elementals?"

I look up in question. "Who?"

"Humans. What you said earlier got me thinking. Do you think they know there are creatures in this world that make up the elements all around them?" He shoves an entire roll in his mouth.

"Well, we're human, and we know."

"You know what I mean. The regular humans, the ones that weren't recruited to be in this mess. Do they have any idea that the wind, or sea, or fire, or earth is alive and can destroy the world they call their own?" He slowly eats a second piece of pecan pie.

"Part of our job is keeping them from learning about this world. Honestly, I think most are oblivious to it. It's better that way. The less they know, the safer they are." I take another bite of chicken.

"You're probably right." He sighs deeply. "I'm getting full."

"I can't imagine why," I retort with a smirk. "I was beginning to think that wasn't a possibility." He laughs softly. "I've wondered the same thing since I first learned about them, the elementals I mean. In fact, I'm not sure I believed in them the first few months of being recruited."

Zeppelin is over and the Eagles come on. Murphy's energy is calming, and it feels good to talk to someone.

Not just to give or receive orders, but to really talk to someone. Be in the same space and just be.

"Tell me about yourself," I blurt, after a particularly expressive air guitar solo.

"Well, let me put this away first." He stretches, leaning his air guitar against the wall beside the bed. "I joined the E.F.U. when I was eighteen."

"What the hell is E.F.U.?" I ask with a smile.

"Elemental Fighting Unit. It's not the official title, but I like it better than Phoenix Unit, or whatever they call us these days. I've tried to make the name official for years, but no one seems interested."

"Imagine that." I laugh.

"I know, right?" He laughs with me.

A loud siren startles both of us. "What's that?" He stands from the bed. The fluorescent light flashes several times before going out completely, putting us in total darkness. "Is this something that happens regularly?"

I grab a flashlight from the dresser. "No. Maybe it's some kind of training?" I open the hall door to see the entire floor engulfed in black. "This doesn't feel right."

"Aye. Something's wrong. This isn't a training exercise." A dimly lit EXIT sign glows above the stairwell. Murphy takes the lead as we move toward the bottom, one floor at a time. Screams from below stop us in our tracks. "Are those screams?"

"Sounds that way." We keep moving.

"Could an elemental have gotten into the compound?" he whispers.

"I doubt it. There are wards everywhere." We reach the bottom floor, stepping into the empty and silent cafeteria. Trays of uneaten food cover the tables. Other than that, nothing looks out of the ordinary. "Where are they?" I follow Murphy to the front door.

"Ready?" he mouths, placing his hands on the door. I nod, pulling weapons out of the vest I managed to grab from my room. He pushes the door wide and we're met with a scene straight from a horror movie. Recruits and trainers are running around the square in what looks like complete mayhem. It takes several minutes to process that the balls of fire on the ground are actually people. A burst of flames flies in front of us, passing a few feet above our heads. "Shit, I hate the fire ones!" Murphy yells.

"Adria, you're here!" the elemental screams, passing over a second time. "I thought you'd never come!" I instantly recognize her voice.

"How does she know your name?"

"It's the bitch from the training building," a random voice answers. I turn to see Hadley, covered in blood and singed clothes, standing at the top of the stairs.

"How did she get out?" Hadley doesn't answer, just stares at the destruction happening before us. "Hadley!" I yell, shaking his shoulders.

"It's the bitch from the training building," he repeats. His eyes are large and empty as he stares blankly.

"Hadley?"

"He's in shock." Murphy pulls the man back into the dorm. "This is the one you use for training, the one who killed your friend?" I nod, watching her turn back in our direction.

"Adria, don't worry dear. I'm coming!" A ball of fire hits the ground next to me, barely missing us.

"We have to lead her away from here. She's going to destroy the compound." Murphy pulls me closer. "We need water. The lake?" He raises an eyebrow. I nod.

"Hey, fire freak!" I yell toward the sky. "If you want me, come get me." Murphy and I take off running with her right behind us in the sky. We pass the building that was her makeshift home, rounding past the obstacle course straight toward the lake. She lands on the same sandy beach of our air elemental battle earlier and her flames extinguish, revealing the beautiful woman I recognize.

Murphy and I stand back to back, ready for her next move. Screams from the compound echo through the stillness. "I told you I'd get free." Her voice is laced with anger and hatred. "Now look at us. We're out here all alone. No one will come to your rescue this time." She laughs.

"What do you want?" Murphy asks.

"Well, that's rude. We haven't been properly introduced, yet you're demanding answers from me." She circles us, reminding me of our earlier fight.

"Name's Murphy."

"He has an accent!" she exclaims. "I love a man with an accent." She moves closer to him.

"What do you want?" I keep my voice low. "You have your freedom, why not just leave?"

Her laugh raises the hairs on my arms. "Oh, I have every intention of leaving." She moves away from Murphy and back toward me. "Our last conversation didn't end on a good note. I wanted to tell you goodbye in my own special way." A blast of flames hits a small sapling beside the beach. It explodes into flames.

"I'm good." I smile. "We were never that close anyway."

"There's that sarcasm that I love." She moves closer to Murphy again. "However, I'm bored with this." She transforms into flames and lifts off the sand. Where her hands were moments earlier, small tendrils of flames lift and point straight at Murphy and me. "Goodbye, dear Adria. Do tell Hannah I said hello."

At the mention of her name, anger fills my core. Like before, tension forms deep inside, only stronger this time. The world slows down as I watch the flames leave her hands, heading straight toward us. The tension releases from my core, forming a large wall of water between us. Her flames hit the water as her energy pushes against mine.

Murphy turns toward me. "Use the water!" he yells, over the roar of the elements. "You can control it, push her back!" I follow his command and focus on pushing the water closer to her flames.

"What is this?" Her fire recedes, pushed back by the water.

"Push, Adria!" Murphy yells from behind. "Control her!" The water creeps toward the flames until overtaking them and eventually overtaking the elemental until nothing but steam remains. The elemental screams before collapsing in defeat.

"Is she dead?"

"Probably." In an instant, the elemental's body turns to nothing more than ash, scattered by the wind. I stare in disbelief. Did I just kill a fire elemental using water that I somehow produced with my body?

"Adria?" Murphy places his hands on my shoulders. "Are you okay?"

Truthfully, I don't know. I look around the scene in complete confusion. "What... what happened?" I hold my hands in front of my face, looking for clues. "Where did that water come from and how the hell did you know I could do that?"

"We need to talk, but now's not the time. We're needed at the compound." He pulls me close to him, keeping my feet steady.

"Are you sure she's gone?"

"Yes. The water killed her. You killed her."

I stop walking. "How? How did I kill her? Fire elementals don't die that easily. The water killed her instantly, like a fly hit with a flyswatter."

Murphy turns to me, brushing escaped hair behind my ear. "I promise I'll tell you everything I know, but we need to get back to the compound. There are people there who need our help." I nod in agreement, following him away from the lake and back to where we started. Questions and confusion fill my mind the entire way.

Seeing the destruction in the compound gets me out of my head and back to reality. Bodies are scattered throughout the square. Most are alive with various degrees of burns and scrapes. Several aren't as lucky. When all is said and done, we lost eight with another fifteen severely burned. Murphy and I stay late into the night, helping clean up the destruction left in her wake.

Not sure where to help next, we find the chief who, other than looking exhausted, is still alive and moving. "Adria, Murphy, thank you for your help. We don't know where she's gone, but it looks like she's left the compound." Director Scott nods toward a fellow trainer. "Jacobs reset the wards, and we've done everything we can for the night. Why don't the two of you get some rest and we'll reevaluate in the morning?"

"Aye," Murphy answers for both of us. Normally, I would kick his ass for that, but tonight isn't normal.

I wait for Director Scott to walk away before speaking "Tell me everything." My voice is low. He puts his hand on my elbow, steering me to the seawall. I ignore the hand he offers and climb to the top. "I don't need help. I need answers."

My patience runs thin as we sit in silence for what seems like an eternity. The square behind us is quiet and the energy of the camp feels back to normal. "Murphy?"

He lowers his head. "I haven't been honest with you." My arms cross in defense. "I didn't come to train with you because my recruits were dying. In fact, I don't have any recruits and I'm not a Phoenix. I came to find *you*." I fight the urge to kick his ass. "I came on behalf of your father."

I jump off the wall, anger fueling my movement. "That's not funny." I never told him about my childhood or lack of family. How could he know I grew up in foster care, never knowing my parents? "Dammit, this is why I don't make friends!"

He holds his hands up in defense. "Please, let me explain. Your father has been looking for you. I followed a lead that led me here, to you. I'm searching for the daughter of Llyr."

I stare dumbfounded. "Llyr? The god of water?

Master of all water elementals? The First Elemental of water? You think he's my father?"

"Yes."

"What makes you think in this vast expanse of a universe, I'm the daughter of a god?" I can't hold in my laughter. "I'm no more special than anyone else."

"How many other Phoenix have you run into that can form a wall of water out of thin air and kill a fire elemental within seconds? If that's the norm around here, please tell me." His tone matches mine.

"That doesn't make me special. I'm smart and on a few occasions, lucky even, but not the daughter of an ancient god."

"I sensed it in you the first moment we met." He jumps off beside me.

"Sensed what exactly?" I ask angrily.

"Power beyond recognition. I sensed... home."

My forehead wrinkles in confusion. "You're not making any sense."

"Elementals can sense other elementals. It's the reason the one from the ocean yesterday spoke to you. He knew." His hands are on his hips as he paces in front of me. "I wasn't sure what I sensed. I thought we'd be safe for a while and I'd have time to figure it out, but with the attack this afternoon and what I just witnessed, we don't have time. I have to tell you the truth."

"You're telling me you're an elemental?" I draw the knife from my belt and get into defensive mode, ready to attack.

He holds his hands up. "Adria, stop. I'm not going to hurt you." He backs up to the wall, ready to protect himself if needed. "I'm not fully elemental. I'm like you, a hybrid. My mother was a water elemental, a siren, and my father is human."

"Hybrid? How the hell does something like that even happen? That guy yesterday had no solid form." I wave the knife in his direction. "Where does..." I don't finish the thought. "That's why you insisted we go to the ocean yesterday. You knew that thing was out there, didn't you?" I hold the knife toward his chest.

He looks down. "I did. But I also knew he wouldn't hurt you. I wanted his opinion."

"His opinion of me, you mean."

"Aye."

"What was his opinion?" I spew, not moving my stance.

He looks me in the eyes. "He told me you were the queen. That's what he called you, wasn't it?"

"They lie Murphy. We're taught that from day one."

"Yes, they do. But he doesn't. He sensed it in you too."

"Then why the hell haven't I been 'sensed' before? I've never been attacked by an air elemental or hailed as a queen by a water elemental until *you* arrived. If I'm the daughter of a god, wouldn't I have been discovered by now?" My words are harsh, and anger fills my tone.

"That's an excellent question, and one I don't have the answer to." He relaxes his stance slightly.

"You stand here wanting me to believe all this bullshit? Just accept it and move on like my life didn't matter. The hell I lived as a child didn't matter?" I pause, feeling the anger growing inside. "The air elemental from today, was he part of your plan too?"

"No, but he was beneficial. The fight tonight confirmed what I already knew. You're the daughter of Llyr, and you are loved more than you know." His tone softens.

Loved more than you know. No one has ever told me they love me and meant it. Growing up, the promise of love was usually met with conditions. I turn, walking toward the dorm. "Leave me alone."

"Adria, please." I don't stop.

CHAPTER 6

I head down the twelve flights of stairs, still angry and confused from last night's conversation. His tall ass better not be waiting on the steps. I may have to stab him for real this time.

Bursting through the doors, I'm relieved to see the stairs clear. I take a deep breath, slowly releasing it through my mouth. The courtyard is clear of any evidence of last night's attack and after the craziness of yesterday, this morning calls for a twenty-mile run.

I descend the stairs two at a time. Rounding the corner to where a tall figure looms in the darkness. Shit. At least he followed rule number one and has his back to the stone wall.

I ignore him and head toward the square. He doesn't speak, instead matches my pace, jogging beside me. I speed up until we're nearly at a full run. He doesn't slow down.

Passing Atticus for the tenth time, I abruptly stop.

Murphy runs a few steps past me before stopping. "Thank gods. You were wearing me down." He bends over, breathing deeply. I ignore him and move to one of the ballistic dummies. Practicing every tactical move I know, I stab the dummy over and over until nothing's left but large pieces full of holes.

"Damn," a deep voice sounds beside me. Out of the corner of my eye, I see him step back, putting space between us. "Can we talk? Please?" I continue stabbing what's left of the dummy without answering and move to a new one.

"Okay, then I'll talk. You listen." He follows me, staying at a safe distance. "There are things you need to know." I move over to another dummy after obliterating the second. "Your mother hid you away. It was the only way to keep you safe, to keep you alive." He sighs before continuing. "At the beginning of time, only the elementals occupied the earth. They were the Firsts, none better than the other. There were four of them and they worked together to form the earth."

I stop stabbing. "I know all of this. Why do you think I spend my life training recruits to fight them?" Switching the knife out for spears, I begin throwing them at a target forty yards away.

He follows me to retrieve my spears. "The First Elementals began creating lesser versions of themselves. The lesser elementals weren't as knowledgeable or powerful and were forced to work, continuing what the Firsts started and building the world for the future. It didn't take long for the lessers to discover each other. Where the First Elementals tolerated and respected one another, the lesser forms did not. Battles began to break out among them in a quest for power."

For the first time, I look him in the eyes. "You're still not telling me anything that a first-year Phoenix doesn't learn." He sighs deeply. I relish the frustration I'm causing him. It's my toxic trait. "I'm listening." I walk to the seawall, climbing to the top. He copies my movement.

"The battles were terrible for the newly created world. Craters, broken-off land masses, and valleys, all formed because of the fighting. The only thing that could stop them was a First Elemental or complete destruction.

"The lesser elementals from fire and water hated each other the most. They began the battle of all battles. Sensing the destruction that was to come, the lessers from air joined water while earth joined fire, for the beginning of a battle that would shape the world we know now.

"Volcanos spewed molten lava over the world, forming new land masses. Lakes and seas swelled with tidal waves that crashed into the land. The earth shook, causing fissures to snake along the land, and the winds formed tornadoes that destroyed the newly formed land below. The Firsts tried to regain control of their lessers many times but weren't successful. They'd grown too strong and refused to release their newfound power. The Firsts knew the importance of unity and equality, so they joined together, calling all of their lesser creations to them. As the Firsts joined their strength, each lesser was drawn into their creator and became part of what originally formed them, the First. Essentially, they were absorbed back into their creator."

I turn toward him. "How do I know you're not just blowing smoke up my ass?"

He looks out over the sea as the sun rises, glistening off of the waves. "You don't. But it's the truth. I swear to you."

"Why do we run into lesser elementals today? If they've all been *absorbed*, where did our friends yesterday come from?"

He rubs a small cut on his cheek left from our encounter. "Over the millennia since then, things have changed. Lessers have been created again, but rules have been set in place and must be followed."

"What does any of this have to do with me?" My tone mimics the frustration I feel inside.

"In the great battle, the lessers of Llyr and Shu, the god of air, joined forces to fight against Brigit, the goddess of fire, and Dagda, the god of earth. The Firsts defeated the lessers, but it wasn't one big happy family. Over the years, rules have been broken, creating too many lessers, and the world is being threatened as it was before. Every news broadcast is full of natural disasters, earthquakes, volcanic eruptions, hurricanes, and the list goes on and on. It's beginning again. The lessers are battling, slowly beginning their uprise." Murphy raises his head to the sun, soaking in its warmth.

"Can't the Firsts just do what they did last time? Absorb them all and start over?"

"They could, but every living thing on the planet would die along with them. It would be utter destruction."

Well, shit. "I still don't understand what this has to do with Llyr thinking I'm his daughter?"

"You *are* his daughter, I'm sure of it." He pauses. "Your mother was human, but not an ordinary human..."

I interrupt, "Let me guess. She had long blonde hair that she would let down from a tower and Llyr would climb, eventually win her over, have his way with her, and boom, I appeared."

He stares at me with what can only be described as a resting bitch face. "May I continue?" Annoyance is prevalent in his tone. I can't hide the smirk from my face.

"When you were born, the lessers were causing problems again. Not on the same scale as before or even now, but problems, nonetheless. By this time the alliance between the Firsts was demolished and they'd been fighting like the lessers. Llyr knew if it was discovered he had a child with a human, that child would be killed immediately. For your safety, he and your mother decided to hide you and Llyr would never know where she took you. She would raise you away from elementals, away from the Firsts, and away from the lessers. You were to be raised as a human."

I jump to the ground in anger. "That never happened, did it? She didn't raise me away from all of that. In fact, she didn't raise me at all. The system raised me, adults who did evil things raised me, *I* raised me!" The energy coils deep inside, threatening to explode.

He jumps beside me. "Adria, I'm so sorry for what you've been through. But look who you've become. You're still drawn into the world of elementals. It's in your blood, in your soul. It's who you are. Inside, you know I'm telling you the truth. You are the daughter of Llyr. You are loved and more powerful than you know."

"Why now?" I hiss. "If he wanted me hidden from danger, why now? Why send people to find me, and how the hell do you know all of this?"

"Because now is the time. The Firsts have separated even more and Llyr fears what he's always known would happen is on the horizon. A battle that will mean the end of the world and every living being is close." He looks down. "And the reason I know all of this is, the island where I live, the island I grew up on, is where you were born and Llyr still lives."

Water begins to form a small wall between us. I don't question where it came from. "How do I know any of this is true?" I spit in anger.

Murphy passes through the water, moving in front of me. His hair is misty wet, and water beads off his training vest. Sliding his hands over his shoulders, he opens them in front of me. "This is how you know. Look around, Adria. Do you see anyone else creating walls and bubbles of water? Did you see anyone produce a wall of water capable of killing a fire elemental last night? This," he shakes the water off his hands, "isn't an ordinary human thing. You're not human, I'm not human, we're hybrids and this world isn't for us."

I turn away, pulling the water with me. Growing up in foster care, I never felt like I belonged, never stayed anywhere long enough *to* belong. Deep inside, I know what he's saying is true, but it doesn't make the hurt any less. "How?" I ask.

"How, what?" He steps closer.

"How could he let me believe I was abandoned, or an orphan, or whatever the hell I thought? I don't even know anymore." My voice sounds sad, even to me. What's left of the wall of water trickles to nothing.

"I don't know." His tone softens. "What's important is he wants you by his side now, he needs you." Murphy moves within arm's length.

Those are the wrong words. A large bubble of raging water forms around the two of us, engulfing us in its roar. "He needs me? Where was he when I needed him? Where was he when in order to eat, I had to beg on the streets? Where was he when I was locked in a closet for weeks at a time without food or water because I didn't take out the trash? Where was he then?" Tears slide down my cheeks as the bubble turns into nothing.

"Adria, I don't have all the answers. I'm sorry for the things that happened to you. Llyr can't make up for the past, but this is where it changes. You know inside that I'm right. You're a hybrid, and one of the strongest in existence. You're the child of a god. The power you displayed yesterday is just a touch of what you're capable of. You need training, you need knowledge, and you need someone who can answer these questions for you. You need your father."

Tears flow without control. I haven't ugly cried since being a teenager. Murphy wraps his long arms around me, pulling me close and letting me cry into his vest. There isn't a label for the vast amount of emotions flowing from my body. I curl my arms into his chest and enjoy the moment of being surrounded and protected.

When the tears stop, I pull away, too embarrassed to make eye contact. The moment we shared felt intimate, and the awkwardness that follows makes me self-conscious. He's telling the truth. I feel it in my bones, in my soul. If I have a family and answers somewhere, I don't have a choice.

"When do we leave?" I whisper.

"After lunch. I'm hungry." He laughs, attempting to lighten the mood.

"That seems to be a recurring theme for you." We walk toward the dorm.

"Aye, 'tis true," he calls after. I trudge my way up the twelve flights of stairs, information swirling through my brain. I don't bother packing. It'll take all of two minutes to throw my few belongings in a trash bag. Instead, I lay down on the bed taking in my four cinder block walls. I grew up in what many consider a prison system, looking around the room, I realize all I did was move from one prison to another. Being a product of the system, I learned how to read a person and their intentions. Murphy's are true. He won't hurt me, and he believes in what he's saying. At least there's one good thing I learned from my childhood. The rest was shit.

I fight the urge to close my eyes. It's still early. Most of the compound is just now awake and eating breakfast. I don't feel like looking or being looked at by anyone. People have stared my entire life. I chalked it up to being Amazon size, but it's different here. Since Hannah died, no one even comes near me. It's like they think I'm bad luck or diseased. Other than the recruit of the month, Murphy's the first person I've said more than ten words to in months. Since he's arrived, they stare at the two of us like we're freaks. Maybe we are.

Why was I never taught about hybrids? I didn't even know that was a possibility. Is it their dirty little secret? Am I a freak of nature? Questions plague my mind as my eyes betray me and close, pulling me into a world of familiarity.

I'm in the grassy square where Hannah and I are sparring, our usual morning routine. She looks different than I remember. Her hair is dark and smooth, and her eyes are larger. The top of her head barely reaches my shoulder, but she looks taller somehow. She does her signature first move and tries to sweep my feet out from under me. I block it every time, knowing that's what she'll do, but she keeps trying, nonetheless.

"Ah, dammit, Adria. That one hurt. How'd you know that's what I was going to do?" She pulls back.

I smile and walk around her like prey. "Because it's what you do every freakin' time."

She laughs. "I guess I need a new opening move."

We continue sparring, throwing soft punches back and forth. "He's right, you know."

"Who?" I ask, knocking her to the ground again.

"He's telling you the truth. You can trust him." I continue stalking her.

"Hannah, if you're talking about that new recruit Michael, he's creepy. He spent ten minutes telling me how he and his hamster have matching outfits." I knock her to the ground again. I don't remember it being this easy to get the upper hand.

She props her arms over her knees but doesn't get up.

"Murphy, he's telling you the truth. You have to go with him. You need to meet Llyr, you're the answer."

"The answer to what?" I sit next to her.

She looks around the compound. "The answer to this war, to the senseless deaths, to fighting them." She points at the building that used to house the fire elemental, the building she died in.

"I'm just Adria, nothing special. I'm not the answer to anything." I pick at a piece of grass while I speak.

"That's where you're wrong." She nudges her shoulder into mine. "You are the child of a god. There's a reason I gave my life for yours. You must go and discover who you really are, plus I'm tired of seeing you like this." She points to my dirty training clothes. "Go be who you're meant to be, go kick some ass." She leans sideways, putting her head on my shoulder.

"Are you really here?" She doesn't answer.

A noise startles me awake. I sit straight up in bed. Hannah? A shiny object on the edge of the dresser catches my eye. When I pick it up, I realize it's the dolphin pin that Hannah and I both wore. The same pin that was on the floor of the fire elemental building. Mine is still attached to my vest. This one is Hannah's. Tears stream down my cheeks. "Okay, I get the message. I'm going." I pin her dolphin next to mine, pack my trash bag, and head downstairs.

More time has passed than I realized, and lunch is being served. Murphy's sitting at our usual table with a plate full of everything. I set my tray of spaghetti across from him. "I'm sorry."

He puts his fork down and stares at me like I've been possessed. "For what?"

"For being a jerk." I start eating, hoping he won't push the issue.

He follows my lead. "Jerkiness forgiven."

We eat the rest of our meal in silence.

CHAPTER 7

"Is this a private jet?" We step onto the streamlined airliner, greeted by a man and a woman.

"It is," Murphy answers. Putting his hand on the shoulder of the man, "This is Daniel. He's our pilot." He moves to the woman standing behind Daniel.

"Hi, I'm Sophie. If there's anything you need, please don't hesitate to ask." Her accent is similar to Murphy's but more refined.

"Sophie's my sister." Murphy wraps an arm around her neck and kisses her on the cheek. "And, she's annoying as hell."

She pulls back with a laugh, slapping him on the shoulder. "Look who's talking, you huge pain in the arse." She dries her cheek with the back of her hand. "Be a gentleman and take our guest to her seat." Murphy follows directions, leading me toward a seat that resembles a small piece of heaven, and is poofier than the clouds we'll be flying through shortly.

I raise my hand like a child in school. He raises an eyebrow, "Question?"

"Do you remember the air elemental from yesterday?" I hope he sees where I'm going with this. "What's to keep him or one of his millions of siblings from attacking the plane and bringing it down? If he could sense 'my power'," I hold up air quotes, "couldn't others?"

"Aye, but the plane is heavily warded, and it belongs to Llyr. Lessers are strictly forbidden from contact with a First, especially one that's not their god." He points to an unfamiliar carving on the top of each seat. "This is the sigil that protects us, it makes us invisible to them." The sigil feels strangely familiar.

"Is this how you got to my compound?" His explanation feels sketchy.

"Aye. I've flown in these jets thousands of times. I can assure you, we're safe." He steps to the back of the plane. "Are you hungry? I can get you something to eat."

"No, I'm still full from lunch." Trusting his words, I sink into the seat, enjoying the feel as the rich leather hugs me from every angle.

"I'm famished, I'll be back in a minute."

"Why does that not surprise me?" He laughs and disappears in the same direction as Sophie.

The speaker above my head beeps. "Good afternoon. This is your captain, Daniel. Please ensure your seatbelt is latched and all belongings are safely stowed away. We'll be in flight shortly."

Murphy comes back carrying three bags of chips and a doughnut. "That doesn't look like airline food."

"It was all I could find. Sure you don't want something?" He tries handing me a bag of Cool Ranch Doritos.

I motion him away. "How many planes does Llyr own?"

"To be honest, I'm not sure." He sits across the aisle from me, struggling to strap his seat belt and not drop his doughnut. "Being the god of water has its advantages."

The smell of rich leather fills my nose. "I would say so."

Sophie sits down several seats in front of us, strapping herself in. "You eating again?" she points to the doughnut.

"You know it. I'm a growing boy." His words are muffled as he shoves chips into his mouth.

Sophie has an easy energy, very similar to her brother's. The plane begins moving, taxiing down the runway. "We're third in line, only a matter of minutes before we're off the ground," Daniel announces over the speaker.

I look around the cabin. Butterflies begin to take flight in my stomach. "What if I'm not what he expects?"

Murphy puts his doughnut down, turning completely toward me. "If you're asking me if he's going to like you, how could he not? You're stronger than anyone I've met, faster than me, and you're his daughter." The plane starts moving and he faces forward. "Gods, I hate flying."

......

I discovered a book on the history of elementals a few

seats from mine and have been reading it for the past hour. My eyes are beginning to cross as I study the lack of published facts about the elemental world. I move around the cabin looking over the vast whiteness of clouds that surround us. Funny how from above, they resemble the ocean. How many of those clouds are lessers waiting to pounce?

Murphy lowered his seat to a sleeping position earlier and has a mask over his face. "He's a good guy," Sophie says, moving toward me.

I smile in return. "Where are we going?"

"He didn't tell you?" My head shakes in response. "Sounds about right." She moves beside me. "Do you mind if I sit?"

"Of course not." I move my long legs out of the way as she sits in front of me.

"We're heading to the Isle of Man."

My forehead wrinkles. "Is this a real place, or an island in the middle of nowhere, like a superhero movie?"

Sophie snorts a laugh. "It's an actual place, with actual people living on it. Have you seriously never heard of it?" She huffs. "You Americans and your limited knowledge of geography. Oh, I mean no offense."

"None taken. You told no lies." I laugh.

"I reckon the Isle of Man is a wee one compared to the UK. It doesn't belong to anyone, at least, not any particular government. It's the home of Llyr and will be yours too."

"What's he like?" The thought of meeting Llyr makes me nervous. That, coupled with the anxiety brewing inside, causes me to notice a stray thread on my pants. I pull on it while speaking.

"Who, Llyr?" I nod, rolling the thread between my fingers. "Well, he's strong, extremely handsome, a little scary, and power just kind of oozes from his pores."

"He sounds charming." My voice is full of sarcasm, making us both laugh.

"Actually, he's quite the charmer." Her eyebrows wiggle up and down.

"Ew, that's not what I need to hear. Are you like him?" I nod my head toward the sleeping giant across the aisle.

"No, I'm much smarter." She winks. "But if you're asking if I'm a hybrid, no. I'm one hundred percent human."

"That's what Murphy called me earlier, a hybrid." I think back on our conversation.

"Aye. Although most hybrids are from lesser elementals getting frisky with a human. You're the outcome of a First and a human. You were not born from lust but from love. Did he not tell you anything?"

"In his defense, he tried. I wasn't very open to communication."

Murphy rumbles under his mask. "I remember being threatened with a knife and a spear, during that conversation."

Sophie laughs. "Sounds like she figured you out quickly."

"Since you're not a hybrid, are you allowed to live on the Isle?"

Her smile is warm. "I am. I work for Llyr. My family

lives on the island, where they've lived for centuries. Our parents own a bookstore right in the middle of the village."

"Is that normal? I mean, humans, living with and knowing about elementals?" In America, humans have no knowledge of the elementals that surround them daily. It's my job to train soldiers to keep it that way. If Llyr's living among humans and they know who and what he is, everything I've been taught is wrong.

"Not that I'm aware of, no. Most humans on our island are unaware of Llyr's true identity. Our family knows because of that one over there." She nudges her head toward Murphy.

An announcement interrupts the list of questions I've prepared in my head. "Please put on your seat belts as we begin our descent to our destination," Daniel's voice rings over the speaker. The plane slowly begins to descend. I don't know if the rumbles in my stomach are from motion sickness or nerves.

Murphy's sitting up and not eating what remains in his chip bag. The look on his face mirrors mine. What does he have to be nervous about? The wheels touch the landing strip, bouncing slightly from the impact. From the window, huge mountains loom in the distance. I catch a glimpse of the sea running parallel to the runway. It's so clear I can almost see the bottom.

We taxi into the small airport, stopping away from the building. I gather my trash bag of belongings and follow Murphy to the door. He turns, stopping both of us. "There'll be a car waiting on us, but Llyr won't be here to greet you. Don't think that means he doesn't care. He's off the island but will return as soon as he can." Surprisingly, I'm disappointed. I didn't expect to run into his arms and cry, but I was hoping to see what he looks like at least. "Are you ready?" he asks.

"Ready as I'll ever be." His hand brushes my arm before leading us down the stairs. The familiarity of the touch eases the tension.

The wind slaps me in the face the moment we hit the tarmac. Not a normal wind, but a blast that almost knocks me on my ass, blowing my hair in every direction possible. I look up half expecting an attack from an air lesser. "Is this normal?"

"What?" he asks, as his curls turn into frizz.

"The wind. I was accosted by the breeze when we got down the stairs."

Murphy laughs loudly. "Oh, I should've warned you. The island is very windy. I've always thought it has something to do with Shu."

"Shu? The god of air?" I shove loose strands behind my ears.

"Yea. I think it's his gift to Llyr." He smiles. "It's a long story." I turn back to the car waiting for us, and it's not just any car. On the tarmac sits an ice-blue, Rolls Royce Phantom.

"Please tell me that's our car! The Phantom is waiting for *us*?"

He turns to look at me. "You know cars? That surprises me."

"Why? I had nothing better to do growing up. Cars are a passion of mine. I borrowed many growing up."

He raises an eyebrow. "Borrowed?"

"Sure." I turn back to the car. "I've never seen one of those in person." Between the wind and the fangirl moment, I trip walking toward it.

A tall man wearing a dark suit greets us. "Miss Kane, Mr. McKenzie. May I load your items?" I hand him my trash bag, which he places in the back, discreetly.

"Thank you, Stephen," Murphy responds. The two of us step into the car. I can't stop touching every intricate detail throughout the backseat. Hand cut, custom dyed leather, hand stitching, plush carpeting, the smell alone is amazing. I rub the seat, enjoying the texture on my skin.

"This car is unbelievable." Murphy stares at me, smiling.

"You're like a kid in a candy store."

"Do you realize how cool this car is? It takes over a year to get one, especially with all of these extras." I open a hidden door, revealing a full bar set up.

"A year for humans maybe. I doubt Llyr had to wait more than a week. Being a First has its perks."

As we drive, we pass structures that are both older and newer than I expected. The architecture here is strange. There are thatch roof houses, next to small wooden cottages, next to what looks like modern builds. It's apparent people from all walks and styles of life live here. The car follows a well-worn road, leading upward and across what looks like an ancient mote covered by a bridge. "We're almost there," is the only thing Murphy's said for a while.

"What if it turns out I'm not Llyr's long-lost daughter? What if you've brought some wayward psychopath all the way out here under the pretense that I'm half First

Elemental?" I squirm in my seat as I speak. "Did anyone stop to consider that?"

Murphy smiles, weakly. "From everything I've seen and know about you, there's no question. You are the daughter of Llyr."

"Okay, but let's say you're wrong..."

"Adria?" he interrupts. I raise my eyebrows in response. "Can we stop with all the what-ifs?" I watch as he squirms deeper into the leather.

"Are you okay?"

He straightens his shirt. "I'm good. Just a little nervous." His voice sounds more formal than usual.

"I can certainly understand that." The car stops, and Stephen opens the door before I have time to register where we are.

I step onto a large expanse of grass and stone masonry. A familiarity hits me instantly. I've been here before. It takes a moment to realize we're standing in front of a castle, an actual freaking castle. It's built on an even smaller island and looks like it once was used for fortification. A stone wall surrounds the entire estate, no doubt erected centuries ago. Stone will keep the earth elementals out, while the water surrounding the island will keep the fire elementals out. Llyr built a sanctuary for himself and the unsuspecting humans on the island.

Stephen walks back, carrying my trash bag. "Miss, follow me." Murphy follows behind, which eases the nervousness slightly. On the outside, the main building looks to have been built during medieval times. Large ornate carvings line the peaks of the roof. Gargoyles of all shapes and sizes stare down from above, guarding everything below. The architecture is old but beautiful. Stephen opens a large wooden door that looks like it could withstand a Viking attack. "Follow me," he repeats.

"Still here, Stephen." He turns to look at me.

"That you are. Sorry miss."

Where the outside looks millennium old, the inside holds the character of old architecture with modern conveniences. The entire home is updated and flawless. Stephen leads us up a grand staircase. The halls split off from the landing, leading in three different directions. "Miss Kane, your room is down here." Murphy stays on the landing at the top of the stairs.

"You're not coming?" I ask, following Stephen.

"This wing is the family wing. Mr. McKenzie isn't housed in these quarters." I stop walking.

"Are you kidding me?"

"It's okay. I'm in the wing next door." He points in the opposite direction. "I'll see you at dinner."

"It's all about the food for you, isn't it?" I smile and continue walking.

Stephen opens another large, wooden door. The beauty takes my breath away. Opposite the hall door, two wide balcony doors stand open, their sheers blowing in the wind. The smell of ocean air hits me instantly. "This is amazing," I whisper.

Stephen walks to a closed door at the far end of the room. "Your closet and bathroom facilities are through here. I believe you'll find acceptable clothing and necessities there." He sets my trash bag of belongings beside the door. "Dinner will be served at eight o'clock, cocktails at seven-thirty. In your honor, tonight's dinner is black tie. Welcome home, Miss Kane."

He exits, leaving me to explore. The walls are covered with ornate wallpaper with flowers the same color as the sea looming beneath. The tile floor has the same texture and look as beach sand. The room is decorated to blend in with the scene outside the balcony. I couldn't have designed something more perfect if I tried.

A large mirror surrounded by lights leans against the wall closest to me. Next to it is a fully stocked make-up area with every kind of product and hair utensil known to man. I run my fingers along each item, touching everything from brush bristles to make-up pallets. Beside the bed is a large desk, holding every Apple product available. My mind flashes to my laptop, hanging on with one screw tucked safely in my trash bag.

The four-post bed is the most luxurious item I've ever seen. Each post is covered in sheers that blow in the sea breeze, giving me romance movie vibes. The mattress and bedding are the same height as my waist. Being six feet, that's an accomplishment. This is nicer than anything I could create in a dream.

I open the door leading to the bathroom and closet. Shirts, pants, dresses, skirts, and even a row of formal gowns stare back at me. Is this real? Drawers full of anything that won't fit on a hanger, line the walls underneath. A quick look at the tags of a few of them and I realize they're my size. When did anyone have time to shop for all of this?

The bathroom is half the size of the bedroom and has double windows above the bathtub that overlooks the sea.

Suddenly aware of how gross I feel, I strip out of my sticky clothes and fill the tub. It fills quickly and I lower myself into the bliss of bubbles and warmth.

Stephen said dinner was black tie. What exactly does that mean? I google the answer on my outdated cell phone and discover that a tea-length gown is acceptable. Good, I don't want to try and walk in floor-length taffeta.

My mind replays the events of the past few days until the water turns icy cold. I wrap a towel around my body and a smaller version around my head. The number of products I used for this bath is probably more than I've used in my entire life. Luxury items aren't prevalent in the foster care system.

Exploring the closet, I find a whole section of tea-length gowns. I choose a royal blue, off-the-shoulder dress that leaves little to the imagination. The front V-neck will most likely touch my navel and I'm okay with that. Although intimidated by the glitz and glam, I like the idea of being flashy. Growing up the way I did, I became the master of fitting in and adjusting to my environment. If they want flashy, I'll give them flashy.

I open my pitiful computer and head straight to the '70s playlist. *Back in Black* blares from the one remaining speaker. Sitting at the make-up table, I don't know where to begin. I've worn make-up before, but never with this amount of choices. My usual routine consists of powder, mascara, and lip gloss, purchased from a drugstore. The number of foundations in front of me would rival any store. I do what every person my age does, I go to YouTube University for help. Imagine my surprise when I discover that you're supposed to prep the skin before applying foundation. There's even something called primer that goes on after prep.

Ten videos and forty-five minutes later, I'm surprised at the face in the mirror. My high cheekbones stand out, but not too much. My eyelids are smoky blue, and I somehow managed not to glue my fake eyelashes to my eyeballs. "I look pretty damn good," I say out loud.

Releasing my hair from the towel, it's mostly dried and in a weird shape. Shit. Using a hairdryer and a large brush, I manage to tame the frizz. Several videos later, my hair's styled in something called "beachy curls". It feels appropriate for the setting.

I pull on the dress, managing to zip it without stretching an arm out of socket and realize I was right, my belly button shows. But damn, this thing fits like a glove, like it was made for me. Choosing a pair of strappy silver sandals, I complete the outfit. I've dressed up before, but nothing like this. "I hope I can walk in these damn things," I say out loud to the stranger in the mirror. The woman staring back at me looks nothing like Adria Kane, the elemental slayer. She's refined, she's clean, and she looks pretty damn good. The Adria on the inside feels like an imposter, wearing someone else's skin.

CHAPTER 8

$\mathcal{I}$ walk down the hallway of the family wing, not sure what will be waiting downstairs. Voices from below make me pause on the landing. The sounds of several men laughing, enjoying time together, resonate up the stairs. A loud whistle behind me startles me. Murphy's by the balcony door with his arms crossed, dressed in a black tuxedo. His hair is clean and perfect curls sit on top of his head. Any evidence of our fight with the air elemental is gone and his face is flawless. It's Murphy, but a much cleaner version. I smile.

"Adria, I'm speechless." Red floods my cheeks.

"That's a first for you, isn't it?" I tease.

He laughs, "Actually, yes." He looks at me from head to toe, taking in each detail, and making my stomach knot.

"Quit, you're making me nervous." I feel like a schoolgirl.

He moves toward me and extends his elbow. "Shall we?"

I wrap my arm around his. "Yes, we shall."

We descend the stairs in true pageantry style. Slowly and methodically, making sure to catch everyone's attention on the way down. The room is full of men and women all dressed similarly to us. "Who am I meeting tonight?" I whisper.

"Tonight's for high-ranking lesser elementals. They've gathered to meet the daughter of Llyr."

We're close enough to the bottom that I can see most of the people in the room are male. I only count half the number of women mixed among them as we get closer. "Where are all the women?" I stop moving.

"Not many reside on the island. The ones that do are here."

"You mean all of the high-ranking lessers are men? What kind of messed up elemental shit is that?" My voice is loud enough to be heard from below.

"There are high-ranking women as well, just not on the island," he whispers his response.

I look at the room of men below. "Why is that?" Pulling my arm from his, I cross them in front of me. "Is this some weird bachelor-type thing? Am I supposed to hand out roses at the end of the night?" Murphy laughs and his teeth glisten. "It's not funny. I swear, if you dragged me all the way here to be auctioned off or something worse, I will kick your ass from here back to California. It wouldn't be the first time."

He raises his hands in surrender. "I promise it's nothing like that. They're here to see the daughter of Llyr, nothing more. These men are here to represent the community of elementals. Most of them are from the mainland. Both women and men hold equal rank in the elemental community, however, most of the women have chosen to be further south. It's nothing to do with Llyr or the lessers."

"What's to stop me from killing them all?" I ask, with a mixture of seriousness and humor. "After all, I've spent the last several years of my life training people to kill them."

Murphy's face turns serious. "The lessers you are trained to kill are not the lessers in this castle. There are ranks among elementals and the people in attendance tonight are not the same as the ones we fight." He pauses, trying to read my face. "Promise me you won't do anything rash. These lessers all support Llyr, your father. They want nothing more than for you to be successful."

"Don't worry. I'll behave." I raise my forehead, "I promise. Tonight is the start of something new. However, I won't keep that promise if this turns out to be some kind of bachelor auction thing." I glare a warning at him. His relaxed smile comforts my turmoil. Wrapping my elbow through his again, I smile for my audience as we near the bottom of the steps.

A shorter man with dirty blonde hair is the first to greet me. He only comes to my shoulder, and I feel the need to bend over when he speaks. He takes my hand into his, kissing the top gently. "It's a pleasure to meet you." He looks me over, but it's not like when Murphy did it. This guy makes it creepy. "I'll have to say, you're more lovely than we imagined."

"Thank you. It's a pleasure to meet you," I answer, taking a step back. Murphy, sensing my discomfort, moves between the two of us and introduces me to each attendee as they step forward. He knows I can handle myself, but I'll give him an A for effort.

I catch myself looking around the room for the one who's supposed to be my father. "He's not here," Murphy interrupts. "He won't be back until tomorrow. His flight was delayed because of weather, or he would've made it for dinner."

"Can't the god of water just zap himself here or something?" I try not to sound like an insolent child. Truth is, I'm relieved.

"Yes, but he made a pact years ago to be as human as possible. He's kept that persona for as long as I've known him." He hands me a drink that's a mixture of pink and blue fizz. "Drink this. It'll take the edge off."

"How do I know this isn't some concoction of roofie and yumminess?" I take the drink from him with a smile.

He returns the smile. "First of all, you don't, and second of all, if I wanted to get you in bed, I wouldn't need a drug." His voice is flirtatious and confident, and I like it. I drink the entire glass in one gulp. He's right. After finishing it, I don't care who's staring at me.

Stephen interrupts, "Dinner is served."

The crowd waits for Murphy and me to enter the dining room, before following behind. More food than I've ever seen covers the table in front of us. "I bet you could eat everything on this table," I whisper in Murphy's ear.

"Don't tempt me." He laughs, pulling out my chair.

Thankfully, the guests talk amongst themselves while eating, allowing me to enjoy my meal somewhat peacefully. I watch as Murphy molds to his environment. He's well-spoken, clean cut and charming. His accent even sounds more refined. Quite the opposite of the compound.

Most of the guests are finished eating when the talking begins to diminish. "Tell us, Miss Kane, what are your plans for our island?" The short man I met first, asks from across the table.

Even though I knew tonight's dinner was about the long-lost daughter of Llyr, I somehow fooled myself into thinking I wouldn't be subject to questions. I take a deep breath and channel my inner beauty pageant queen. "Well, sir—"

"Commander O'Brien," Murphy intercedes.

I nod in understanding. "Commander O'Brien, since this is quite literally my first evening on the island, I don't have any long-range plans other than learning my way around this beautiful island and castle. In the future, I would love the opportunity to learn about each of you and your families and how my father and I," those words feel foreign leaving my lips, "can best be of assistance to you."

"Here, here." The crowd erupts, lifting their glasses toward each other.

"Why have you just now come to us? Where has Llyr been hiding you this entire time?" a taller man near the end of the table asks. I grip Murphy's hand silently asking for the right words.

He clears his throat and stands, "Miss Kane has only

just gotten here ladies and gentlemen and is no doubt in need of a rest. I'm sure she'll need a few days to acclimate to her surroundings before answering questions that are better left for Llyr." The men raise their glasses, toasting the invisible air around them.

"Agreed, Mr. McKenzie," Commander O'Brien answers.

The rest of the table mimics him with their proclamations of, "Agreed."

Murphy pulls out my chair and offers his hand. "I think it's time to bid them good night. They've seen enough," he whispers as I stand.

"Please excuse us, ladies and gentlemen. It was a pleasure to meet you all. I look forward to learning more about you and this beautiful island."

Murphy leads me from the room, through open back doors, and out into the night. It isn't until we're away from the castle and out of earshot that I breathe again. "Thank you. I felt like I was going to suffocate in there."

"Aye, me too." He pulls me to a stop. "You were amazing. Don't take this the wrong way, but if someone would've told me you could handle a room full of lesser elementals and keep them at bay a few days ago, I'm not sure I would've believed them."

"No offense taken. The version of me at the compound was the saddest part of me. This version is still in the process of molding to her environment and figuring out what the hell that means."

Murphy takes my hand into his. "I will do everything I can to make sure you don't have to be that person again." His words bring tears to my eyes.

"Dammit Murphy, do you know how long it took me to get this smoky eye look? Don't make me cry off an eyelash."

He laughs, wrapping my arm through his and we walk on the seawall, which is a task in heels. "Remember not too long ago, sitting on a wall similar to this one, overlooking a sea similar to this one, and you telling me about the elementals?"

"Aye. Seems like two years ago." We walk in silence, breathing in the salty air. "I'm so glad to be home." He breathes deeply, filling his lungs. "I hope one day this will feel like home to you too." I don't answer, just enjoy the view. Both of them.

We walk our way around the entire seawall, exploring the small island that's home to the castle. Murphy points to every strange-looking plant, and every ancient stone, telling me their secrets, their stories until we've made a complete circle and end up back where we started. He helps me off the wall and pulls me to his front. Both of us stare at each other awkwardly.

Murphy takes a deep breath and steps back. "You look beautiful tonight."

"Thank you. You clean up pretty good yourself." He wraps my arm through his again, leading me to the open doors of the terrace. The crowd has dispersed, and the two of us make our way up the stairs.

"Six o'clock?" he asks with a smirk.

"Of course. Just because we've changed compounds, doesn't mean we stop training." I turn toward my room. I feel Murphy's eyes on me all the way down the hall and to my door. "You'd better not be looking at my butt," I say, walking into my room. I hear a deep chuckle from the landing.

The balcony doors are still open, welcoming the sweet smell of the ocean below. I quickly change from my gown into sleep shorts and a tank top. They're made from silk and feel like I'm wearing a soft hug. The full moon is high in the sky, shining its reflection on the water below. The image in front of me looks more like a painting than real life.

Propping my feet on the balcony railing, I think how different my life was twenty-four hours ago. I lived in a cinder block prison, with no friends, nothing to call my own, and I was miserable. Tonight, I'm in a lavish castle, the daughter of a god, and have every earthly desire I can imagine at my disposal. I even have a friend, I think. What if this all disappears tomorrow, what if it's some kind of trick and I've fallen right into it?

My childhood taught me to be skeptical. Nothing nice was given without expecting something in return. Is that what's going on here? I look back at the room behind me. Fully furnished and stocked with every item imaginable. Maybe this one time, I need to let my ego rest and enjoy the moment. Not everything good eventually becomes bad.

Chill bumps cover my arms as a cold breeze comes from nowhere. Thankfully, the wind isn't as bad at the castle as it was at the airport, but it's still more than in California. On the corner of the balcony sits a basket of blankets. I pick out the fluffiest one and wrap it around my shoulders. Tears silently stream down my cheeks as I mourn the life I've lived, versus the one I could've lived. I have a choice to make. Do I sit and pity myself for the past, or do I live for the future? The combination of the world's softest blanket and the breeze from the sea sends me into a world of dreams.

I open my eyes and I'm surprised to see Hannah sitting next to me, wrapped in a similar blanket. Her hair is styled, and her make-up is flawless. She looks like she attended the dinner party with me. "Hannah, what are you doing here? Is this real or a dream?"

"Yes," she answers, stretching her legs out to reach the railing.

I laugh at her attempt. "You're going to have to grow a few feet for that."

"Shut up," she says, with a smile. "You and your spider monkey legs suck." I watch as she scoots her chair forward, putting her a few inches in front of me, but able to reach the ledge. "There, that's better." Her tiny feet still barely reach their destination. "This is beautiful." She sighs.

"That it is," I echo. "You know how much I miss you?"

"Yep, I'm pretty unforgettable. That's why I'm here. You just can't let me go, can you?" She smiles. "I may be gone from this world, but that doesn't mean I'm going to stop bossing you around."

"I'm dreaming, aren't I?" My voice is soft.

Hannah looks around the balcony. "Who knows? But this is real, right? 'Cause I'm digging this view." She motions at our surroundings.

My forehead wrinkles. "Unless I've been dreaming for twenty-four hours straight, this is real."

We both stare into the shadows of the ocean. "You deserve this." I don't respond. "Adria, look at me." Reluctantly, I turn my head. "This is where you belong. You deserve this. It doesn't matter what your past holds, this is where the universe has decided to put you. You deserve every bit of this and more. Don't let the bitterness of your past ruin your future." I close my eyes as she speaks.

"What if he doesn't like me?" My words are barely louder than a whisper.

"Who? Murphy?" she huffs. "He *was* staring at your butt earlier. I don't blame him, it was smokin' in that dress."

A loud laugh escapes my lips. "No, Llyr. What if I'm not what he's expecting, not what he wants? What if he's... disappointed?"

Her tone changes to serious as she takes her feet off the railing and turns toward me. "He's loved you since before you were born. Your past isn't going to change that. First Elemental or not, he's your father, and with that title comes unconditional love. How could he ever be disappointed in you?" Tears stream down my cheeks now as I sit quietly, relaxing in the chair.

"I feel like a freak," I answer. "I'm the love child of a human and an ancient god. What does that make me?"

Hannah's petite hand caresses my cheek. "It makes you pretty special."

A vibration on my wrist startles me. I open my eyes to the sun rising over the horizon. I put my new watch on last night and set an alarm for five-thirty. The chair where Hannah sat is empty. "I love you Hannah and I'm sorry," I say to the emptiness.

A crow lands on the railing, cawing loudly. The caws remind me of Hannah, telling me to get my ass up and out to train. "Okay, okay. I'm going."

I find a pair of leggings and a matching tank top in the closet. Out of the countless pairs of sneakers, I choose some that match the pink leggings. I take time to brush my hair and braid it before putting it in a bun. Normally, my bun looks like a cinnamon roll, today, I make a fancier version.

Walking into the hallway, I'm not surprised to see Murphy waiting on the landing. He's dressed for a run, but like me, wearing nicer clothes than at the compound. "Morning sunshine," he says, handing me a cup of something steamy.

"Ooo, this is a steamy cup of deliciousness." I take a small sip. Chocolate, vanilla, coffee, and something that tastes like cream greet my tongue. "Oh, my gods. What is this?"

"Vanilla bean latte with chocolate sprinkles."

"Is there a Starbucks on the island?"

He smiles. "No, but there's a 'Murphy's Coffee and More' in my room."

"*You* made this?" I take faster sips.

"Aye."

Half of the cup is empty by the time we reach the bottom of the stairs. "So, do I put my orders in at night, or... how does this work?"

He laughs but doesn't answer. The cup is empty by the time we enter the courtyard. That was the best coffee I've ever had. I hope he knows I'm serious. He can't tease me with the world's best coffee and not provide it daily.

"I thought I'd introduce you to more of the island with a run." He takes the empty cup away, throwing it in the bin, as he called it.

"I did some research this morning. The main island is over seventy-five miles of land. I don't think I'm quite up for that." Pulling my arms in front, I begin stretching.

"Aye, me either. How about we just explore the village and port area?" His smile is wide.

"It's a plan," I squat down, stretching out my knees. "You're staring at my butt again."

Murphy doesn't answer, just starts running.

CHAPTER 9

e run in silence for a while, and just like before, neither of us gets winded. The island is breathtakingly beautiful. Murphy takes me on several back roads that couldn't be seen on our drive in. The homes are a mixture of medieval, country, and modern. "Does the island have trouble making a decision on style, or are some of these as old as they look?"

"That's a good question." He smirks. "The island has been inhabited by humans for over eight thousand years, but elementals have been here since before time. Over the years since, the island has been in the hands of the Irish, Norseman, Scottish, English, and Dutch, not necessarily in that order. In my opinion, the island has a Celtic feel."

"That's why the architecture is so diverse, it makes sense. Who's the governing body now?" My new watch vibrates on my wrist. A quick glance tells me it's proud of me for exercising and I earned an award. Yay, me!

"Do you remember who your father is? Unofficially,

he's in charge and has been since before humans were here. Officially, the people who live here are citizens of the United Kingdom and have all of the privileges that come with it." He jogs off the sidewalk, taking us down the main road.

Most of the village streets and main buildings are made of stone, impenetrable for earth elementals. Several buildings not made of stone have protective sigils carved into them or hung on their doorways. "Sophie told me most of the humans that live here don't know who or what Llyr is, but I see protection sigils all around the island. How can they not know?"

"Most people don't see what's right in front of their faces. Or if they do see it, they ignore it. It's either a gift or a curse of humanity. I've yet to decide." Not so long ago, I was one of those naïve, unsuspecting humans. "Llyr doesn't hide his presence, as evident with the car that picked us up at the airport, but he hides under the pretense of being descended from the oldest inhabiting family on the island. His ancestors can be traced back to 2,000 B.C." He laughs. "Ancestors my arse. It was him the entire time."

"Murphy?" I ask, slowing my pace.

"Hmm?" He matches me.

"If Llyr's been here since the beginning of time, does that mean I have siblings? Surely my mother wasn't the only human he ever got frisky with." My lip curls in disgust.

"That, lass, is a question for Llyr. I don't have an answer for that one. I can tell you that a child between a human and god is forbidden." We slow to a stop.

"You're saying I'm the product of something that's forbidden?" I'm not sure why that surprises me.

"That seems a bit harsh." He faces me.

"Why would it be forbidden?" I ask, stretching my hamstring.

"I don't know. It's just something that's always been." He copies my movement, stretching beside me.

Hearing I'm the product of a forbidden act brings up feelings I'm not prepared to deal with right at the moment. Feelings that remind me of my childhood. I brush them aside and take a deep breath.

"Ready to head back?" He walks beside me. I nod.

A quaint shop in front of us catches my eye. Like most, the building is built from stacked stone. Small bunches of herbs are hanging upside down from each of the windows. The smell of freshly baked bread hits me like a load of bricks as we pass. A sign above the door reads, *A Little Slice of Heaven*. I don't bother to ask, just head inside. He follows me. The glass case is full of muffins, every flavor of pastry known to man, and freshly baked rolls, bread, and bagels on every tray. The smell is heavenly.

"Good morning," an older woman greets us with a smile. Her accent is similar to Murphy's, with a more British feel to it. "Would you care for a slice of bread?" she opens the case, releasing the smell into the world.

My eyes grow huge. "Yes, please!"

"Two then?" I look at Murphy with questioning eyes. He nods. "Would you like some fresh butter on top? Just churned yesterday."

Oh, my gods. My mouth salivates at the thought. "Yes,

please." She hands us the slices, still showing the warmest smile I've seen for a while.

"Charge it to Dr. Smith?" she asks.

My forehead wrinkles in confusion. "Yes, thank you," Murphy answers, ushering me toward the door. "I'll tell you later," he whispers, on the way out.

Once outside I can't stop a laugh from bubbling up. "I'm assuming Llyr is Dr. Smith. Llyr Smith? How original is that?"

Murphy smiles beside me. "Close. He goes by Dr. Kyler Smith."

I stop, giving him my signature 'what the hell' face. "Kyler, I like. It's creative, and although it gives a first grader who eats glue and boogers regularly vibe, it works. But Smith? He chose the most common name on earth as a surname."

"Aye, easier to blend in that way."

I take a bite of the bread. My mouth has a tiny orgasm and I fight the urge to moan. "This is amazing. No wonder Llyr wants to live here. This beats compound food by a landslide."

We walk to the town square where a large fountain sits in the middle. I've finished my bread and want more as Murphy leads us to a park bench. I watch as humans pass, mostly on foot, a few on bicycles. "The humans that live here are protected by Llyr and his lessers. They're safe. They don't question who or what he is because they're smart enough not to." He points to a small bookstore across the street from the bench. "See that store?" I nod. "That store is owned by my family and has been for years."

"Sophie mentioned that on the plane. Is she there?" I ask, excitedly.

"I doubt it. Since she's started working for Llyr, she rarely gets a chance to stay overnight." My excitement flees.

"The island is beautiful. I understand why everyone seems so protective of it."

"It's your home too, Adria. You belong here." He slides his hand next to mine on the bench. Not close enough to touch, but close enough his energy pulses toward me.

"I never had a home longer than six months growing up. I never belonged anywhere." His hand slides over the top of mine.

"Now you do." I nod in response. Overcome with emotion, I'm unable to speak. We sit, our hands touching for several minutes, neither moving until the silence becomes awkward. I reluctantly stand, throwing my bread wrapper in a nearby trash can.

"How far are we from the castle?" I stretch out again.

"Just a few kilometers." He mimics my movements.

I stare at him dumbfounded. "How many football fields would that be?"

He returns the stare. "You Americans will do everything you can to avoid using the metric system."

I laugh, "Yep!"

"About two miles. Does that help?" His voice is riddled with sarcasm.

"Actually, it does. Thank you." I begin jogging past the fountain.

He joins me quickly. "If you're going this way, you might want to add on several more football fields."

I resist the urge to punch him in the shoulder. "Then, by all means, lead me the correct way, kind sir." He turns, jogging in the complete opposite direction.

The tops of the castle come into view as we approach the bridge. "The castle is beautiful."

"Aye, it is. The Norse built it around the tenth century."

"Vikings built the place where I slept last night?" I've always loved history.

"Aye. It's changed a lot since then. But she still has the same bones."

We cross over the bridge that reminds me of a medieval moat into the main grounds. An emerald green Rolls Royce Phantom sits in the driveway. Murphy stops, pulling me with him.

"What?" I ask, confused. He nods to the car.

"That's Llyr's car." My stomach drops. We look around for any signs of life, finding none.

"Why am I so nervous?" I run my hands down my sides, making sure my clothes are in place and neat.

He grabs my elbows and faces me toward him. "You look beautiful. He's going to love you, how could he not?"

Damn right! I take a deep breath. "Okay, let's do this. Do you think he's inside?"

"Most likely. Probably in meetings." He motions me up the stairs, waiting at the bottom.

I turn around confused. "Oh, hell no. You're not staying out here. I'm not doing this alone."

"Adria, it'd be better for me to wait here." He looks anxious.

My arms cross in rebellion. "Then I'm not going in. You're either with me, or I'll meet him later." He sighs, realizing there's no escape and follows me up the stairs.

The double doors open to the vast foyer. Voices ring from the nearby study. Stephen appears out of nowhere saying, "There you are Miss. I'll let him know you're here." Butterflies take flight.

"Shouldn't I go change or fix my hair or..."

"Adria?" a deep voice interrupts.

A man equal to Murphy in height enters the foyer. His energy rushes me like a linebacker during the Superbowl. His smile is warm and covers his handsome face. He looks to be in his early forties, with no wrinkles or blemishes. High cheekbones accentuate his narrow face and chiseled jawline. His blonde hair shows no signs of gray and is styled as if he stepped out of a magazine. He's wearing skinny jeans with holes in the knees and a fitted t-shirt showing off muscles similar to Murphy's.

He stops several feet from me. "You look just like her," his voice cracks.

My forehead wrinkles in confusion. "Who?"

"Claire, your mother." Hearing those words knocks me back a step. Murphy senses my unsteadiness, and moves behind me, sliding his hand around my elbow.

"Murphy, thank you for finding her. You may go." Llyr dismisses him in an instant and my heart sinks. My eyes plead for him to stay.

"I'll be in my room if you need me." He smiles,

squeezes my elbow, and leaves me alone with the god of water.

Llyr's smile is infectious, and I return it without intention. He wraps his arm around my shoulder. "Come. Let's talk." He leads me into the room he came from.

Standing by the window is a man just as tall as Llyr. He turns with a smile. His hair mirrors the color of Murphy's, but instead of curls, it's shoulder-length and straight. His eyes are the color of amber. "Adria, this is my assistant, Earwyn."

Earwyn walks toward me with a sideways grin. "Good to meet you. I've heard much about you." His accent sounds like he could be from Alabama, or possibly Georgia.

"You're American?" I ask, surprised.

"I am. Tennessee's where I call home originally. Now I have the pleasure of living on this beautiful island, with these good folks." He sticks his large hand in my direction. I shake it, not sure what else to do.

"Adria Kane," I answer. "What have you heard about me?"

"I'm not sure I know what you mean?"

"You said you've heard much about me. From who? Murphy's the only one I know, and you just got here." I stare into amber-colored eyes, refusing to back down.

He lets out an uneasy laugh. "Nothing specific. It's just something I say when I meet someone new. Sorry to make it awkward." He pulls his hand away. "She's your kid all right." He turns to Llyr.

"Adria, please sit down. We have much to talk about." Llyr motions to a ridiculously soft-looking couch against the wall. I expect him to sit behind his desk, but to my surprise, he sits at the other end of the couch. "I'm so sorry my plane was delayed in Asia. With all the issues there, I wasn't able to get away any faster. I apologize for not being here when you arrived."

I don't know what to say, so I choose silence.

Llyr continues, "Words can't express how happy I am to have finally found you."

I ignore the sting his words cause. Has he been looking for me? I wasn't that hard to find. Instead of responding, I focus on keeping my face void of emotion.

"I do hope you found your room acceptable." He crosses his legs in front of him.

"It's more than I ever imagined. Thank you." Our interaction feels formal and stiff.

He motions to Earwyn. "I've asked Earwyn to oversee your training while here at the compound." At the mention of his name, Earwyn moves toward us.

"Oh, no, that won't be necessary," I interrupt. "I'm perfectly able to keep up my training on my own."

"Then I'll let you train me," Earwyn adds with an awkward laugh. His energy is dark and heavy, and I don't like it. I turn back to Llyr.

"I'd like to keep working with Murphy. I know he wasn't at the compound to train with me, but we worked well together." Earwyn laughs a second time, taking a sip from his brandy glass.

"Of course," Llyr answers. "I didn't mean to imply you weren't capable." I study the man who's supposed to be my father. I don't know what I was expecting when we met, but this is not it. Maybe I've read too many fantasy books. If this *was* a book, I would've run into his arms as he wrapped me in a fatherly embrace that instantly bonded us through the tendrils of time we'd missed. So far, this has been awkward and uneventful.

"Can I propose a toast to the returned prodigal daughter?" Earwyn raises his glass in the air. Prodigal daughter? Does he think I left to go sow my oats? I watch as he and Llyr clink their glasses together.

"It's wonderful to have you home," Llyr says. His energy is pure, and his words are true. Even still, emotions sit on the brink of my subconscious. "After all these years, we finally found each other again."

Anger builds inside. He's the damn god of water with an entire army at his command, yet a young girl in the largest foster care system in America can't be found. Llyr senses my energy shift and stands.

"I know what you're thinking." He moves toward the bar across the room. "You're thinking the same thing I've thought for years, how is the god of the sea so incapable?" He pours himself another brandy. "Care for a drink?" he holds an empty glass in the air. I shake my head. He sighs before continuing. "The thoughts you're thinking right now are nothing more than I've thought myself."

Anger explodes from the depths of my soul. Anger for the loss of my childhood, for the hell I endured, and for this man standing in front of me. "You're nothing like me and you have *no* idea what I've been through."

Llyr sets the glass of brandy back on the bar. "You're right, I don't. For that, I'm truly sorry." He sighs, sitting on the arm of the couch. "I'm not sure what all Murphy's told you..."

I interrupt, "He told me you and my mother hid me away for my *safety*."

He looks down at an invisible memory. "She was amazing, your mother."

"I wouldn't know, would I?" My words are laced with venom.

Llyr pauses, letting my words sink in. "I've been looking for you since, well, since I learned of her death. The two of us agreed, for your safety, she would raise you away from elementals, away from the dangers that this world holds, and away from me. I gave her enough money that the two of you would never want for anything and she left."

Dammit, I will not cry. I stare at a dark spot on the ornate wooden wall trying to distract myself from the tears.

He continues, "I thought she was alive and raising you in the safety of mundane life. I took peace in that. When I found out she was... gone, I set out to find you. Part of our agreement when she left was to change your name, your birth certificate, and anything that could tie you to me." He runs a hand through his hair. "Clues poured in for years, rumors of what could've been you, but nothing ever panned out, until now."

Anger still boils beneath my skin. "Whatever plan you and the woman you call my mother hashed out sucked. I wasn't raised in safety, in fact, I wasn't raised by anyone. I was passed around from foster home to foster home, never having my own bed or my own room. Going days without a solid meal, eating from trash cans. Being treated like an object, rather than a person. If I am your daughter, the daughter of the god of water, how the hell could you let me live like that? Nothing you thought I would face here can compare to what I lived through. How can a freaking god not have enough power to find his own daughter?" I stand in anger.

He stands too. "Adria, nothing I say or do will make your past any easier. I do know if you stayed here with me, not just your mother would be gone. You would be too. My enemies have tried every method to hurt me over the millennia. It was a risk, but I'd do it again."

His words sting. He'd put me through all of that again. I cross my arms in rebellion. "Yes, you had a horrible childhood, but you're alive. You're here now, with me, and all of this is yours." He motions around him. "You will never want for anything again. I'll make sure of that. You've grown into a strong, capable woman who I'm proud to call my daughter." I can't fight the tears any longer. "Adria, a million apologies won't make up for the past, but we can have a future together. The kind of future your mother and I dreamed of for you." His voice is soft and sincere. "I'm here for you. You are my first priority in everything I do." He steps toward me. I step back.

"I'm done talking." I don't want to hear any more of this bullshit. I'm about an inch away from flooding the entire castle.

"Of course." His voice is full of emotion.

I don't say anything, just leave and escape up the stairs to my room. Murphy's sitting on a puffy couch on the landing. "Are you okay?" he jumps to his feet as soon as I hit the top step.

My words don't work. I nod, and fall into his arms, laying my head on his chest. He wraps his arms around me, offering comfort. "I'm sorry. He can be a bit much."

"I carry a lot of baggage," I whisper.

"Don't we all?" He laughs. "Come on, I'll walk you to your room. Don't tell Stephen." He keeps an arm over my shoulder and the two of us walk slowly down the long hallway.

He opens the door to the room of my dreams. "This is nooiiccceee," he says, mimicking a viral video. He's trying to lighten the mood and I'm grateful. "I'm going to send a complaint to Stephen first thing in the morning. This is why I'm not allowed in here. It makes my room look like a cheap motel." He walks around touching all of my new electronic devices and picks up the new laptop, opening and closing it repeatedly. "Look at that, the top isn't coming off."

"Shut up." I take it from his hands. "You keep doing that and it *will* come off." He walks out on the balcony, breathing in the fresh sea air. "I need a shower. Will you stay here while I jump in real quick? I don't want to be alone right now." After the explosion of emotion, I just experienced, being alone is the last thing I need.

"Aye." He sits in Hannah's chair. "I guess I can suffer with this view for the cause."

I take the shortest shower of my life and throw on a clean pair of leggings and an oversized sweatshirt. True to his word, Murphy's suffering, looking over the sea. I sit beside him. "You smell like flowers and pine." He sniffs the air.

"Thank you?" I'm not sure if that's a compliment, but

I treat it as one. "Thanks for staying. That got a little intense downstairs."

He huffs a laugh. "Llyr's had a lot of time to perfect his intensity."

"I guess. Maybe it's just me. I've never had a family, never been more than a monthly check my entire life. To come here and be given all of this, it's a bit overwhelming." I look around me. "Do I even deserve this?"

Murphy turns quickly. "You deserve every bit of this and more. No child deserves not to feel love or not to have a warm bed to sleep in and a belly full of food. Aye, this is overwhelming, but never question whether you deserve it. You're more deserving than most."

"See, this is why you're growing on me. Despite your monstrous size, you're a good guy." He laughs at my admission.

"I'm growing on you, huh?" He crosses his long legs at the ankle. "I tend to do that. As far as size, elemental blood makes us grow a bit larger than humans. Have you not noticed you're a rather tall drink of water yourself?"

I never put the puzzle pieces together. "Seriously? That's why everyone here is so tall. Well, except for that little man, O'Brien."

"Aye." He laughs. "It's in the blood. O'Brien's must have skipped a generation."

Murphy doesn't push me to speak, instead, he just sits with me and I'm grateful. His energy is calming, and I don't feel the need to keep a conversation going. We sit in the same energy until the sun begins setting over the horizon. "Where did the day go?"

"Where our legs are long, the days are short." He smirks.

"No... for real?"

He laughs loudly. "I'm lying, lass, however, days are a wee bit shorter up here." I hit his shoulder playfully. He winces in pretend pain.

"I don't want to go back down there tonight," I announce after several more minutes of silence.

"Aye, I'll stay with you, if you're okay with that." He scoots his chair closer to mine.

"It should be close to dinner time. Won't you starve from not eating?"

"That's a strong possibility." He wraps a blanket around my shoulders.

We sit side by side, neither speaking as the moon rises high in the sky. Soft snores interrupt the quiet. Murphy's asleep. I cover him with a matching blanket and lay my head on his shoulder.

Several hours later I wake up, no longer outside but tucked under the covers of my bed with Murphy sitting in a chair next to the bed, sound asleep.

I watch him sleep for a few minutes and a warm vibration forms in the pit of my stomach. He really is a good guy.

CHAPTER 10

*M*orning comes much too early. Murphy's chair is empty, meaning sometime during the night, he returned to his room. I get dressed in one of the many matching leggings and tank top outfits, match my running shoes to the outfit, and set out for a run. I can't help but smile when I see Murphy standing on the landing with a cup of what I hope is his delicious coffee.

"Is this from 'Murphy's Coffee and More'?" I take the cup from him.

"Aye, 'tis. Your internet order was received last evening right before closing." I take a huge gulp, it's even better than yesterday.

"I seriously think you've missed your calling. If this hybrid thing doesn't work out, you need to open your own shop. This coffee *grounds* me." I raise an eyebrow at him.

"Ah, I see what you did there." He smiles. "That made

me laugh a *latte*." I almost spit the coffee out in response. "Ready?"

"Yes, I need a run." We get to the bottom of the stairs when Earwyn steps out of the study.

"Adria, Murphy." He nods toward us. "I was just about to go for a run. Care to join me?"

Is it selfish to say no? I don't want him to join us. Running is a me and Murphy thing. "We were just about to do the same thing," Murphy answers.

"Well, we'll just all go together then." Earwyn pats Murphy on the back. Both men are the same height, and their hair is so close in color, it could be dyed from the same box.

The three of us run several miles. Unlike yesterday, the energy is heavy. The two men don't like each other, and that becomes more obvious the further we go. They seem to compete for my attention, each trying to outwit the other on facts about the island, about elementals, and their history. Our jog has turned into a pissing contest and I'm getting tired of being the prize. I fall back, letting them lead the way while taking turns telling me every mundane detail of every street, building, and blade of grass we pass. They're so busy competing for who has the most knowledge, they don't notice when I turn in the opposite direction.

The castle is to my left. As long as I keep it in sight, I'll be fine. The further I go, the houses become spread out, until there's only one or two every half mile or so. The home styles this far out have become mostly thatch-roof homes, reminding me of pictures I've seen of medieval England. The sound of the sea rushing against the cliff banks helps take away any anxiety about meeting Llyr. Several cars have passed, but no one has stopped or hit me. I laugh out loud at the thought.

The ground becomes less grassy and rockier the further away from the village I get. The narrow road has changed from pavement to gravel, and the pebbles don't feel great on the bottom of my feet. I leave the path and head to the cliff. Below, white waves crash against the mountain in a show of force. Choosing a large boulder, I climb to the top and let the sounds lull me into an almost trance.

"Am I his daughter?" I whisper to the sea.

The waves continue pounding the rocks, but don't respond. The peak of the highest part of the castle is barely visible from where I sit. Last night's conversation about my mother, about my life, plays on repeat in my head. There's no denying I have a connection with him, I felt it instantly. Again, I ask. "Am I his daughter?"

The waves stop crashing and what was a wild, thunderous sound now goes silent. "My queen," the sea whispers. "Search your heart, you know the truth." Holy shit! I stand, almost falling off the boulder. Did I imagine that? Did the sea just answer me?

As quickly as they stopped, the waves return to their assault on the rocks below. I do know. Why else would I have flown across the world with a man I barely met to meet another man I've never met? Llyr's my father, it's time to accept it. Whether a curse or blessing, the jury's still out.

"Adria!" a deep voice calls behind me. "We lost you!" I

look back to the road to see Murphy and Earwyn jogging toward me.

"Oh, yaaaay, you found me." My voice oozes sarcasm. Neither man seems to notice.

"Are you okay?" Earwyn asks.

I stand up, brushing the sand from my legs. "I'm fine. I just got tired of the two of you and your pissing contest." I jump off the boulder and start jogging back the way I came.

"What pissing contest? I haven't done that since I was a kid." Murphy's voice sounds confused.

"She means the two of us were competing for her attention," Earwyn fills in the blanks. "It's American slang."

"Ah. I would've won the other," Murphy says, making me laugh. Thankfully, neither speak and I lead them back to the castle grounds.

"Llyr will want you to join him for lunch," Earwyn announces, looking at his watch. "Lunch is served at noon." He walks into the main entrance, leaving Murphy and me alone.

He runs a hand through his messy curls. "I'm sorry about earlier. Earwyn and I aren't great together. Probably because we're family."

I look up confused. "He's your family?"

"Aye, cousin. Our fathers were brothers."

"That explains the hair." Stretching out my hamstring, I lift my leg high in the back.

"Is his mother an elemental too?"

His eyes get big. "Aye, a fire elemental. His father

moved to America after he was born, so we didn't meet until a few years ago."

"Wait. Did you say Earwyn's mother was a fire elemental?"

"Aye, that's one reason I don't like the bastard. I hate the fire ones." I stare at him in disbelief.

"Am I the only one that sees an issue with that?" My eyes are as big as saucers. "He's the assistant for the god of the sea, yet his mother is a fire lesser? Isn't that a conflict of interest?"

Murphy huffs in agreement. "When it comes to that situation, I find it better to mind my own business. He's family, but that doesn't mean I have to like him."

"What's the other reason?"

He lowers into a hamstring stretch. "He's an arse."

I laugh out loud. "Your family likes living on the edge, don't they?" He laughs as the two of us enter the castle. "I'll see you at lunch," I say as we separate on the landing.

"I won't be at lunch. That invitation was for you alone."

"I'm the daughter of the god of water. I'll say who can or can't come to lunch with me. I'll be damned if I'm going to sit across the table from him without you there. You're coming. End of discussion." I turn, walking into my room without giving him a chance to argue.

I take a hot shower, clearing any remaining sand and dirt from the run. Taking a minute to ramble through the closet, I find an adorable, shorts-length romper. Blue vertical stripes run in contrast to the turquoise fabric. The colors remind me of the sea, most likely on purpose. A pair of brown, strapless sandals complete the ensemble.

I dry my hair, styling it similar to the beachy curls I did the first night here. Two YouTube videos later and I'm wearing "light, everyday make-up". At least that's what I searched for. One look in the mirror tells me I've accomplished the simple, yet stylish look I was aiming for.

A soft knock on my door interrupts my AC/DC music fest. "Yes?"

"'Tis me. I'm sorry to bother you." I open the door to see Murphy standing there. He's dressed in khaki pants and a blue button-down shirt, his hair controlled and soft.

"You're not interrupting me. I was just about to head down. Wanna walk together?"

"That's what I came to tell you. I will not be welcomed at lunch." Murphy looks awkward.

"That's ridiculous," I answer, thinking he's teasing me.

"No, it's not. Llyr and I don't see things... eye to eye. He allows me to live here, but that's where our relationship ends."

"Is that why Stephen said you weren't allowed in my wing?" I remember the first night we arrived.

"Aye."

My hand props on my hip. "That's just dumb. Whatever happened between the two of you is in the past. I'm here and I want you with me."

His smile warms my heart. "Llyr isn't going to feel the same."

"Consider this my first act of rebellion. I don't give a damn how he feels. You're my only friend and I won't leave you to eat alone while I'm stuck in there with your cousin and my... my father, whom I barely know." I wrap my arm through his and pull him down the hall. He doesn't object but is moving slower than normal.

We enter the dining room where Llyr and Earwyn are waiting. "Adria, it's good to see you." He looks at Murphy and nods.

"I hope you don't mind, I asked Murphy to join us." The tension in the room is palpable and it's not coming from me.

Llyr smiles weakly. "Of course." He motions to two empty seats at the table. "Earwyn was telling me about your run this morning."

It's clear Llyr is trying to make small talk and I owe it to him to try and not be a complete brat. Instead of the typical sarcastic answer that would normally pop from my mouth, I decide to be more open-minded today. I smile and answer, "The island is beautiful. I could run the same path every day and never get bored."

"I agree. Except for the running part." He laughs, easing the tension. His energy is soft and loving. "I've been to every nook and cranny on this planet, but this is where I call home."

Thankfully, the conversation stays light as the history of the island, the history of the castle, and the history of elementals are spoken about. Stephen serves lunch, which consists of soup and sandwiches. Dipping my grilled cheese sandwich into the bowl of broccoli and cheese soup has been something I've done since I remember eating. Llyr mimics my movement without noticing I'd done the same thing. "You dip your sandwich into your soup?" I ask.

"Of course. How else can you eat grilled cheese and soup?"

"That's what I'm saying. There is no other way." He smiles warmly.

"In all the years I've hunted elementals, I've never seen one eat human food." I think back to the fire elemental at the compound. She never ate food, anyway.

He sits back, patting his invisible stomach. "Lower lesser elementals can eat, but most choose not to. High-level elementals will choose to eat on occasion and most First Elementals don't eat at all, but I'm different. I like to be as close to humans as possible, therefore, I relish a good meal every now and then. Especially one that's not seafood.

"I thought this afternoon, we could spend some time together. There are things we need to talk about, things I need to explain." Just when the tension was melting, dread fills me at the thought. I nod in agreement.

"How about two o'clock?" Earwyn intercedes.

Llyr turns to his assistant. "Earwyn, this will be a conversation between me and my daughter, alone."

Earwyn looks slightly offended. "Of course." He bows his head. "If you'll excuse me, there are some matters I need to attend to." He looks at his cousin. "Murphy, care to join me?"

Murphy's face says he does not care to join him, but he stands anyway, following his cousin-twin out of the room.

"Please," Llyr holds an arm out for me, motioning me to a large sitting room, one I haven't had the opportunity to explore yet. I choose the softest chair in the room. It's at this moment I realize I have an obsession with soft things. He sits in a chair that mirrors mine, both facing a huge fireplace. The room is decorated in dark mahogany wood. Floor-to-ceiling windows line the wall opposite to where we sit, flooding the room with light. The combination of warm wood, light streaming in from outside, and ornate, soft furniture makes the room feel comfortable and inviting.

"I've done some thinking about our conversation last night." He pauses.

"I'm sorry for the way I acted."

He raises his hands. "No, please don't apologize. It's me who owes you an apology. You have every right to be angry. Hell, I'd be angry too. What you went through, what I could've stopped, I get it." His calm energy turns nervous. "I see now that what your mother and I thought we were doing to save your life, was wrong. At the time, it seemed like the only answer." I don't speak, just stare into the empty fireplace.

"She was the most beautiful thing I'd ever met. She was smart, fierce, and strong. In all the years I've lived on this planet, I'd never met anyone like her. Before her, humans were nothing more than weaklings, a thorn in my side. Clogging up my oceans with trash, killing the animals that take refuge in it. They were a nuisance." He pauses in thought. "We met when she was around your age. I was on a business trip to Los Angeles, and she was a server working the convention I was attending. She was beautiful, but there was something else about her that I sensed instantly."

"Wait, you go to conventions?" He smiles at my question.

"I tell you about your mother, and you're stuck on the fact that I go to conventions." He laughs. "You remind me so much of her. Even in your mannerisms." He smiles at me. "She would sit in that same chair, with her legs curled underneath her, listening to me drone on about something she cared nothing about." He pauses. "It's the same way you're sitting now." Suddenly self-conscious, I fight the urge to lower my legs. "And to answer your question, yes, I do go to conventions. Dr. Kyler Smith is well known in many organizations having to do with the preservation of the oceans."

"What was different about her?"

"Hmm?" he raises his eyebrows.

"You said you sensed something about her when you met." He sighs and sits back in the chair.

"Elementals can sense other elementals instantly. I'm sure Murphy mentioned that to you." I nod in agreement. "It's what I sensed in her."

I lower my legs, scooting to the front of my chair. "My mother was a hybrid?"

He waits before answering. "She was more than that." I sit impatiently waiting for more. "Originally, I assumed she was an offspring of a lesser of some sort. I made a point of sitting near her during the convention, making sure she was the one who served the tables where I sat. Nothing I did to gain her attention worked. She did her job and ignored everyone around her."

That's something we have in common. I'm the master of ignoring the world. "After several days of trying, I convinced her to let me buy her a drink at the hotel bar. We hit it off instantly. She had a power to her that drew me in." I don't rush him to continue. "It took many attempts and a lot of convincing, but she eventually opened up to me, and over time we fell in love.

"It wasn't until several years later that we discovered who she truly was. She lived here, at the castle. In fact, she's the one who decorated this room." He looks around, gently rubbing the arm of the chair. "We were happy. She knew the truth about me and was okay with the lifestyle." He stands, rubbing his hand along a nearby table. "Love between a First and a human is something that's just not done. The child that can occur is something that's forbidden."

"Murphy mentioned the forbidden child part," I whisper. I can tell there's more to the reason, but don't push for an answer.

"Most hybrids don't have the powers of their elemental parent. They retain certain aspects, but no real power over the element itself. The human genes overpower them, putting them in sort of a dormancy. She grew up not knowing anything about her family or her heritage."

"That sounds familiar," I interrupt him. He physically winces, and I feel guilty for the slash.

"During the great battle, Shu sided with me to fight the lessers that tried to destroy the world."

"Shu, the god of air?" Llyr nods. "Murphy told me about that too. Shu sided with you over earth and fire."

"Yes. We were good friends once."

"What happened?"

"Each of the elements has sought to gain control over others in the years since. Shu and I parted ways thousands of years ago over nothing in particular. It was his lessers that attacked that day." He pauses at the memory. "They flew from the sky, landing in the middle of the village and in the castle courtyard. I was on the island fighting the few who landed there, and Claire was here alone. By the time I made it back, two lessers had her in the courtyard and were trying to carry her away. She produced a wall of wind from her hands, pushing the lessers back to the edge of the seawall. They were terrified and knew immediately who and what she was. The two of them bowed, prostrate to the ground in front of her, begging her for forgiveness. In that instant, I knew what was different about her. She wasn't a hybrid at all, she was the child of a First."

"Shu?" I whisper, already knowing the answer.

He nods. "There was no other answer. I was in love with the daughter of a First."

"Did he know?" I fight tears.

He shakes his head. "Not that day. I killed the lessers so they couldn't share their findings."

"My mother was the daughter of the god of air and I'm the daughter of the god of water. What does that make me?"

"Something more powerful than any of us, than any of the Firsts."

I sit dumbfounded. "That's why you sent me away." Tears fall down my cheeks.

"Yes," he whispers. "If Shu were to discover you exist, I don't know what he'd do."

CHAPTER 11

The sun beams through the open balcony doors, waking me. After my conversation with Llyr yesterday, I hid in my room for the rest of the day. I didn't even set my alarm this morning. My mind is a mess of emotions and I'd make horrible company.

Crawling out of the soft bed, I hear a knock on my door. "Murphy, I don't feel like company right now. I'll find you later."

"It's Stephen, miss. Your father had to leave on business this morning. He asked me to wake you if you slept past ten o'clock."

Ten o'clock? What the hell? I haven't slept past six o'clock in years. I look at my watch to confirm he's not making the time up. "I'm up. Thank you, Stephen."

"He left word for you to train with Earwyn and Murphy today. They're waiting downstairs."

I roll my eyes in response. "Tell them unless they have coffee and doughnuts, I'm not interested."

"I believe I saw something resembling coffee in Mr. McKenzie's hand."

I sigh loudly, making sure it can be heard through the door. "I'm coming."

"Yes, miss. I'll let them know."

"Stephen?" I yell through the door.

"Miss?"

"Thank you. I know it was you who picked out all of these clothes. They're perfect."

He's silent for a moment. "You're welcome, miss." The fading crescendo of footsteps tells me he's left.

I pick out matching leggings, a tank top, and shoes, pull my hair into a messy bun and head down the stairs. Murphy's smiling, and Earwyn looks annoyed that he's had to wait on me.

"Good morning, sunshine," Murphy lightens the mood. He holds the coffee out, luring me forward.

"I feel like this is some sort of a trap." I smile, taking the coffee.

"Ah, you got me. I'm luring you to my secret lair using nothing but my coffee and charm."

I laugh. "Your skills need tweaking. This is a weak way to kidnap someone."

"Noted. Next time I'll add a muffin to the offering." I raise my eyebrows in agreement.

Earwyn's not impressed with our banter. "Shall we?" His voice void of emotion.

The three of us walk into the open courtyard. The story Llyr told me of Claire using the power of air to repel the two lessers comes to mind. It happened right here, in the same courtyard we're about to train in. I want to tell

Murphy everything, but not when Earwyn's around. I don't like his vibe.

"Llyr asked me to work with you on defensive moves." Earwyn leads us to an obstacle course he's set up in the courtyard. He made good use of his time while I slept. "We'll begin with this course. It may be more advanced than you're used to, but it's a great way to assess your skills."

Murphy looks at him like he's dumb. "You do know what she did before coming here? Right?"

Earwyn ignores him. "I've set this course so that you must defeat each obstacle before you can move to the next. Each dummy has a piece of silver strapped to its chest. You must retrieve the silver from all five to succeed."

"Where are my weapons? I need my knives and daggers."

"In a true fight with an elemental, mortal weapons are useless. Knives won't penetrate them and are of no use. You have to defeat them with your wit and use items that are around you." The more Earwyn speaks, the more he annoys me.

Four awkward-looking men stand off the side of the course. I can tell instantly they're lesser elementals. "Why are they here?" I nod my head. "Does Llyr know you brought them to the island?"

He sighs, "They're each controlling the environment of the dummies, and Llyr trusts my judgment."

I glare toward the lessers. This sounds fun. "Okay, let's do this."

Earwyn smiles. "Good. Impress me."

That's the wrong thing to say. "I'm not doing

anything to impress *you*. What I do is for survival. Training only helps heighten those skills." Earwyn takes a step back and motions to the beginning.

"Don't try for speed, more for skill," he adds. That's about the dumbest thing I've ever heard. If you aren't quick, you die. I ignore him and assess the first obstacle. The dummy is sitting in the middle of thorn bushes. Obviously, this will be earth. The thorns completely surround the dummy, blocking all sides. I step closer and the thorns grow before my eyes. They cover it completely, camouflaging it from view. Dammit. I can't reach inside without my arms getting destroyed.

On the ground next to the seawall is an old stone, probably from an original wall that surrounded the castle. I smile, remembering natural stone is an earth elemental weakness. Using the stone, I hit the thorns as hard as possible, breaking them free of the dummy. I grab the silver and move straight to number two.

Two is surrounded by swirling water, moving faster than the eye can see. "Is this even a challenge?" I ask. Closing my eyes, I imagine the water coming to life. Moving of its own free will. I imagine the water separating, opening a path around the silver. When my eyes open, nothing has changed. I try again and meet with the same outcome. What the hell?

"Everything okay?" Earwyn's tone is condescending. I ignore him and try again. Nothing happens. If I can't alter the element, maybe I can join it. I take a few deep breaths, releasing them slowly from my lungs. Instead of separating the water, I focus on becoming part of the rushing water. As soon as my hand touches the surface, the once roaring, supernatural water flow releases, allowing my hand to pass through easily. I reach inside, taking the silver from dummy two. Behind me, Murphy releases a deep breath.

Three is sitting all alone, not covered by anything. I look around for clues of what element this will be. Air and fire are the two that remain. I step toward the dummy and watch as it becomes engulfed in a wall of flames. I reach deep inside, calling on my element and met with nothing. I try again, but still, nothing happens. This is beginning to piss me off.

The flames reach higher, overtaking the head of the dummy. Unable to produce water, I remember seeing a small bucket next to the seawall from when Murphy and I walked around my first night. I run toward it, filling it with water from the small fountain in the center of the courtyard as I pass and pour it on the flames. The water weakens the flames, and I'm able to grab the silver. Murphy laughs loudly. "Somehow, I don't think that's what he had in mind." I flip him off as I move on to number four. He laughs deeply in the background.

A soft breeze lifts the loose hairs from my neck as I approach this one. Of course, this is air, but how? I look around for what will be waiting for me. I look at the lesser standing to the side. It's not hard to tell which one he is. His hair is windblown and he's staring nervously. From the looks on the faces of these four lessers, they're terrified to be here. I wonder what Earwyn's done to them.

Instead of focusing on the dummy, I focus on the lesser. I stare at him until he becomes even more uncomfortable. I move toward him. "Adria? That's not part of the course." Earwyn warns and I hear Murphy laughing in the background.

I move in front of the lesser, standing eye to eye with him. The look in his eyes makes me question Earwyn's tactics. He's terrified. Placing my hand on his shoulder, I whisper in his ear. "Let me through."

The lesser closes his eyes, "Yes, mistress."

"Thank you," I answer. He opens his eyes and nods knowingly.

Returning to the dummy, I take the silver off without issue.

"What kind of magic was that?" Murphy asks. "What did you say to him?"

"I promised him some of your coffee." I laugh.

"Aye, that'll do it." He returns the laugh.

I approach dummy five. The first four were the elements. This one is most likely a combination of them all. "What am I supposed to do here?"

"That's for you to figure out." It's official, I don't like him. Murphy's right, he is an ass.

I walk around the dummy like a lion stalking prey. All at once, all four elements work in tandem. Briars surround the dummy, while wind whips them against my skin. A pool of water covers the ground turning it instantly to mud and the briars burn without being on fire.

I don't see any weakness. All four are working together to keep me out. Llyr's words come to mind. "Something more powerful than all of us." I close my eyes, feeling the magic that surrounds me. The call of the water that coils deep inside, the air that sends an invisible breeze through my body, the fire that warms my arms and legs, and finally the earth, firmly planted beneath my feet, grounding me to the world around me.

Both times I've tried to call on water this morning have been unsuccessful. What's different? I think back to killing the fire elemental at the compound. Nothing happened until she mentioned Hannah's name, snagging something inside me. Maybe I need a trigger? I focus on the times I've used the element and the emotions that gave me control. I picture the air elemental and Murphy unconscious. I picture the fire elemental and the havoc she wreaked on the compound. I think about Hannah and her final moments.

A low rumble forms at my core. Goosebumps cover my body as I focus on pulling the four elements together, forming them into one. I envision a whirlwind of water forming above. In an instant, the sky turns black, and thunder pounds through the sky. Reaching my arms high above me, I call on the power of my creation. I pull it to me, to the castle, to the dummy, to my soul. My hair whips around my face as the storm creeps onto the island, and closer to me.

"Adria!" Murphy yells from behind. "Stop!" The power that flows through my body is indescribable. "You're going to destroy the island!" he calls again, this time directly behind me. "Please stop." He wraps an arm around my waist. The jolt of his touch brings me back to reality and I release the energy with a small explosion, knocking everyone and everything down within fifty feet, leaving me standing in the vortex of power, alone. The dummy is laying on its side. Kicking it over, I remove the silver, giving me all five pieces and five defeated dummies.

I turn around to the men behind me. Both are soaking wet and Earwyn is lying on the ground, covered in debris. Karma's a bitch.

"Adria," Murphy whispers. "How did you do that?"

I smile. "I don't know, but it felt great."

"You formed a freaking hurricane." Long arms wrap around my back and pull me tight. "A freaking hurricane."

Earwyn doesn't seem as excited as his cousin. He's brushing leaves, dirt, and pieces of what looks like grass off his uniform. I hand him the five silver pieces. "Is that all you've got?" My arrogance is a farce. Truth is, this was much harder than I expected and showed me how much I need to learn.

He clears his throat. "That's all for today. Your father will be back this evening. Dinner will be served at eight o'clock and is black tie."

"I do hope it's as fun as dinner the other night." I use as much sarcasm as possible. "Is this dinner to find me a suitable match?"

Earwyn doesn't care for my humor. "I believe dinner tonight is an introduction of you as his daughter. Nothing more." Why do I feel like a child being scolded?

Earwyn cleans up the course, while Murphy and I spar for most of the afternoon. After making me promise not to suck him into a hurricane, we stay at a stalemate most matches. Neither gaining the upper hand.

The sun is beginning to set, and I realize my muscles are more sore than usual. "I think I'm going to get ready for dinner. Care to join me?" Murphy looks at me with surprise and a smirk. "Not like that, dumbass."

"Well, in that case, I'll be happy to escort you in."

"That's what I meant." I wrap my arm through his and the two of us enter, heading up the stairs. "See you at dinner?"

He smiles deeply. "Aye. See you at dinner." I walk away, fully aware he's staring at my butt.

I open the window above the gigantic bathtub, drop a few bath bombs into the warm water, and lower myself into bubbles of ecstasy. The water takes away the aches and the view takes away frustrations. I relax completely, letting my body sink into the abyss.

"Is there room for me?" Hannah sits on the edge of the tub.

Her voice startles my eyes open. "Hannah? No, and that's a little creepy." I splash her with the water. "Did I fall asleep?" I look around the room for clues. Everything looks the same.

She shrugs. "Probably." She's dressed in torn jeans and the alien hoodie I kept. "Llyr loves you."

Folding my legs into my chest, I wrap my arms around them. "I know."

"Then why do you act like a spoiled child when you talk to him?" I splash water her way again. "You know I can't feel that, right?"

"Gods, you're annoying." She's right though. I am acting like a spoiled child.

"You know I'm right. He's your father and he loves you. I've never known any father that doesn't make mistakes. Granted, this was a huge mistake, but that mistake made you the person you are today. He's right when he says you would've been dead."

I look up in surprise. "What?"

"You would've died if your mother hadn't taken you away from here. There wouldn't have been anything he could do to save you." I draw my legs closer.

Llyr said the same but hearing it from Hannah hits differently. She looks around the bathroom. "This bathroom is bigger than the bedrooms in the compound."

"Hannah?"

"Hmm?"

"Do you, I mean, have you met anyone else... anyone else that's not here anymore?" My words stumble from my mouth.

"You mean, have I met other dead people?" She smiles. "Of course! I've met loads of them."

"Have you met her?" I ask, almost afraid of the answer.

"Who? You're going to have to be more specific."

"Claire? Have you met my mother, Claire?" The words whisper from my mouth. It's the first time I used her name as my mother.

Hannah's demeanor changes and she sighs. "I have." Her voice is soft and sad. "She's just as amazing as Llyr said she was, and he's right." I look up, waiting for her to continue. "You look just like her."

"Can she come to me like you do?" I lay my head on the side of the tub.

"I don't know."

"Are you really here, or just a figment of my imagination?" I huff, "Maybe I'm delusional."

"You're delusional alright. Anyone with half a brain would've jumped on that tall hunk of a man by now." I smile, grateful she's lightened the mood.

"You realize the top of your head would be even with his stomach, don't you?"

"Shut up." She splashes water on me. "To answer your question, I'm here but not here. I go where you go, see what you see, do what you do, and will always be here to knock a little sense into you as long as you need me."

"I know. I love you for that." As quickly as she appeared, Hannah was gone. I'm out of time to soak. Climbing out reluctantly, I'm nervous about dinner tonight. If Earwyn's right and it's an introduction of Llyr's daughter event, I will be on display the entire night and all eyes will be on me, judging my every look, every bite, every breath.

Several videos later, my hair is styled in something called a loose fishtail braid. The long braid swoops over my shoulder with wisps of curls on each side. I copied the make-up look from the first night, changing up the smoky eye to match the green dress I pulled out of the closet earlier.

Unlike the first dress, this one is form fitted on the top while the bottom sprays out like a mermaid tail. Perfect for the environment. In the compound, and for pretty much all of my life, I never had the chance to dress up, wear nice clothes, or go to fancy dinners. I feel like a fish out of water, no pun intended. This is the kind of closet and clothes most girls dream of. I never thought anything like this was a possibility for me.

I strap on a pair of green sandals with at least a three-inch heel. On the rare occasion I've worn heels, I'd never gone for anything very high. Being six feet tall barefoot makes me a giant in heels.

I add a crystal necklace with a large green stone in the middle and matching earrings. The colors match perfectly with the taffeta of the dress. The woman staring back at me in the mirror looks nothing like Adria. The old Adria was a scared little girl wearing hand-me-down clothes and shoes with holes in the soles. She was the girl who no one wanted or cared about. She's gone. This is the new me, and it's time I embrace who and what I am. I'm the child of a god and tonight will be my introduction to the world.

I take a deep breath, looking back in the mirror. I run both hands down my thighs, smoothing out invisible wrinkles. It's time.

I'm disappointed Murphy isn't waiting on the landing and come very close to banging on his door, but I have no idea which room is his. In true Adria style, I'm sure I'd pick the wrong one.

I head down the stairs alone. Three-inch heels and stairs are not best friends, and I slowly work my way to the bottom.

I hear laughter as I descend, then silence greets me as I reach the end. The room is full of men and women, all dressed similarly to me in their evening wear. Llyr greets me, helping me down the last step. "You look stunning," he whispers for my ears only. "The picture of elegance."

I try not to laugh out loud at the irony of his words. Elegance has never been a word used to describe anything about me. "Aye, she is," says a deep voice behind me. I turn to see Murphy staring at me with a sideways grin.

He's dressed in black tuxedo pants and an emerald green jacket. Our outfits match so well, we look like we're going to prom. His bowtie has dark green starfish randomly placed around it. "You look rather stunning yourself." I return the smile. Murphy nods his head to Llyr and follows as my father leads me into the sitting room. All eyes are on me and strangely enough, I like it. Normally, I avoid being the center of attention at all costs.

There's a full bar with workers serving drinks to eager guests. "Would you care for a drink?" Llyr asks.

"In a minute, maybe. Thank you." He turns me around to face the crowd.

"Many years ago, I met the most beautiful creature who's ever stepped foot on this planet. She had a heart of pure love and strength that was unsurpassed. Not long after, she was taken from me." His voice is heavy with emotion, causing him to pause. "We had a child together. It's taken me longer than it should have, but I've found her." I glance at Murphy. The look in his eyes is warm and gentle. "May I present, Miss Adria Kane Smith, my daughter?" The crowd erupts in applause. "Please enjoy a cocktail and join us for dinner shortly. I hope that you will take a moment to greet Adria and welcome her to our little slice of heaven, the Isle of Man."

He kisses me on the cheek and whispers, "These people are human." I nod knowingly. No speaking of elementals. He moves toward a group of older men and joins their conversation. He's a master at his art and I watch as he weaves his magic throughout the room.

The first person to greet me is a woman who looks to be in her late fifties. She extends her hand to me with a warm smile. "I'm Isabella O'Cain. It's a pleasure to meet you." Her accent is a mixture of Irish, English, and something I don't recognize. "Your father has been a complete blessing to this island. We're so fortunate to have him, and now you, here."

I return her warm smile. "Thank you. I'm excited to be here." She moves over to the bar, leaving me open for the next person. A small line has formed, and my stomach settles into knots for the immediate future.

I go through the same motions with at least twenty other guests before Murphy comes to my rescue. "Excuse me, Miss Smith, would you care to join me on the terrace?" He takes my elbow, gently guiding me away from the makeshift receiving line. Fresh sea air greets me instantly.

"Thank you. I was getting overwhelmed by all of them. How am I supposed to remember all those names? Each one told me how wonderful Llyr is and how he saved the island."

"That's true. Without his support, there have been times in the past when the island would have not been able to fight invaders. Human or elemental." He's standing so close, our arms touch. Neither of us moves.

"The stone and sigils?" I remember seeing them scattered throughout the island and village.

"Aye, but that's just one small thing he's done." He points toward the village where the tops of the homes and stores are barely visible. "Over the years, many governments have tried to conquer the island, and every time they're overrun by the humans that live here. Llyr makes sure each family is armed and well-trained on how to protect themselves and their homes. He's made their safety his main priority on the island."

"What happened between the two of you?" I turn toward him.

He looks down, rubbing his hands together. "I think that's a story better left for another day." I don't push, and instead, we turn, watching the sun set across the vast horizon. "Llyr was right. You look stunning tonight." I lay my head on his shoulder.

"So do you." He lays his head on top of mine.

"Did you notice how we match? I feel like I should've handed you a wrist corsage while Llyr took awkward pictures of us in the garden." I laugh loudly at his words.

"Exactly what I was thinking. We look like we're going to prom."

He gets quiet. "I'd be honored to take you to the prom, Miss Kane." He turns toward me, extending his hand. "May I have this dance?"

I take his hand, stepping toward him. Instead of dancing, we stare at one another. His eyes glance to my lips as a cold wind blows from the sea. Our relationship has done a one-hundred-and-eighty-degree turn from the compound. My life has turned upside down, yet he's been the constant the entire time.

Murphy wants to kiss me, and I have no objection. In these heels, our mouths are the same height. He leans in just as the back door opens. "Dinner is served." Earwyn's standing at the door with an annoyed look on his face.

Murphy stops but the look in his eyes gives a promise of more. Goosebumps cover my arms as we turn and enter the castle, arm in arm.

The energy in the dining room is light and airy as we enter. Stephen has outdone himself tonight. Meats, vegetables, and salads of every kind line the mile-long table. Llyr stands as we enter, pulling the chair next to his out. "Please, sit." He motions to the empty space. Earwyn is sitting opposite me, and Murphy takes the empty seat next to him. Course after course is brought to the table as guests talk quietly to one another. "You did well earlier," Llyr says. "You handled our guests with elegance and grace."

Hearing his words of praise feels good. I can't think of the last time anyone praised me for anything I did, except surviving. I smile in return. "Aye, she did," Murphy adds.

"Yes, she did," Earwyn adds his two cents. "Although, I think there's much we need to work on." He continues slicing his steak.

I watch the two men in front of me. Earwyn never looks up from his plate. Each move is precise and calculated as he slices into a small potato. His motions are almost robotic, zombie-like. Murphy's the opposite, eating double helpings of everything on the table, smiling at conversations he overhears, and talking to the woman next to him. He catches me watching and wiggles an eyebrow in response. The motion sets off butterflies in my stomach.

"Adria? Did you hear Mr. Buchanan?"

"What?" I look up, startled. I turn in the direction of a slender man seated a few seats down. "I'm sorry Mr. Buchanan. I must have been in a daze." The crowd laughs softly. "What was the question?"

"No apology necessary," the man says. "I just simply stated that my wife and I," he motions to a round woman beside him, "would love the opportunity for you to visit our store in town. Maybe sign a few autographs and hold a few babies. You know, that type of thing." He sits back in his seat.

"Mr. and Mrs. Buchanan, I'd be honored. Thank you for the invitation." I nod at the oddly paired couple.

"See, I told you she'd do it!" the woman says to her husband.

Llyr stands, putting his napkin beside his plate. "In due time Adria will be more than happy to oblige any requests, within reason. However, let's save those requests for a later date. Tonight is reserved for her just meeting you all." I sigh in relief.

The crowd lifts their glasses in agreement. "Thank you," I whisper as he sits next to me.

"Thank *you*." He clinks his glass to mine. "Thank you for returning here, returning home."

CHAPTER 12

The watch on my wrist buzzes, waking me from a glorious night's sleep. Thoughts of the terrace rush to mind bringing a smile. Did Murphy and I almost kiss? The sun's peeking over the horizon, yelling at me to get out of bed. Llyr's bringing in someone to work with me and asked if we could meet earlier this morning. I'm excited about the possibilities.

I match my leggings, tank top, and shoes. It's hard to believe that a week ago I only had three outfits to choose between. Now, I have workout clothes in every color imaginable. I brush out the braid from last night and arrange my hair into a French braid, the only braid I don't need a tutorial for. Murphy's waiting at the bottom of the stairs holding his signature homemade blend and a muffin. "You stepped up your game today."

"Aye, you said adding a muffin to the mix was the best way to lure you." He smiles.

"I could get used to this."

He raises an eyebrow. "Good."

"Good morning, Adria." Llyr greets me with a smile. He motions toward a tall, older man with dark hair and dark eyes. His long braids hang to each side of his narrow face. He's indigenous and has a quiet confidence about him that's both intimidating and awe-inspiring. "This is Payne. He's going to do some training with you today."

"Hi." I wave awkwardly.

"You're American?" he asks, his accent very midwestern.

"I am. You?"

He nods. "Montana. I'm not sure what I was expecting, but it certainly wasn't an American." My smile fades immediately. What the hell's that supposed to mean? I wrinkle my forehead in question, making Murphy smile.

"Payne is here to broaden our understanding of your gifts," Llyr answers my unasked question. I can sense that he's an elemental, but not his element.

"Shall we?" he asks, motioning to the courtyard. I finish my breakfast and lead the way outside.

Earwyn and Murphy follow, both dressed for training. "Are we going to jog?" I begin stretching.

"No," he answers quickly. "We're going over here." He points to the seawall. "You two find something else to do," I smirk at him telling the two giants, in no specific terms, to buzz off. They follow his order and stretch out for a run.

I climb to the top of the wall watching them exit the courtyard. Payne lowers both palms toward the ground and rises into the air. He flies to the top of the wall and sits beside me.

I stare in awe. "Did you just fly?"

"Somewhat," he answers, making himself comfortable. "Your father and I have been friends for a long time. We've been through a lot together. He's asked me to work with you on the air part of your skills. Before you ask, yes, I know about Claire and who she truly was."

I lower my head. Hearing her name from someone other than Llyr strikes a nerve. "I sense you have the gift, although different than usual, it's there."

I scrunch my forehead. "What do you mean, different?"

He pauses. "I'm not sure how to explain the feeling. It feels suppressed, unused."

I tell him about the small hurricane I produced yesterday. "Wouldn't that have been me using air and water?"

He doesn't seem impressed. "Yes and no. I've seen powerful water elementals produce a hurricane on command. With the amount of power I sense in you, if you would've tapped into the air aspect of your gift yesterday, this entire island would be gone."

I stare at him. "Are you freaking serious?"

"Freaking serious," he answers, mocking my words.

"Llyr said I was more powerful than any of them."

He breathes deeply. "He's right, and that's what confuses me. I sensed your power the moment I crossed the bridge to the castle. Any high-level lesser elementals would surely be able to sense the same. How have you managed to survive this long without someone or something discovering you?"

I think back on the insanity of my life. Maybe I was bounced through foster homes for protection. If that were the case, that would mean Llyr would've known where I was earlier. "I don't know. I had a regular run-of-the-mill, traumatic childhood, joined the military to escape prison, was drafted into the Phoenix organization and now I'm here. My life's been in danger many times throughout the years, but there's only been one elemental that almost killed me." I think back to how Hannah died so that I could live.

He looks up in question. "Which element were they, the one that almost killed you?"

"Fire," I whisper. "My friend died that day to save me."

"Interesting," he answers. "Could your friend have known who you were?"

I shake my head and laugh. "I doubt it. I didn't even know who I was until a week ago. How would anyone else?" He doesn't respond. "So, how do I use air?"

"That's a question I don't have the answer for. I've never trained anyone like you before and likely never will again. First, we need to discover how you access water."

I shrug. "I don't know." He frowns. "It just happens. It starts almost like a roaring deep in my stomach, that bursts to the surface."

"What happens when it bursts?"

How do I explain something that doesn't even make sense to me? "The first time it happened, I was surrounded by a ball of water and the fire elemental was scared away. The second time, Murphy was hurt, and I thought he was going to die. The third time, I killed the fire elemental."

Payne looks up in question. "You killed a fire elemental? The one who killed your friend?"

I nod. "She had it coming," I recall her words about Hannah.

"Hmm..." he moans, crossing his arms in front of his chest. "So, you've only used water three times before yesterday, when you created the hurricane?"

"Yes. I figured out yesterday it responds faster if I'm angry or scared."

"All of the times you've controlled your element have been under distress?" I nod. He jumps down from the wall. "Okay, that's enough for today."

What the hell? I stare at him confused. "Have I done or said something wrong?"

He scratches his head. "Not at all. I need to do some research and reading. We'll train tomorrow morning. Do me a favor?" he asks, standing below. "Don't tell anyone about air, not yet, at least." I nod.

Just as I jump from the wall, Earwyn and Murphy enter the gate from their run. Nosey about how Payne was training me, they only jogged a mile or so.

"I'll see you tomorrow morning, Adria. It's going to be a pleasure to work with you." He bows his head, turning toward the castle.

Murphy jogs to my side, while Earwyn looks on. "What's the scoop on him?" I ask, nodding my head toward Earwyn. "I don't like his energy. I don't think he trusts me any more than I trust him."

He looks at his cousin. "I don't think trust is his problem," he says, with a sideways grin.

"Then what the hell *is* the problem? He's always

glaring at me." I look over at the sour look he's sharing. "See, he looks like someone broke his favorite crayon."

Murphy laughs. "I think that look is meant for me."

"Why would he not like you? You're cousins."

"Family has nothing to do with it, he's just an arse." He turns his back toward Earwyn.

I laugh, "I bet he's a blast at family reunions."

"That's something we've never done, but I can imagine nailing him with a water balloon would be quite fun." He wiggles his eyebrows. We walk around the seawall and away from Earwyn's judgmental eyes.

"Tell me about your family." Murphy's energy changes at the mention of them. "I'm sorry if I've pried too much. Sometimes I'm too nosey for my own good."

"No, you haven't." We continue walking around the terrace. "I don't know where to start," he admits. He turns toward me with a smile. "You met Sophie on the plane."

"Your sister?" I remember how fun and light her energy was.

"Aye, we were raised as siblings, but we're not related by blood. Her parents took me in when I was orphaned on the castle steps." I stop walking.

"You were left on the castle steps?" Thinking about all the whining I've done about my childhood, I realize how selfish I must have sounded.

"Aye. Llyr knew instantly that I was a hybrid and needed to be raised here, on the island. He knew of a family that had lived on the island for generations and didn't have any children of their own. He took me to them, and they welcomed me in."

"I'm so sorry." I take his hand into mine.

"I'm not. They gave me a life I wouldn't have had otherwise. A few years after they adopted me, Sophie was born. I grew up working at the bookstore in town and training here at the castle. I was given an ideal life." He smiles, remembering his childhood.

"Do your parents know... what you are?"

"Aye. It became hard to hide after a while. I have a strong affection for anything that has to do with water. My parents thought I'd drowned on more than one occasion." He laughs at the memory. "It wasn't funny then, but now, it's quite hilarious."

"I don't think that's funny. Your poor parents." I hit him on the shoulder. "Have you met your birth father?" My questions are getting pretty nosey.

"No." He doesn't elaborate, and I don't push any further.

We continue walking around the perimeter, neither speaking. We approach the courtyard from the other direction to find Earwyn busy setting up what appears to be a sparring ring. "Should we help him?" I ask, praying he says no.

He sighs deeply. "Probably."

"Perfect timing," Earwyn says as we approach. "Adria, care to work on your sparring skills?" He motions to the far side of the mat.

"With you?" I don't know why that surprises me.

"If you're okay with that." He gives me a smile that doesn't reach his eyes.

"As long as you're okay with a broken leg."

"I like your spunk. Murphy, keep score," he tells his cousin.

Murphy laughs. "I don't think that'll be necessary. You don't stand a chance, cousin. I do wish I had some popcorn though."

"Hush, Murphy. You're next." He wiggles his eyebrows in response, making me laugh.

Earwyn states the rules as if I've never sparred before. "If at any time you feel nervous or anxious, raise your hand and I will instantly stop. Nothing that will actually hurt the other person is allowed. Think of it as flag football."

I nod and the two of us move around each other in a choreographed dance. Neither making the first advance. Getting bored, I throw a simple punch in his direction. He dodges it with little effort. I repeat the move several times, trying to get a feel for how Earwyn thinks and what style he uses.

He leans very heavily to the right, throwing all of his defense moves in that direction. His right hand always leads each move. A quick study of his feet tells me the same. He favors his right side. I change my style and begin throwing punches to his left. He's much slower and more awkward on that side. We've only been sparring a few minutes, but he's given me all the information needed to defeat him, or so I think.

Switching his weight to the other side, he drops low, kicking what I thought was his weaker leg underneath me, knocking me to the ground. I hit hard, the air escaping my lungs.

"Adria?" Murphy calls, from the side.

"I'm fine," I answer, trying to catch my breath. Earwyn extends a hand to help me up. I ignore him, rolling to the side and pushing myself up. "Again."

Earwyn nods and we begin our dance once more. I watch as his apparent weakness changes from one side to the other. He's trying to trick me, and it pisses me off. I lunge toward his left side, making contact with his shoulder. He doesn't flinch. I copy the move on his right side, receiving the same reaction. He's strong, stronger than anyone I remember fighting. Everyone has a weakness. My job is to find his.

Murphy's pacing, bouncing from side to side, clearly wanting to help. *Find the weakness, find the weakness,* plays through my mind on repeat. Earwyn throws punches at me, none making contact. He drops low, attempting the same move that brought me down earlier. This time, instead of letting him make contact, I drop low, kicking both feet out in front of me, and make contact with his chest, knocking him back ten feet. He lands on his back but is up in a matter of seconds. He flashes a smile that unnerves me. He liked that. He's back in front of me before I have time to digest what happened. The calm demeanor he showed moments ago is replaced with anger. His amber eyes flash to shades of red and his skin has turned an ashy shade of white, as he throws punches at a relentless speed. I'm blocking them but tiring quickly.

Wherever I move, Earwyn follows, kicking and punching with everything he has. My speed is the only thing keeping me alive as I dodge most of them, returning punches when I can.

"Dammit, Earwyn, that's enough!" Murphy yells, from the sideline. "You've proven your point!"

The glow in Earwyn's eyes says otherwise, as he continues his assault. Anger builds inside me and the pressure of the element I control threatens to explode on him. Murphy said hybrids usually can't control their element, but I sense something more from Earwyn. He's angry, not just at me, but at something bigger than me. I feel his fire on the verge of exploding.

I throw my leg out, kicking him hard on the ankle. He falls to the ground with a loud thud. I jump on top of him, straddling his hips with mine, and holding his arms to the ground. He's strong and pushes me off to the side. Before I can move, he's on top of me, copying the move I just held him in. "What are you going to do, water baby?"

"That's enough!" a deep voice calls behind me. In an instant, Earwyn is off of me and standing to the side with his head bowed. The picture of perfect submission. "Are you all right, Adria?" I look to see Llyr holding out a hand to help me up.

Ignoring his hand, I jump up, aware of my aching muscles. Brushing dirt and grass from my leggings, "Yes, I'm fine."

"What kind of training is this, Earwyn?"

Earwyn waits before answering. "I wanted her to feel what real combat was like." His voice is calm, cool, and collected, and his eyes have returned to their normal amber hue. Anger pours off of Murphy, his energy is heavy and dark. I walk beside him, hoping to help it release.

Llyr looks at me. "I wanted to tell you I won't be at

dinner tonight. I have a meeting off the island." He looks at Earwyn. "You will accompany me."

"Yes sir, if you'll excuse me." He bows slightly in my direction and walks to the castle.

Llyr watches him walk away. "I'll see you tomorrow." He nods before turning toward the castle.

"Did that bastard hurt you?" Murphy asks when we're alone.

"Just my pride." I laugh off the anger. "And a few sore muscles."

He turns to face me. "I've never seen anyone move so fast. He would've killed you if Llyr hadn't walked up." I can't remember the last time someone was able to defeat me that badly while sparring.

"I don't know if he would've killed me, but he was determined to win." I rub my shoulder, the location of his last hit. "Did you notice how he changed?"

"Aye. I saw his eyes."

"What do you think that means?"

"I don't know, but I don't like it." He nods toward the sparring area. "Feel like continuing with me?"

I stretch my back and hamstrings, loosening up tight muscles. "Sure, if you think you can handle it." He smiles a wicked smile.

Murphy and I spar until the sun begins to lower into the sea. Neither of us gets the upper hand on the other, we stay equal through each round. "Would you like to meet my family?"

I can't hide my surprise at his question. "Yes, I would." We move into the castle and to the second-floor landing.

"Can you be ready in an hour?" he asks.

"Sure."

"Wear something comfortable, our meals are less formal than they are here." He laughs softly. "I'll meet you here in an hour." He walks away.

"It's a date," I answer, instantly regretting my choice of words. "I mean, it's a plan. I mean... I'll see you in an hour." I turn in embarrassment and rush toward my room.

An hour later, Murphy's wearing a pair of black jeans that look like they were sewn onto his body and a plaid button-down shirt with sleeves rolled up to his elbows. Damn, I like this version.

His eyes sweep up and down, assessing the tight jeans and fuzzy pink cut-off sweater I found in the closet. I chose a low heel bootie to finish the outfit and managed to fix my hair without the use of a video. My goal was a simple beach curl, accented by light makeup and soft pink lips.

"You look... beautiful," he says.

"So do you. Are those jeans painted on, or is there actual fabric there?"

"If we're going to go there, you might want to look in the mirror." He raises his eyebrow.

"I'd thought I'd make it easier to see my butt." I laugh.

"Aye, makes sense. Thank you for thinking of me." He extends his elbow toward me, and I accept as we walk down the stairs.

The castle is quiet as we exit into the courtyard, choosing to walk to the village instead of taking a car. Stars shine brightly in the clear night sky, illuminating the path magically. The smell of the sea warms my soul. I haven't yet let go of his arm, and he doesn't seem to mind.

We approach the fountain in the heart of the village. "Are we going to the bookstore?"

"Aye. They live above it." He leads me to a hidden door beside the storefront, revealing a set of stairs. The smell of deliciousness hits me instantly.

"Oh, my gods. That smells spectacular." He leads me through another door at the top of the stairs.

We enter a quaint room that instantly reminds me of Hogwarts. Dark mahogany bookshelves line the hunter-green walls, giving a dark academic vibe. My eyes are immediately drawn to the wall of books, organized by the color of their spines. Colorful prints cover the rest of the walls similar to an art gallery. Against the far wall sits an overstuffed, burgundy couch, perfectly accented against the wall color. Ahead of me, a large bay window overlooks the fountain in the village square. A wrinkled blanket, a half-read book, and soft pillows line the bench underneath, showing signs of a wonderful reading nook. "This is beautiful," I whisper.

A short woman bounces in from the kitchen. She's wearing capri pants, tennis shoes, and a colorful t-shirt. Her apron says, "World's Okayest Cook" and I know right away I'm going to like her. "You must be Adria!" she exclaims, wrapping her short arms around my waist. "It's a pleasure to meet you!"

Her enthusiasm is addictive, and I smile at her welcome. "I am. Thank you for the invitation to dinner, Mrs. McKenzie."

She waves her hand dismissively. "Mrs. McKenzie was

my mother-in-law, gods rest her soul. She was the most stubborn human ever put on this earth. My name is Bonnie, and you're welcome anytime."

"Murphy! I've missed you, son." He bends down, kissing her on the forehead.

"I've missed you, too." She wraps her arm around his waist, barely coming to his shoulder.

"This boy of mine. I'm not sure he'll ever stop growing." She pops him lovingly with her towel. "Your father will be back in a minute. He had to go to the market for more wine. What kind of hosts would we be without wine for our guests?"

As if on cue, the door opens, revealing a tall, lanky man with salt and pepper hair. He hands his wife a bottle of wine. "Sorry, I'm late."

"You're not late. We just got here." Murphy shakes his dad's hand and gives him a half hug. Even though his father is tall, he barely reaches Murphy's nose. "It's good to see you," he says with a smile.

"You too. Who is this lovely creature you've brought into my home?"

I smile, shaking his hand. "I'm Adria. Thank you for opening your home to me."

"We'll see if you feel the same after eating Bonnie's cooking." She slaps him on the shoulder.

"You hush. You're still here, alive and well." She turns back into the kitchen.

"Barely hanging on," he whispers.

"I can hear you," Bonnie calls from the next room.

"I'm Ethan." He shakes my hand again. "We're pleased to have you here." Their warmth with each other is something I dreamed of as a child. The look on Murphy's face echoes my thoughts. He loves them dearly.

"I'm going to see if Bonnie needs any help," I say, nodding toward the kitchen.

He nods, as Ethan is telling him a story about a book that he'd ordered that turned out to be over five hundred years old.

Bonnie's standing in front of a stove that looks straight out of the nineteen fifties. She's humming as she cooks, and her energy is infectious. "Can I help with anything?"

"I've just about finished the bangers and mash, how about making the salad?" She points to the items on the table. "If you'll cut those up and put 'em in that large bowl we'll be ready to eat soon."

It's been years since I've tried to cook anything, but how hard can it be to cut vegetables and mix them together? I begin the meager task, making sure to cut everything the same size. Bonnie spoons huge scoops of potatoes in a bowl and tops it with several sausages. The smell is heavenly. I finish the salad, putting it on the table next to the main meal. "We make a pretty good team." She says with a smile. "Will you rescue Murphy and let them know dinner is ready?" I laugh and nod.

Murphy's sitting on the couch while Ethan's telling him about the stack of books in his lap. Murphy doesn't look bored. He's intently listening with a smile on his face. "Dinner is ready."

"Ah, I'm starving," Ethan says, walking past me. Murphy places his hand on my back, escorting me to the table.

"This looks and smells amazing. I've missed your cooking." Murphy kisses his mother's head again.

Ethan looks shocked. "What are they feeding you up there then?" Bonnie pops him with the towel again as he opens the wine, pouring each of us a glass.

We sit down for what's most likely the most memorable meal of my existence. Their family dynamic is something I've craved my entire life. The food is good, but the company is better. They talk about Murphy and Sophie growing up and how Murphy would scare them any time he got near water. They talk about how they discovered the truth about him and elementals and how Ethan's dedicated his life to separating legend from fact about hybrids and their history. The meal ends with Bonnie dragging out photo albums with pictures of Murphy and Sophie through every awkward stage of childhood. Murphy's hair stands out in each picture. Bright red curls, sometimes messy, sometimes smooth, but always there.

I look around the table as they banter back and forth. Tears threaten to fall at the amount of love I feel from them toward each other. Murphy was like me, abandoned, but he was found. Llyr won't ever be able to show awkward pictures of me growing up, but we can start now. For the first time in my life, I feel like I belong to something, to a family.

We walk back to the castle in silence, my arm wrapped tightly through his. Crossing over the bridge to the small island I stop walking. "Thank you."

"For what?"

"For everything. The wonderful meal, spending time with your family, making me feel welcome. Even if it was for a short time, they made me feel like I belonged, and I'm grateful. It's something I've dreamed of my entire life. Having a family that embarrasses you with awkward pictures, talks about all your weird stages in life, but most of all loves you more than anything. Your family is... perfect." The word seems inadequate.

"Aye, they are." He turns to look at me. "So are you."

I fight the urge to look down. I've known him barely a week, but there's no denying our connection. The energy between us is pulsating and his eyes echo my turmoil inside. Murphy steps toward me, sliding one hand to my cheek and the other to my waist. Every crash of the sea, the caw of a seagull, cricket singing their song, resonates deep inside. His eyes move to my lips, and he slowly moves his head toward mine. My eyes close in anticipation. His lips touch mine, gentle, soft, yet firm. Instinctively, I turn my head to the side, giving him more access. My lips part as he gently touches my tongue with his. Sensations flood me, head to toe. The kisses are soft, almost exploratory, neither pushing past boundaries. The arm around my waist slides to my back and under the hem of the sweater. His skin touching mine brings even more heat. Before long, he's breathing harder than he has on any run we've been on. I untuck his shirt in the back, sliding my hands inside the ridge of his jeans to touch his skin. Goose bumps form from our connection. Our kisses turn desperate. I want to be closer to him as my hands explore the rock-hard chest next to mine.

He pulls away, breathing heavily. "I'm sorry, Adria." He turns away from me.

"Don't be." I move toward him.

"I need a minute to... get it together." He walks several feet in the direction of the village. He's breathing in through his nose and out through his mouth before turning around with a huge smile. "What the hell was that?"

"Well, in America, we call it a kiss." I return the smile.

He runs his hand through his curls, making them frizz out. "That was not like any kiss I've had before."

"You're welcome?" I tease, moving toward him.

He holds up his hands. "No, don't. I don't think I can control myself if you get that close to me again." He's walking in circles with his hands on his hips. "Gods, you do things to me. I've never felt anything like that, with anyone." He continues running his hands through messy curls.

I wrap my arm through his, turning us toward the castle. "You do things to me too." I lay my head on his shoulder. "It's late. We have early training. I promise this is as close as I'll get."

He looks down at our connected arms. "Do you know how badly I want more?" We enter the castle and up to the landing. We stand face to face, neither speaking for several minutes. "You better go to your room, before something happens that we might regret."

I reach up, kissing him on the cheek. "I would regret nothing." I turn, walking to my room. He physically groans.

CHAPTER 13

I take my time getting dressed and make sure my hair looks extra cute today. Butterflies take flight as I open the door anticipating Murphy to be on the landing. My heart sinks when he's not. Instead of heading downstairs, I walk to the open balcony doors, overlooking the sea. The rising sun glistens off the breaks in the water, resembling glass. I breathe in the scent, filling every cell.

A voice directly behind me wakes me from my sea-induced trance. "Beautiful."

"Yes, it is," I answer. A cup of deliciousness is shoved in front of me before I turn around. "Is this what I think it is?"

"Yes ma'am. Straight from the barista. He didn't get much sleep, so it took some convincing today." Murphy steps back to an acceptable distance.

His smile is warm, causing my stomach to jump a little. "Ready to let me kick your ass?" I ask, walking down the stairs.

"I believe you're confused, Miss Kane. As I remember yesterday, each match ended in a stalemate."

"Did last night end in a stalemate?" I turn toward him.

"Touché, Miss Kane."

Payne is waiting at the bottom of the stairs. His long braids are tied together at the end. He's dressed in sweatpants and a sleeveless shirt and looks like he's prepared for battle. "Good morning. It's a pleasure to see you again."

"Good morning," I respond.

"I've done some research and have a plan that I believe will work for you."

Murphy looks at me in question. I shrug. On cue, Earwyn walks out of the study. He's not dressed in training gear and I'm grateful.

"I thought you went with Llyr?" I ask, confused.

"I did. He sent me to retrieve some papers he left on his desk." Earwyn's demeanor is different and worse than yesterday. His energy feels even more off.

"What kind of papers?" I ask, nodding toward the briefcase in his hands.

'I don't know, nor do I care. My job is to retrieve them, then return to Llyr on the mainland." He shifts from one foot to the other.

"Will Llyr be back tonight?"

"*We* should be." I don't remember asking about him, but okay.

"Shall we?" Payne interrupts our conversation, motioning to the courtyard. "Mr. McKenzie, I think this morning might be better spent with a jog." That's a polite way of telling him to go away. Murphy nods in agreement and begins to stretch.

Payne leads me out of the courtyard and down to a small, sandy beach surrounded by rocks. "Please." He motions to one large enough to sit. "There are no books written for someone with the ability to control two elements. Truth be told, there's never *been* someone with the power to control two elements."

"What does that mean?" I ask, trying to understand what he's saying.

He looks down, "I don't know."

"You do know you're talking in circles?"

"Yes, I'm sorry." He pauses. "I've come across very powerful lesser elementals before, but none with the ability to control more than one element. I don't know if you'll be able to access them at the same time or harness the power of one over the other." He looks at me. "Adria, the power that you have the potential to draw upon is limitless, and as a lesser, that scares me."

"Why?"

He paces through the sand. "I don't fear what you can do, but what others will do when they learn of you."

I haven't thought about that. I'm a huge threat to elementals everywhere. Not just lower-level lessers who wreak havoc on the world, but higher lessers and even Firsts. "Then I need to learn now, instead of later. I need to protect myself and the ones I..." I hesitate before finishing the sentence. "The ones I love."

"I agree. You said your power over water forms in your stomach and is released through your skin." I nod in agreement. "Your stomach area is the home of your solar plexus chakra. It's responsible for our control over ourselves and how we affect our environment. It makes sense that water would use this chakra to give you control over it. You are water, you are half elemental, not just any elemental, you are the daughter of a First." He walks toward the sea.

"I believe that the air element part of you is controlled by your throat chakra." I touch my throat without thinking. "The throat chakra is responsible for how we communicate, how we present ourselves verbally. In your case, I believe it's how you will have the ability to control air."

"Do I just tell the air where to go?" I know it sounds dumb as soon as I say it.

"If it were only that simple." He smiles. "We have to figure out what your triggers are, then learn how to control them." Okay, that sounds simple enough.

"How do we start?"

"You said when you controlled water you were under stress or danger. That tells me you learned how to control it on a cellular level and made it easier to call on when you're under threat. We're going to start with water and work on that control first." He looks over the sea. "I chose this small cove and beach because the water is shallow here. I want you to use it and form a wall of water."

I look over the sea like there will be instructions on how to complete this task waiting for me. "A wall of water?" I ask, hoping I heard wrong.

He nods, pulls his hands behind his back, and looks over the sea. I follow his gaze and breathe deeply. Long breaths in through my nose and out through my mouth. I focus on an area about twenty feet away. I envision the water rising, forming a wall in front of us. Nothing happens.

I try again. Still nothing. "Have you started?" he asks.

"Twice now," I answer.

"Try again. Focus your intention on what you want to happen. Not on how it will happen. Don't think like a human. The human ego will take over and tell you a wall of water isn't possible. Think like an elemental. Give power to it. You control water, you are the water."

I focus again, and again, but nothing happens.

A large rock falls ten feet to my left, startling me. "Where did that come from?"

"Focus," he says. "No matter what happens, you must stay focused." I try again, and another large rock falls two feet to my right. "Ignore it," he says. "Focus on your task. You must not let anything distract you."

"Are you throwing rocks at me?"

"Quit thinking about the rocks. Focus that energy on your task." He stands quietly behind me. This time a rock hits me in the shoulder.

"Ow, dammit. How's that supposed to help me focus?"

"If this were a battle, you wouldn't have time to focus. You must protect your life at all costs. When word gets out of who you are and the abilities you possess, you will never be safe. Your saving grace will be your gifts."

A small whirlwind starts behind me. Back home we called them dirt devils. It grows, drawing strength from the sea breeze. Small rocks and sand have joined into the storm, helping it grow in size and power. "What will you do, Adria? Will you let this continue to grow, or will you stop it? You have the power to end it now."

The storm continues to grow as it moves closer. The wind picks up my hair, slapping my ponytail into my face. Sand whips across my face, leaving what feels like small cuts. "What will you do, Adria?"

I center my focus on my stomach, drawing every bit of strength I have deep inside. I call on the hurt from my childhood, the pain of losing Hannah, the sadness of spending years alone, the warmth I felt from eating with Murphy's family, and the emotions from our kiss. Everything that makes me who I am. The power builds deep in my core, begging to be released. I focus all of my intention and energy on forming a barrier between me and the storm Payne produced. Releasing the energy feels like letting a part of me go. I open my eyes to see a twelve-foot wall of water rising from the sea. Using my energy, I pull the wall toward me, bringing it onto the beach and to the storm raging behind me. I release the power holding the wall in place, and the storm instantly dissipates.

I look at Payne. Both of us are drenched. "Good," he says, his voice monotone. "Again." We complete the same exercise at least ten more times. Each time the storm changes slightly, and each time the wall gets easier to produce.

My body aches in ways it never has before. Muscles deep inside my stomach are sore, feeling like I've done crunches all morning. "Eat lunch and we'll continue afterward," he says, walking through the sand. I follow him off the beach, my feet feeling like they weigh a hundred pounds with each step.

Murphy's sparring with a dummy as I round the corner into the courtyard. His moves are calculated and precise as he swipes. It's clear he's a force to be reckoned with and seeing him brings life back into my tired body. "Hey. Why are you wet?" He says, running toward me.

I smile weakly, "Training."

"Ahh. I heard a rumor that Stephen's serving fish and chips on the terrace in twenty minutes." He raises an eyebrow in question as we walk into the castle.

"Perfect. Just enough time to dry off and change. Meet you down there?" I slowly ascend the stairs. I've never felt this weak after training. I don't even remember being this tired on the first day of Phoenix training.

Back in the safety of my room, I brush the knots, sand, and dirt from my hair. It needs washing, but there's no point if we're going to continue after lunch, it'll only get filthy again. I change into a dry workout outfit and head down to the terrace.

Murphy's standing by the ornate stone railing, overlooking the water. "Beautiful," I mimic his words from this morning. He turns.

"Yes, she is." His playful words make me giddy, bringing energy back into my exhausted body. Being near him feeds my energy and I shamelessly pull all I can from him.

Stephen has the table set and the food is already in place. I'm not hungry, but the company is great. I move the food on my plate around, making it look like I ate more than I did.

"I know that trick." He motions toward my plate.

"Sorry, I'm just not hungry. Payne has me working

muscles and brain cells I've never used before." I set my fork down.

"It's clear he doesn't want anyone to know how he's training you."

I shrug. "I guess."

"The dummies don't put up as good of a fight as you." He smiles.

"You mean they don't kick your ass?"

"I thought we discussed this earlier. Each of our matches has ended in a stalemate."

"Did you block the time at the compound?" I ask, flashing a smile.

"You mean the time you tried taking advantage of me on the sparring mat?" He steals a fry from my plate. "And in front of all those innocent recruits?"

"Is that what that was? Me taking advantage of you?" I push the whole thing toward him. "You can have them all. I think I'll throw up if I eat anything else." He pulls it over and finishes my fries.

"Aye, you sensed my innocence." I spit out my water in a laugh.

"Something tells me you haven't been innocent since childhood." He wiggles his eyebrows.

"I really enjoyed the meal last night. Your parents need their own reality show. It could be about books and cooking."

He laughs at my words. "I don't know about the reality show part, but they are great, aren't they? I'm very lucky." He looks up quickly. "I didn't mean to sound insensitive."

I hold up my hand. "Not insensitive at all. If we were

both going to be abandoned, I'm glad one of us ended up with a loving family."

Murphy sits back in his chair. "Llyr and I have had our disagreements over the years, but you ended up with an amazing family too, it just took a bit longer. He's a good man and he loves you dearly."

"I know." I look down. "Being with your family last night helped me realize that. I guess it's better to be loved later in life than never. When I was young, I thought I didn't deserve to be loved."

He reaches over, taking my hand into his. "Everyone deserves love. You deserve the world..."

"Adria, we should continue." Payne interrupts what was about to be a moment. I roll my eyes in response.

"See you at dinner," I say, following my trainer off the terrace and into the courtyard.

Out of Murphy's sight, Payne turns, knocking me back with a blast of wind. I fly through the air, landing ten feet away on my butt. I stand up quickly, ready for whatever he throws at me next. I reach for my knife and remember weapons won't work. In the moment I take to figure out what to do, Payne hits me with a second blast of wind, this time lifting me through the air and slamming my back into a tree. Like a cartoon, my body literally slides down the trunk. Shit. I fight to stand up, but Payne knocks me down a third time.

Pain and anger fill every cell. "Stop!" I yell.

"What are you going to do, Adria?" He raises his hand toward me again and I react. Pushing a wall of water straight at him, I meet his air halfway. Element against element, water against air. I manage to stand up, walking toward the wall of water. Raising my hands, I push with every ounce of energy I have. His air slowly begins to recede, pushed back by my water. I focus more, pulling the last bit of strength from my core, I force the water to overtake the air, and Payne is drenched. His air is gone, and I collapse in exhaustion.

He walks past me. "Good. We'll train more tomorrow." I can't move. I lose consciousness in the middle of the courtyard, water slapping against the rocks below is the last thing I hear as I drift into a sea of nothing.

My eyes open to soft, turquoise blankets and walls. An arm is wrapped around me, and I'm a little spoon to something solid behind me. I wiggle my way free and off the bed. Murphy turns in the other direction, sound asleep. I'm in my room and Murphy's beside me. This seems sketchy.

My body still aches, but not like before. I look in the mirror and realize I'm still wearing the clothes I had on earlier. That's a good sign. My hair looks like I combed it with a toothpick, and what little makeup I wore is smeared under my eyes. I step into the shower, letting the water massage all the sore areas. The heat feels amazing. It takes three rounds of shampoo to get all of the sand and dirt from my hair. I let the conditioner soak in while the heat continues to rejuvenate my tired bones. Putting on a pair of fuzzy pajamas, I slip back into the bedroom and into bed with Murphy. I snuggle up to his back, enjoying his energy. He turns, facing me.

"You smell better," he whispers.

"I bet." I laugh. "How did I get here? More importantly, why are you in my bed?"

"You carried me up the stairs and tried to have your way with me, again. I'm beginning to think you're obsessed with me. I fought you off, of course, but fell asleep before I could leave." His voice carries a smile.

"Too bad I don't remember any of that, sounds entertaining." He reaches over, lacing his fingers through mine.

"Believe me, it would be memorable." He smirks, while I snort a laugh. "Truthfully, I found you in the courtyard. You were passed out and alone. I brought you up here and you've been asleep ever since."

"How long was I out?" He looks at his watch.

"Looks like just over fifteen hours."

"Oh, my gods. Guess I was tired."

His voice changes to serious. "Did Payne do this to you?"

"No, I did this to me. I overpowered him, but it took every last bit of my energy. I must have passed out."

"And that smug arse just left you lying there, in the dirt?" He props his head on his hand.

"Maybe he's a sore loser." Murphy's energy changes to anger. "Despite his teaching skills, he helped me. I was able to access my ability faster and stronger than ever before."

"How's leaving you in the dirt, passed out, helping you?" He still sounds angry.

"That I don't know, but I trust him. He pisses me off, but I trust him."

"That makes one of us," he answers, laying his head on the pillow.

"Will you stay with me?" I fight to keep my eyes open but don't want him to leave.

He wraps his arm around my waist. "Murphy's Coffee and More won't be able to open tomorrow if I do."

"Damn, that's a hard choice." Making him laugh. "I think I can go one morning without your signature blend. I may not be fit to be around, but that'll be your fault."

"It's a risk I'm willing to take." He pulls me closer. At that moment, clarity hits me. I feel safe with Murphy. That's what his energy provides. For the first time in my life, I feel protected and safe. I fight tears at the realization.

I fall asleep wrapped in his arms.

CHAPTER 14

"Maybe if you'd block using the correct stance, I wouldn't have been able to knock you down so easily." Murphy jumps back to his feet.

"Easy there, Mike Tyson. You do need a coffee, don't you?"

We've been sparring for hours. Payne is a no-show and my muscles are grateful. "I'm sorry. You can't say I didn't warn you."

Earwyn and Llyr still haven't returned from whatever they're doing and for some reason, it doesn't sit well with me.

"Let's take a break." He walks toward a large oak tree, enjoying the shade.

I breathe deeply. "That's the best thing you've said all day."

He pulls out a small, wrapped piece of bubble gum from his pocket. "I offer this in peace." He bows before me and hands me the gum like a knight making an offering to a king.

I accept the gum and sit on a large root. "I'm being a bitch." He wisely stays quiet. "Thank you for taking care of me last night. If it weren't for you, I'd probably have spent the night on the ground."

"Still pisses me off. Where's that bastard anyway?" He looks around the tree.

I laugh. "He's not a leprechaun." Murphy throws a small piece of a leaf, hitting me on the shoulder. "Do that again." This time a larger piece flies through the air. Without much focus, the leaf is batted out of the air by water.

He looks confused. "Did you do that?" He picks up a stick, throwing it at my head. The same thing happens, and the stick is met with a small wall of water and deflected.

"Bloody hell." He smiles, picking up a small rock, and raising an eyebrow in question. I nod, giving him permission. The rock is tossed at my leg but met with water before it's an inch from his hand. "Maybe the leprechaun is helping you."

"It's getting easier." On cue, Payne appears around the corner of the castle. "Shit," I mumble.

Murphy looks around. "What?"

"Looks like my reprieve is over." I stand, moving toward the lesser. "Do me a favor. If you find my body lying somewhere, take care of it."

He stands by my side. "If I find your body lying alone again, I'll take care of him." He nods toward Payne with a fierce look in his eye. Payne shifts back and forth, almost like he hears Murphy's threat. Murphy doesn't take his eyes off the man, as I walk slowly toward him.

"We need him too." He motions toward Murphy. His energy is off, and I don't like it. He almost seems nervous.

"Murphy!" I call back to the tree trunk. He doesn't waste a minute joining us. Payne leads us around to the back of the castle, on top of the seawall.

"Look." He points to a small group of rocks on a secluded part of the island. I see nothing out of the ordinary, just rocks and sand.

"What?" I shrug.

"Llyr's not on the island. His presence, or lack thereof, has been noticed by others. Those rocks you see are not what they appear to be." I squint, trying to make out anything different. Murphy copies my movement. "Keep watching," he says.

Movement catches my eye. "Did that rock just move?"

"It did," Payne answers.

"Shit, earth lessers. How are they here? The island is heavily warded against all kinds of lower-level lessers. Earth lessers shouldn't be able to get past the wards or altered stone." Murphy asks the question I want to know.

"That, I don't know, but with Llyr and Earwyn gone, the three of us are all that stands between this island and their attack." He nods to the rocks.

"Where are all the lessers I met the other night? Isn't there more than the three of us on the island?" I ask, looking between the two of them.

"Most of the lessers live on the mainland, not the island. It's just us," Murphy answers.

"Seriously?" I turn back toward the movement. "How are we going to defeat that?"

"We have the advantage here," Payne says, floating down off of the wall. I'll never get used to that.

"Adria," Murphy fills in the blank.

"Yes. We can't risk news of her abilities getting back to other lessers."

"Understood," Murphy says. "We'll make sure they don't leave."

I watch the rocks fight to climb on shore. "They haven't beaten the wards completely, but they're close."

"I'll meet you down there," Payne says, lifting into the sky.

"Aye." Murphy and I run out of the courtyard, heading toward the shore. "We don't need to engage them."

"I agree. We need to figure out how many there are." We run at full speed, past the village square, past his parent's bookstore out to where there's nothing but land and sea surrounding us. "They're smart choosing this part of the island. They won't be spotted as quickly out here."

We approach the cliff at the edge of the island, high above where the rocks below are working their way up the bank. From above it's impossible to see any movement. The island forms a small peninsula and thankfully we're surrounded by sea. "How's Payne going to get here? It took us a while to get here at a full run."

"I don't think that'll be a problem," I point to a burst of energy moving quickly through the sky. "Here he comes now." A wall of air lands next to us. His entire body has completely transformed into wind.

He forms a wispy version of himself. His body is swirling wind while the familiar features of his face seem to solidify. "You know what must be done," he says.

"Aye, but how do we kill this many? And without weapons?" Murphy asks.

Payne looks at me. "Weapons are useless," I remind him.

"I know, but they make me feel better."

"I'll assess from the sea. You two stay here, don't let them see you." Payne forms the shape of a white cloud and floats off the side of the cliff.

Murphy stands in awe as my teacher camouflages himself in the sky. The ground beneath us buckles slightly. "Did you feel that?" he asks.

"Did they breach the land?" He looks around for signs of anything out of the ordinary. The ground buckles a second time. I've lost Payne's cloud in a scattering of hundreds.

"There's no other explanation." Murphy puts his back to mine as we circle, looking for any signs of danger. A rock the size of my head flies out of nowhere, heading straight for us. In an instant, I deflect it with water. "Where the hell are they?" he shouts.

"Shh, listen." A low rumble starts from the edge of the cliff, gradually crescendoing. "Here they come." Murphy and I both crouch into a fighting position, preparing for whatever's about to top the cliff.

Five boulder-shaped lessers appear over the lip of the sea, heading straight for us. Neither of us speaks, knowing what's about to happen and our role in it. The first one comes straight at me. He's at least eight feet tall. Smaller rocks form the illusion of arms and legs, and a large rock sits where his head should be. He opens a mouth, revealing two rows of sharp stones, resembling teeth.

"Water babies." His words are slow and pitched deep. I don't wait for more words, using all my strength, I roundhouse kick him straight in the gut. He flies back a few feet and looks surprised. Two other lessers are attacking Murphy. He punches, kicks, and pushes them back toward the cliff. While my first friend works on getting up, two more move toward me. I copy the kick with them, pushing them back. All five are on their feet within minutes, heading toward us again.

In an almost identical style, we repeat the same moves as before. "We can't keep doing this," I shout. "They'll keep coming at us until we have no more strength."

"Aye! Where's Payne?" He says, pushing several back to the cliff. "Can you use water to push them off?"

I focus on pulling the power of the water. It comes immediately, and I focus a wall of water on the lessers that are now back on their feet and moving toward us again. The water forces them back but it's not strong enough to push all five over the edge. "They're too heavy. The water won't hold them long."

"Shit!" Murphy looks behind us. "They're coming up the other side!" I look to see at least twenty more earth lessers climbing over the edge of the cliff on the other side of the peninsula. "We have to get out of here. There's no way we can hold off that many. We need to get to the village and get the humans to safety."

"Wait!" I release one hand from the wall of water, turning it toward the large group topping the cliff.

Another wall of water forms, surrounding each group of lessers. I feel my energy draining like a gas tank on empty.

"You're doing it!" he shouts as he runs through the wall of water, toward the large group behind us.

"Murphy, I can't protect you!" I yell after him.

"I'm not helpless." He kicks and punches his way through the group, knocking a few down along the way. I don't know how much longer I can hold them off. Murphy continues to take out as many as he can until the wall can't hold any longer. What once was a wall of water has turned into a trickle. The first five easily pass through, heading straight toward me.

After knocking back as many as he could, Murphy joins me in the center. "We can't defeat this many. We have to go!" He's right. I can't hold them all off. I'm not strong enough.

The skies change from a beautiful shade of cerulean blue to black in an instant. The lessers stop moving, staring into the black above. "This can't be good," Murphy whispers.

Landing in a thud beside us is Llyr. He's wearing a three-piece suit and not a hair is out of place. He looks like he just stepped out of a photo shoot. "Halt," he commands, his voice deep and resonating. "You are violating the wards and thus violating the treaty set forth by your First, Dagda." The lessers bow down in fear. He moves to mine and Murphy's side. "These two and this island are under my protection. Any attempt to come onto this island or to harm them will result in immediate disposal." For the first time, I feel Llyr's power and see him in a different light. I see him as a god. A whirl of air lands next to him and Payne bows before him.

"I brought them here, sire," Payne says, bowed to one knee. Anger emanates from Llyr.

"You brought the lower earth lessers to our island? Why?" Llyr's changed from the loving father I've experienced to the god of the sea.

Payne stands back to full height. "I wanted Adria to experience what a real fight was like. I hoped it would awaken what's buried beneath." His words echo Earwyn's.

Llyr turns to the lessers. "Go, and never return." The lessers jump back to the sea where they came from. "I trusted you Payne, and this is how you return that trust? Not only did you put Adria's life in danger, but you risked starting a war with no resolution?"

I stare at the two men, not sure how to feel. I understand Payne's purpose, but Llyr's right. This could've started a war between the elements. Is my finding my power worth that?

Payne doesn't respond. "Murphy, take Adria back to the castle." Murphy wraps his arm around my waist, and we begin the walk home. I'm too exhausted to run. Llyr calls after us. "Murphy, thank you."

I look up, trying to read his face. Murphy looks relieved. Whatever's happened between the two of them has deeply affected the man helping me walk. Llyr's words eased the tension slightly.

"I failed back there." My words spill out of my mouth in frustration. "I should've been able to hold them off."

Murphy stops walking. "Were you fighting somewhere I wasn't? From what I saw, you held off at least twenty earth elementals with nothing but water." He smooths a stray hair and pushes it behind my ear. "Earth elementals are the worst. They're wicked strong and have barely any weaknesses. The fact that Payne chose them to train you makes me dislike him even more. The bastard just floated in the sky and watched them attack us."

"I don't like his technique, but he's helped me. However, I agree this might have been overkill." We walk a little further. "There's something I need to tell you." Murphy raises an eyebrow. "You know I'm a hybrid. Being the daughter of a First makes me stronger, allows me to use the element, control it, bend it to my will."

"Aye. That's why I came to find you."

Payne warned me not to say anything, but Murphy's been the one constant by my side since this all started. Right now, he's my person. I take a deep breath before continuing, "Not only am I half water First Elemental, I'm also one quarter air First Elemental." Murphy stops walking.

"What? How's that possible?"

"Well, when a mommy and a daddy love each other..."

"Adria," he interrupts sternly. "This isn't the time for jokes. How's that possible?"

I pause. "Claire, my mother. She's the daughter of Shu."

Murphy stares at me dumbfounded. "Claire, the wife of Llyr, your mother, is the daughter of Shu, the god of air?" His words are slow and methodical. I nod. "So that makes you a combination of two First Elementals." He walks in a slow circle, scratching his head. "Holy shit. No wonder Llyr's pissed. Payne could've started a war between water and air."

"Payne's trying to awaken the air part of my abilities. That's why he pushes me so hard. I've only touched the surface of water, but in combination with air, he says I'll be unmatchable. More powerful than a First."

"That's why he brought the lessers here today? He thought putting our lives in danger would awaken that part of you?" I nod in response. "If Llyr allows him to continue training you, no way in hell will he be alone with you again. From this moment on, we're a package deal."

My energy has perked up enough that I'm able to walk on my own without stumbling. "I kind of like the sound of that." He smiles warmly.

"Come on." He wraps an arm around my shoulders. "There's a hot tub on the terrace that's calling my name. I think every muscle in my body hurts."

"Sounds perfect."

......

Thirty minutes pass while I dig for something appropriate to wear. I've gone from owning no bathing suits to having to choose between at least fifty styles and colors. I ramble through the drawer, finding a modest black bikini. The bottoms are high-rise and feel a little less hoish than the set that resembles a ball of string. The last time we swam, I wore undergarments for gods' sake. Does it really matter in the grand scheme of things? After our kiss, being alone with him in a hot tub makes me nervous and excited at the same time. There's no denying our attraction to one another, but it feels like more. Like we're connected somehow. Maybe it's the element of water that connects us, or maybe it's his easy energy that comforts me when we're together, but being with Murphy excites me and I feel like a schoolgirl thinking about him.

Choosing black flip-flops and a simple flower coverup to match the suit, I head toward the landing. I've walked around the pool and hot tub but haven't taken time to swim since arriving. Sadly, Murphy isn't waiting on the landing.

Slowly flopping my way down the stairs, the bottom floor looks empty. "Llyr? Earwyn? Stephen? Anyone?" No one responds.

The terrace is empty too. Did I beat Murphy down? He better not be asleep.

I crawl into the hot tub, relishing every moment as the hot water soothes me from the outside in. "Oh, wow," I moan, lowering all the way down to my neck.

"You didn't wait for me." I open one eye to see Murphy standing next to the hot tub wearing a colorful hat and holding what appears to be an adult beverage.

"I'm guessing from the hat, that's a margarita?" He hands the fishbowl-sized drink to me.

"Yes ma'am, 'tis. It's where the 'more' part of 'Murphy's Coffee and More' comes from." He takes off the huge hat.

"Aww, I kind of liked that," I tease.

"I'll put it back on for you, senorita." He smiles a crooked grin while attempting a horrible Hispanic accent.

I laugh at his weak attempt. "You're a huge goofball, and I'm here for it." He sets the hat down, climbing into the hot tub. His groan mimics mine from earlier. "I know, right?" We sit in silence, watching the sun set over the sea.

Murphy reaches over, taking my hand into his. "Is this okay?" I squeeze his fingers in response. He scoots closer to my side. "I've been thinking about what you told me earlier, about Shu being your grandfather." I lay my head on his shoulder. "I've met Shu several times, he's very resourceful."

"What are you saying?" I ask, watching my free hand float in the jet stream.

"I don't know." He sighs. "Has Llyr said why it took him so long to find you?"

I look up at him in question. "He said he received clues throughout the years, but nothing ever panned out." I shrug, "I was switched from home to home so much, I'm guessing I was lost in the system."

"I would buy that if Llyr was human, but he's not. He has access to bottomless amounts of money, unlimited staff at his disposal, and half the world in his debt." I back away to see him better.

"What are you saying?"

"I don't know. Something feels 'off'." He takes a sip of his margarita. "What if someone else was pulling the strings and keeping you hidden in plain sight, but just out of Llyr's reach?"

"I guess anything's possible. I've learned that in the past week, but who would do that? No one else knows I'm Llyr's daughter, and only you and Payne know about Shu."

He turns to me. "Does Shu know about you?" I set my drink down.

"You think Shu had something to do with it taking so long for Llyr to find me? You think he kept me hidden from Llyr?"

"No, maybe? I don't know. The pieces of the puzzle don't fit. Llyr loves you and would never do anything to hurt you. But Claire is Shu's daughter. Maybe Shu found out about you after it was too late to save his daughter and kept you hidden."

"Why would he hide me from my father? What would be the purpose of hurting his granddaughter?"

"Because Shu blames me for Claire's death." Llyr walks onto the terrace. Murphy moves to an acceptable distance. "When Claire and I met, neither of us had any idea who she was, especially who her father was. It wasn't until years after she left that Shu found out about her."

"Who told him?" I ask.

He sighs deeply. "I did. He had the right to know he had a child and a grandchild. He discovered Claire's death and your whereabouts long before I did. He was the one responsible for hiding you in the foster care system and keeping you just out of reach."

Anger fills me at the thought of my grandfather keeping me hidden. "Why didn't you tell me this before?" Tears threaten to fall. "He made my childhood a living hell and you didn't tell me?"

Llyr looks down. "He's your grandfather. I didn't tell you because I didn't want you to blame him."

"Why the hell not?" I yell. "He's the one responsible. Yes, I blame him."

"You deserved to think the best of him. He's had a rough couple of centuries. He's hurt and angry, which made him unstable." Llyr's voice is soft and calm. "Sometimes anger overpowers blood. He wanted to hurt me more than I'd hurt him." Murphy squeezes my hand tighter.

I refuse to break down over a man I've never met. I let the pain transmute into anger. "Why would her death be your fault?" I ask.

He wipes his cheek. "Because I sent the two of you away."

"That's bullshit." I slide forward on the seat of the hot tub. "Tell me why he blames you!"

Llyr sits on a chair next to the hot tub. "Because it was one of my lower lessers who killed her." I fight the urge to blast him with a wall of water.

"A water lesser was responsible for her death. How?"

"It doesn't matter now. I took care of it."

I stand up in the hot tub. "How?" I yell.

He sighs. "She'd taken you swimming at the beach. You always loved the water. He simply pulled her under."

"My mother, married to the god of the sea, drowned? Is this some weak attempt at a joke? Does anyone else see the irony in this?" I release the energy and blast him with a wall of water. Llyr doesn't budge. "Where is the lesser who did it?" I blast him with another wall.

"Adria," Murphy warns.

I continue walking toward Llyr, blasting him with water. I'm not hurting him, but my anger doesn't care. "Because of your lesser, my mother died, and I was raised by people who took advantage of me, made me do things I didn't want to do, and have never felt love a day in my life?" My pitch matches my anger.

Dark clouds form above me and begin to swirl. "Adria," Murphy warns again. "Get in control."

"I am in control!" I shout, just as a bolt of lightning strikes the sea behind us. Llyr does nothing while I pummel him with anger. I walk closer, still blasting him with water and resentment until only a foot separates us.

"I want him dead!" The voice coming out of me sounds foreign to my ears. Llyr wraps his arms around me, pulling me to his chest.

"I killed him," he whispers. Anger instantly turns to tears. I lay my head on his chest and curl in his arms. His energy fills me from head to toe and the connection between us is instant. "I'm so sorry," he says. "I let you down. I let Claire down." I don't say anything, just take comfort in his hug.

CHAPTER 15

*M*urphy left Llyr and me alone on the terrace after he realized I wasn't going to kill the god of the sea. We didn't talk about the future, the past, or anything significant. We just sat together, staring at the stars. He put his arm around me and pointed out constellations and how they'd changed over the millennia. It was mesmerizing. We talked until the moon was high in the sky and Llyr excused himself to bed.

Disappointment strikes when Murphy's not waiting on the landing. I didn't expect him to wait but wouldn't have minded either. On my door, I find a sticky note. "Third room on the right. Please come when you're done. I need to see that you're okay." Pulling down the note, I head toward the opposite wing.

"One, two, three," I whisper, walking down the hall. Nervous butterflies take flight as I knock softly. The door opens before I knock a second time. Murphy pulls me into the room, taking my hands into his.

"Are you alright?" he asks, looking me up and down. "He didn't hurt you, did he?"

"No, I'm fine. We just talked."

He brushes loose hair behind my ears. "Adria, I'm so sorry."

"Thank you, but it's not your fault, and honestly, I'm okay. It needed to happen, and now I have answers. Granted it doesn't make it any easier, but it gives me a little peace to know why he wasn't able to find me. Only a god could hide me from a god." I lace my fingers through his, leading him onto the balcony. Remembering Llyr's descriptions of the stars, I point toward a cluster high above. "Did you know that's Pegasus, and the cluster on top is Andromeda?"

He looks up. "I did."

"Llyr told me the history. Would you like to hear it?" I ask, staring into the night sky.

"Aye." He wraps an arm around my waist.

"Ancient Celtic tradition says that Pegasus was Llyr's horse and that's why he was able to move around so quickly." I point to waves, crashing against the rocks below. "It's why even today, when a wave crests, the whitecaps are called white horses."

"I didn't know that." He pulls me closer.

I point at Orion's belt. "That. Do you see that?" Murphy pulls my arm down and turns me toward him.

"Are you sure you're okay?" he whispers. "In here?" He touches my head. "That was a lot of heavy information you received."

I take a deep breath. "I promise. For the first time in

my life, I have answers. I know who I am. I have a family who loves me and... I have you."

"Aye, you do." He puts his palms against each cheek, lowering his lips to mine. Warmth fills my core, and my lips open in response. His tongue touches mine, asking for permission. I wrap my arms around his neck, giving him full access. He moans deeply, lifting me into his arms and carrying me to the bed.

I've been with men before, but with Murphy, everything feels different and new. He lowers himself to the side of me, keeping his mouth on mine through the entire walk. He lifts his lips from mine, moving to my neck as he leaves a trail of want in his wake. His fingers lace through mine as he brings more of his weight down on top of me, eliciting an embarrassing moan. My body is on fire.

His hand slides away from mine, tracing my arm until he reaches the hard nipple waiting for his touch. My back arches in response. His tongue and fingers match tempo as he takes his time with each. His hand continues down my side to my butt. He grips the closest cheek and pulls until there's no space between us. Evidence of his arousal presses against my abdomen.

"Adria," he whispers while still kissing me. "We should stop." His hand continues to caress my ass, as he pulls my leg over the top of him, resembling our first sparring match. "You should stop me. I don't have the strength to do it myself."

"Maybe we shouldn't stop?" I straddle him, feeling him completely.

"Gods, Adria." He sighs into my mouth, rubbing his hands along my thighs.

Dammit, he's right. I'm not ready. As badly as I need the distraction, I don't want this to be something that changes our relationship. When we do this, and we will do this, I want it to be special. I want it to mean something to both of us. I kiss him deeply one last time, and he groans in my mouth. "You're right. I want this to be special, not a quick stress relief. You mean more to me than that."

I roll off of him, keeping my hand on his chest. "I need a moment," he says through deep breaths. "Don't move. I need to think about baseball or algebra. If you move, you'll distract me." I snort a laugh. "You're distracting me."

Minutes of silence pass before I dare move or speak. "Are you okay?" I run my fingers up the mountains of muscles on his chest.

"I'm not sure okay is the word, but I'm better." He turns toward me with a smile. "You do crazy things to me, woman."

"You do things to me too." I smile back.

"Ah, dammit. You're distracting me again." He turns away.

"Should I leave?" I whisper.

"No. Please stay. I promise I'll be good."

"What if I'm not?" I tease.

"Adria!" he groans. "You're killing me." He kisses my forehead gently.

His bathing suit is hanging low, and I resist the urge to help him take it off. "You're right. Now isn't the time. When the time is right, I will have my way with you, because you were correct earlier. I am a little obsessed with you."

He slides a long finger over my cheek. "Aye, I knew it." He gently caresses my neck, tracing circles around each freckle. "You're beautiful. I don't think I've told you that before." I smile in response.

"You have, several times. But, thank you. I don't think I'll get tired of hearing it." My heart flutters with his words. "You're an honorable man."

"Aye, sadly," he says, rolling on his back.

I slip into his closet, grab a plaid button-down and crawl into the right side of the bed, because everyone knows that is the only side worth sleeping on.

"What are you doing?" he asks, wrinkling his forehead.

"Oh, I'm sorry. I thought you wanted me to stay."

"Aye, I do. But that's my side of the bed you're lying on." His voice is playful.

"I think you're confused, dear sir. Guests and daughters of gods always sleep on the right side of the bed. Since I'm both a guest and a daughter of a god, that gives me dibs." I crawl under the cover, pulling it up as high as possible.

He stands beside the bed, staring at me. I open an eye, waiting for a snarky response. "It's a good thing I'm in a generous mood," he says, crawling over me to the other side. He slides under the cover beside me, pulling my back to him.

Evidence of his arousal hits me in the back. "Are you sure me being the little spoon is the best idea right now?" I fight the urge to reach behind and wrap my hand around him.

"No, just don't wiggle." He buries his face into my

neck. "I'll be okay." I lace my fingers through his, bringing our joined hands to my stomach.

"Good night," I whisper, wrapped in a Murphy cocoon.

Soft kisses on my neck are followed with, "Good night."

.....

"Adria?" Hannah's voice calls from the balcony. Murphy's asleep beside me, still the big spoon to my little one. "Come outside," she whispers.

"Hannah?" I crawl out of bed, following the sound of her voice. I find her curled up in a balcony chair. She looks behind me at Murphy.

"Yes girl, it's about damn time." She gives me an air high-five.

"Oh, no. We didn't..." She holds up her hand, interrupting me.

"Whatever, Adria. You're in bed with a gorgeous man that I would've jumped on weeks ago and you're wearing his shirt. The evidence is pretty substantial."

I laugh. "It is, but we didn't." She looks out over the sea, ignoring my protest. "Why are you here?" I ask.

"Don't trust him." Her voice is shallower than before.

I turn to the bed behind me, watching him sleep. "Murphy?"

She doesn't answer for a minute. "The other one. Don't trust him."

"The other one... Earwyn? What are you saying, Hannah?"

"He's jealous and he's not on your side." Her answers are vague and confusing.

"Jealous of who? Me? Murphy?" Turning back toward my friend, her seat is empty. "Hannah?" Wind blows the hem of the shirt while I stare in confusion. Am I dreaming? I ask the question over and over until long fingers slide down my side to my butt, waking me up.

"Good morning sunshine," a deep voice whispers. Goosebumps cover my body in response.

"If you do that again, I will not be held responsible for my actions." I turn, facing him. "Every American woman dreams of being woken by a man with an accent whispering in her ear and grabbing her ass."

Murphy laughs. "Looks like I've missed my calling then." He leans down, kissing me on the forehead. "I could get used to waking up with you beside me. I'd rather under me, but beside me will work for now." I slide my arm around his neck pulling him toward me. Slow kisses turn fierce quickly. He rolls on top of me, separating my legs with his, sliding down where our skin meets. He slowly rocks his hips into me, eliciting a moan that can probably be heard down the hall. The only things keeping our skin from meeting are bathing suits. The hardest part of him touches the softest part of me, and I want more. I crave more.

I'm met with a brief moment of clarity and slide out from under him. "Remember our talk last night?"

"Aye, I do," he answers.

"I don't want to rush things with you." I run my hand slowly over his abs.

"I don't want to rush things with you either. I want to

take my time and explore every inch of you." He brings my hand to his lips, kissing each finger.

"I need to leave." I jump out of bed, still wearing his shirt.

He sits up and breathes deeply. "That's probably for the best, but dammit I don't like it. We make dumb decisions together." He stands, pulling me to his front, kissing my cheek gently. "We'll continue this when the time is right." His voice is soft and seductive. I nod, resisting the urge to continue what we started. He steps away looking me up and down. "Damn, that shirt looks ten times better on you than me."

"I should go." I point awkwardly at the door. "I'll return the shirt later." Just before stepping into the hall, I lift my borrowed shirt and the bathing suit bottom, revealing a naked butt cheek. I close the door and run down the hall toward my room, trying not to giggle too loudly on the way.

A cold shower helps ease the tension building inside. I choose a particularly tight pair of leggings that ride up in all the right places, a tight tank top, and light makeup. An hour later, I'm dressed and ready for the adventure of the day.

A smiling Murphy is waiting on the landing, holding coffee and a doughnut. "I saw no evidence of 'Murphy's Coffee and More' in your room."

"A true artist never reveals their secrets." We walk down the stairs.

"I think you took that slightly out of context. Coffee isn't an art."

"Maybe," he answers, with a smile. "Tell that to my

barista." He whistles low as we get close to the bottom. "I'm a fan of those pants you have on." I can't hide my smirk.

Llyr's waiting at the bottom of the stairs, alone. He's wearing traditional training gear, like what we wore at the compound. "Good morning. I trust you slept well."

I look at Murphy, trying not to giggle like a schoolgirl. "I did, thank you. Where's Payne?" I look around the foyer for my missing trainer.

"Payne tried his way, now we try mine. I'll be training you for the time being if that's all right with you of course." I smile.

"Sounds great." Llyr looks past me to Murphy.

"I'd like your help if you don't mind."

"Of course, sire," he answers with a slight bow.

"Shall we?" he motions to the door.

"Should I put on training gear?" I ask, shielding my eyes from the light.

"I don't think so," Llyr answers. "The kind of training I have in mind is more mental than physical. Why don't we go for a walk?" He leads us past the seawall onto the rocks surrounding the castle walls. "In the beginning, only the four of us existed. This island was the first we created together."

I stop walking. "This island was the start of everything?"

"I didn't know that," Murphy admits.

Llyr looks around with pride. "All four of us lived here, together, in perfect harmony for many millennia. Rather out of greed or pride—they go hand in hand—we decided to build more and more until we created the world before you. We created the beauty of this planet. It was perfect, set forth for all to grow. Eventually, out of loneliness and boredom, lessers were created. It was the lessers who began the first wars, not the Firsts."

"Murphy told me about the great battle while we were at the compound," I answer.

"I'm grateful to him for that." He looks at Murphy. "He's been a constant steadfast, and the person responsible for returning you to me. I never properly thanked you for that." Murphy bows his head.

Llyr continues, "After we absorbed all the lessers, a pact was made to prevent anything like that from happening again. It didn't take long for that to be broken. Dagda and Brigit began to form lessers within a century. Shu and I eventually did the same centuries later, only this time, we made sure rules were developed and enforced. Peace reigned for many, many millennia. Over the past thousand years, turmoil is beginning again."

"Murphy told me about compounds being overrun in different parts of the world."

"I'm afraid that's true," Llyr answers. "In the great battle, eventually the four of us had to come together to defeat the lessers, but before that Shu and I stood side by side against Dagda and Brigit. Now, even that connection has weakened."

"Because of me?" I ask.

"Our separation happened centuries ago, but his finding out about Claire made our connection even weaker than before." We continue climbing the rocks, moving our way around the island. "If we have to battle against lessers again, I don't know if Shu will side with me. If he joins earth and fire, that's a battle I can't win."

"How many lessers do you have?" I ask, looking over the open water.

"Roughly, two hundred thousand."

"That's a huge army on your side."

"Aye," Murphy answers. "Except Brigit has over ten million." I stop walking.

"Is that accurate?" I ask Llyr.

"It is."

"What are the chances of there being another great battle?" I continue walking again.

"Earwyn is meeting with them now. Tensions are running high between us all."

"Does Shu know I'm here?" My foot slips on a slippery rock. Murphy catches me.

"No, and it's going to stay that way unless we have no other choice." His voice sounds more stern than usual.

"What if I want to meet him?"

"Absolutely not," Llyr and Murphy object in unison.

"He's the one who kept you hidden for years. He did that to hurt me. If he knew you were here, I don't know what he would do." Llyr glides his hand over my cheek. "I lost you once, I won't lose you again."

"Living in those foster homes was hell, being homeless was a living nightmare, but that life made me strong, made me fierce. I am who I am because of that life. I had to fight for survival. It's taken me a while to realize it, but maybe it was the best thing that could've happened to me." I can't believe those words came out of my mouth. "Let me meet him. I'm his granddaughter."

Llyr turns to the sea. He closes his eyes and turns into a twelve-foot wall of swirling water before my eyes. He raises what are most likely his hands, and chants something in a language that feels familiar, but just out of reach of understanding.

Hundreds of lessers rise from the water, moving toward us. They bow in unison at the god before them, my father. One breaks away from the group, heading in my direction. "My queen," he whispers as he bows before me. I recognize him as the lesser from the compound, my first experience with a water elemental.

I bow my head in response. "Good to see you again, my friend." He joins the others.

"My children, it's good to see you. I know you've been here guarding this island for centuries and I'm grateful. I fear the time has come when we will need to broaden our numbers and be ready for attacks from all elements." He motions toward me. "My daughter, Adria, is here and will guide you. I ask that you protect her with your life."

A whisper of approval comes from the mass of water before us. Chill bumps cover my skin. "They're magnificent," I whisper to Murphy.

"Aye," he responds.

Llyr lowers his arms, and the lessers disappear into the sea below. "Call them," he says to me. My eyes feel like saucers. "Your soul knows the words. Trust." He turns back to human form and stands behind me. "Lift your arms and call them to the surface."

I take a deep breath in, blowing it out loudly. How the hell am I supposed to summon lesser elementals in an ancient language? I raise my hands as directed and close my eyes. Llyr whispers in my ear. "Etach spak dune."

"Etach spak dune," I echo. The water stirs under my command.

"Again," he demands.

"Etach spak dune," I repeat, louder. Again, the water stirs.

"Once more."

"Etach spak dune." The lessers rise from the sea directly in front of me.

"Perfect," Llyr whispers. "They're yours to command."

I bow my head to the mass of water. "Thank you, my friends." I release the imaginary string I was holding, and they disappear into the sea like before.

"I just did that." I smile at the men behind me. Both return the gesture.

"Call upon them to form a storm." I don't question how. Feeling into my core, I pull the energy I've used for water walls. Picturing a storm in my mind, I command the lessers to do my bidding. In an instant, a waterspout forms out in the sea. "Good, now control it." I move my hand back and forth watching as the storm moves in the same direction. I push forward and the storm moves away, pulling in, and the storm moves closer. "They're at your command," Llyr says in my ear. I release the energy, pulling my hand to my side, and watch as the storm disappears in a moment.

Llyr laughs deeply. "Magnificent."

"That was pretty amazing," Murphy says.

"That concludes lesson number one. Why don't the

two of you go on a run around the island and we'll meet again after lunch for lesson two."

"Thank you," I say to Llyr as he works his way up the rocks.

"I'm sorry I didn't train you from the beginning. I trusted Payne, but he clearly had tough love training in mind." I laugh at his choice of words.

"After lunch."

CHAPTER 16

"That was both terrifying and hot at the same time," Murphy announces, running beside me. We've left the village, running to the far end of the island where we encountered the earth elementals earlier.

I laugh. "It was amazing. I could feel the power of those words. It felt like only the tip of an iceberg. Like I was on the verge of a huge discovery." We top a small hill at the bottom most tip of the island. The sun is high in the sky. The mixture of elements around me strengthens me, filling my soul. I pull energy from the water, the air, and the earth that surrounds us.

"You're beaming," he says. "Your skin is glowing."

"So are you." He moves to me, taking my hands into his. I don't wait for him to act, I kiss him deeply, pulling our hands behind me. The energy between us is electric. His tongue brushes against mine and he moans into my mouth.

"Adria, you're making me feel all kinds of things and

the top of this hill is not the place for what's going through my mind." He pulls away.

"It's the energy of this place. My body's on fire."

"As much as I would *love* to extinguish those flames, we have to get back. Llyr trusts me with you. I don't want to mess that up, again." He steps back.

"Again?" I ask.

"Come on, I'll tell you as we head back." He starts jogging but doesn't speak for a while and I don't push the issue. The village square's within eyesight before he finally breaks the silence. "I was Llyr's right-hand man. The one that he took to meetings, etc."

"Like Earwyn?" I ask. "You were his assistant?"

"Aye."

"What happened?"

"Earwyn worked for Brigit."

I interrupt again. "Brigit, the goddess of fire?"

"Aye, the goddess of fire."

"So, the twin cousins were twin assistants?"

"You going to let me tell the story or keep interrupting?" He smiles with his words. I slide a hand over my lips, mimicking a zipper, sliding it into my pocket, and motion for him to continue. "I received intel that Brigit had created a new kind of lesser." I raise my hand to ask a question. Murphy rolls his eyes but responds. "Yes?"

"A new kind of lesser?" My eyebrows raise in question. We stop running as we approach the fountain in the square.

"Aye, I learned through my informant that the lessers Brigit had been creating were different. Not like any lessers we'd seen before. These were monstrous, and destructive, the kind that kills humans for sport. Llyr went straight to Brigit, who of course denied any creation. Trusting me, trusting my word, Llyr forced her hand and made her show him everything she'd done. He found nothing, no evidence of anything I'd told him." He sits down on a bench surrounding the fountain. "Brigit's a crafty bitch. I knew she was lying but couldn't prove it."

"Llyr believed her?"

"Aye, with Earwyn's convincing of course."

"That's why you don't like him." Their dislike is obvious, even to the clueless.

"Just another reason on a growing list," he agrees.

"Why is he here? If he worked for Brigit, and he's a damn fire hybrid, why does he now work for Llyr?" I scrunch my forehead in confusion.

"When Llyr forced his way into her world and found no evidence of my accusations, she was angry. In order to keep the peace between fire and water, she insisted that Earwyn, loyal to her, would work in Llyr's home in return for peace."

I can't hide my shock. "What the hell? Earwyn's a spy for Brigit, and Llyr knows it?"

"Not long after coming here, Earwyn renounced his loyalty to Brigit and pledged allegiance to Llyr." I jump to my feet.

"And Llyr believed him? Did you believe him? I don't believe him, and I barely know him." I pace around the circle of the fountain.

Remembering Hannah's words last night. "I don't trust him."

"At first, I didn't either, but as much as it pains me to

say it, he's given me no reason to think he's not being truthful. I've looked for evidence all over the world, anything to prove Brigit was lying and using Earwyn to spy, but she's smart and has many people on her payroll."

"That's the tension between you and Llyr?" I ask, stopping in front of him.

"Aye. After that, he took any responsibility away from me and gave it to Earwyn, the slimy bastard."

"Until you found me..." I finish his thought.

"Until I found you," he echoes.

"So, I'm your redeeming grace."

He stands, moving toward me. "You're much more than that. In fact, you're much more than I bargained for when I set out to find you." His pupils dilate as he moves closer.

"I knew the moment I met you there was something special about you, besides the elemental blood. My soul sang when I met you that night in your commander's office. You were pissy and annoyed, but I saw through the façade. I saw you, the real you, and felt a connection like no other." The streets are covered with people going about their everyday lives. If not, I might have thrown all inhibitions out of the window and jumped his bones right here.

Murphy's breathing fast as he cups my face into his hands, gently rubbing his thumb along my jawline. His actions speak volumes and I'm overcome with emotion. Goosebumps cover my arms. He closes his eyes, resting his forehead against mine. "Thank you for finding me," I whisper.

"Thank you for being found," he whispers back. We

stare at each other a few minutes longer before I interrupt the moment with a question that's been gnawing at me.

"Why do only some of the lower-level lessers attack humans?" I sit on the familiar bench next to the fountain. "Until coming here, I assumed all lessers were like our fire friend at the compound or the air elemental that attacked us. I never realized there were high-level lessers who don't set out to kill everything in their sight."

Murphy sits at the opposite end of the bench. "Just like there are good and bad humans, there are good and bad elementals. The ones we came in contact with are not good. Most likely lower-level lessers who have nothing more than death and destruction on their minds."

"I don't know how to feel about that," I answer, sliding my hands under my legs. Murphy wrinkles his forehead in confusion. "What if I've killed or trained someone else to kill an elemental who was not inherently bad?"

"Have you ever killed or fought an elemental who didn't attack you first?" he asks.

I think back to my years at the compound. I shake my head. "No."

"Then your actions were justified and understood. Now that you know the truth about lessers, I have no doubt any action you take will be the last resort." He stands, pulling me up with him. "It's lunchtime and Llyr will be expecting us." I follow him back to the castle grounds and into the house. Stephen has an amazing-looking salad and sandwich waiting for us in the dining room.

"Stephen," I call as he exits the room. He stops to look

at me. "Thank you, this looks delicious." He smiles broadly.

"My pleasure." I make a mental note to thank him more often. Paid or not, he needs to know he's appreciated. He bows, leaving the room.

I enjoy each bite of my lunch, making sure not to overstuff my stomach. I don't know what our afternoon training will be and throwing up is an embarrassing option. "Where's Llyr? He should be hungry too."

"Llyr doesn't eat every day," I remember him dipping his sandwich in his soup and telling me the same thing. "Lessers usually don't eat anything, especially the lower-level ones. Their energy sustains them."

I think back to the compound. "You've told me that before, but the fire lesser at the compound would eat anyone she could get her hands on." He stares at me like I have two heads.

"She did what?" he asks, confused.

"The fire lesser from the compound, the one I killed. She would eat recruits or trainers. She wasn't picky," I repeat.

"Are you saying she ate humans?" His face turns pale. "Are you sure?"

Flashbacks of charred flesh flash through my mind. "Yes. I thought that was normal for lessers. At least it was normal at the compound."

He stands from his chair. "Adria, I need you to be one hundred percent sure about this. You're telling me the fire elemental at your compound, the one you killed on the beach, ate human flesh?"

I stare at him in confusion. "Yeah. Why are you acting creepy?"

"Come with me." He leads me out of the door and into the courtyard. Llyr's in the far corner, sitting on a bench overlooking the water.

"Ah, perfect timing." He stands as we approach. "Ready for lesson two?"

"Adria, please tell Llyr what you told me."

I don't understand what's going on, but I do as asked. Llyr has the same look on his face as Murphy. The two exchange knowing glances. "What the hell's going on? Why are you two acting weird?" I look between the two of them.

"Lessers don't eat anything, especially humans," Llyr answers.

"Someone should have told that bitch in the compound then. She ate quite a few recruits over the years." Not to mention Hannah. Sitting down on the bench, I focus on pushing that thought away. "What does this mean?"

"It means I was right all along. Brigit did create new lessers. One's that were more dangerous than ever." I watch the two men pace back and forth, each hashing out details in their minds.

"Where's Earwyn?" I ask. Neither man answers. "Llyr, where's Earwyn?" I repeat.

"He's meeting with several higher-level lessers from each element." Llyr stops pacing. "I left early to be with you."

I stand, looking both of them in the eyes. "Am I the

only one that doesn't think that's what he's actually doing?"

Llyr looks at me. "What are you thinking?"

It's my turn to pace. "Earwyn's in a meeting with high-level officials of each element, except water."

"There are higher-up water lessers there too." He interrupts. "O'Brien is there, along with several of his family."

"I remember him from my first night here. He asked me what my plans were for the island and Murphy shut him up politely." I stop moving. "I don't trust Earwyn. He's worked for Brigit before and was forced to come here and work for you."

"He pledged his allegiance toward water," Llyr answers.

"Nothing personal, but I've never been a fan of O'Brien. He's only supported the element with the most benefits for the moment." Murphy runs a hand through his curls. "As far as Earwyn goes, he's my cousin and we're connected by blood, but I agree with Adria. He's hiding something. I've felt it for years but never found any evidence. He knows the secrets of the island. He knows Adria's here. He knows everything about your defense systems and how to override them, and now he's off the island with others who would benefit from that information." The skies darken above. Llyr's visibly angry.

"How could I have been so foolish?" Llyr asks.

"Does he know about me?" Llyr knows what I'm asking.

"He knows you're my daughter, but not Claire's true identity."

"What about Shu? He knows who I truly am."

"Yes, but he doesn't know you're here," he answers.

"If he has lessers in the meeting with Earwyn, he may by now," Murphy says, pacing in a circle.

"Dammit to hell. I'll be back," Llyr says. Turning to Murphy, "Get the island ready for attack, prepare the humans. If I'm not back by nightfall, you know what to do." The two men share a knowing look. He turns to me. "Adria, I love you." Llyr literally blinks out of existence.

"Llyr?" I yell. "Murphy, what just happened?"

"He's gone. We have to get the people to safety. Follow me." We climb to the top tower of the castle. The bricks look old and a few crumble as we carefully climb. At the top is a large bell, straight out of medieval times. Murphy pulls with all his weight, and the bell slowly swings to one side, then the other, filling the tower with ear-piercing overtones. I cover my ears in response. He rings it for several minutes, making sure everyone hears before we head back down.

"They'll know what to do when they hear it. Llyr set up underground passages and bunkers years ago in case something like this were to happen. Each home has a door to the passage and the bunkers are hidden deep underground and heavily warded. The humans will be safe. Come on, we need to check the island wards." He leads me to a garage I've never been in. Inside are cars of every make, model, and year. I think I've entered heaven.

"How did I not know this was here?" I say, looking around the room of luxury cars. "Oh, my gods. This is a McLaren F1!" I stop in my tracks.

"Adria, we don't have time for a fangirl moment. We need to check the wards." I swat him away.

"I don't think you understand the significance of this car. Only one hundred of these were ever produced. They sell for over twenty million dollars." I run my hand across the hood. "How did I not know this was in here?"

Murphy stands next to me. "I hate to interrupt your love affair, but we need something easy to get around in. Come on." He pulls me away from magic on four wheels to a group of motorcycles. "Can you ride?" he asks, handing me a helmet.

I climb on top of a bright red Ducati. "I borrowed one of these once. In fact, it's what helped get me here."

He huffs a laugh. "That sounds like a story I want to hear. We need to check the wards, make sure they're secure."

"What do I look for?" I have no clue what the wards even look like.

"They'll look like a sigil. Most of them are in plain sight, carved on large boulders. There's one on each solar point of the island, North, South, East, and West. I'll check south and east while you check north and west. Each sigil matches the point where it sits."

"Okay." The bike roars to life. I've forgotten what it feels like to have that much power between my legs. I laugh at the innuendo.

"What?" Murphy asks.

"I'll tell you later." I wink. "What happens if one of the wards is gone?"

"Come find me, we'll figure it out." I lower the shield on my helmet, release the clutch, and fly out of the garage toward the north end of the island. I push the bike past one hundred miles an hour. The last time I rode one of these I was outrunning someone. Technically, I still am. I focus on the road in front of me. One tiny rock at this speed could throw the bike off and make me wreck before I know what happened. It only takes a few minutes to reach the northern point. I find a large boulder sitting exactly where Murphy said it'd be. Carved on the boulder is a symbol similar to waves crashing into land. Instinctively, I know the symbol is Llyr's and it stands for water. I assess the rock, looking for any damage or cracks that would make the sigil not effective. I don't see anything. It looks perfect. I jump back on the bike and head for the western one. After several attempts and not finding it, I turn on the compass on my watch and follow it to the exact location of the western ward. A large boulder sits on top of a cliff, surrounded by nothing but water and stone. The sigil is the same, but as I approach, I realize it's damaged. A large crack separates the sigil into two pieces.

"Shit," I say out loud. Looking over the cliff, everything looks normal. I don't know what to do.

"Etach spak dune," I shout over the water, repeating the words Llyr taught me earlier. Nothing happens.

Stretching my arms wide, I repeat the words. "Etach spak dune!" The water swirls as hundreds of lessers form their shapes below.

"How may we be of service?" they whisper in unison.

"This ward is down," I shout. "We have reason to believe the island will be under attack soon. Protect the island and don't allow any lessers to breach this point. I will return."

"Yes, your highness," they whisper.

"Thank you, my friends." I jump back on the bike and push the Ducati faster, speeding toward the village and Murphy. Hopefully, he'll know how to fix the ward. Entering the village, the usually busy streets are empty, homes look abandoned, and stores are closed. Thank gods Llyr had an escape plan already in place. I fly past Murphy's parent's store and home. The lights are off and a metal gate covers the entrance, relief floods me.

Heading south, I don't see Murphy anywhere. Maybe he's still checking the sigils. Pulling out my compass, I follow the arrow to the southern point of the island. The boulder is easy to find, and the sigil looks complete. Fresh tire tracks grab my attention. He's been here but gone. Something's wrong. I feel it in my bones. I push the bike to speeds well over one hundred twenty miles an hour heading to the eastern ward. This bike is built for a track, not rocky roads. Speeds like this on terrain like this are a death wish.

A vibration on my wrist alerts me I'm only a few miles away from the eastern point of the island. I see the fight before I approach. Shit, Murphy's under attack. Lesser elementals have breached the cliffs and are being held off by a wall of water. "What the hell?"

Parking the bike on the ground, I run toward the fight. Earth and fire lessers have Murphy surrounded but he's holding them off with water. He has the freaking power of water. I produce a tidal wave as I run, clearing off one side of his wall and lessers. I pass through his water with no resistance. "Are you okay?" I yell.

"Aye." We stand back to back, each producing our

own wall of water, pushing the lessers back. The fire lessers can't fight the water and have left the fight, heading toward the city. "Don't let them get away!" he shouts.

I pull from my core, calling on the parts of me that have begged to be set free for years. I call on the pain of my childhood, the love I've discovered on the island, and everything that's made me who I am. In a scream, I release the energy, producing a huge explosion of water, rocks, and sand. The world goes silent. Murphy's still backed up against me. "What was that?" he asks.

"Me." Keeping our backs together, we circle looking for any signs of movement, neither spotting any. "Are they gone?"

"I think so. Whatever you did was powerful enough to overtake them all. It was like a nuclear bomb of energy." He turns to face me. "The eastern sigil is destroyed." He points where a boulder once stood. Nothing's left but pebbles.

"The western one is cracked, but not destroyed. Water lessers are guarding it."

"There's no way to fix this one. Are the humans safe?" he asks.

"Yes. The village looked deserted." He sighs deeply. "Your parents' store looks abandoned, I checked."

"Thank gods." He walks to the edge of the cliff. "They'll be back. We can't stay here."

"How much time do we have?"

He walks back to me with his hands on his hips. "A few days maybe? I don't know how many escaped if any. As soon as it's discovered the island is vulnerable, they'll return. We have to get to the castle."

I grab his arm as he starts walking. "Are we not going to discuss the elephant on the island?"

He turns to me. "I should've told you. I'm sorry."

"You're sorry? You're the one who told me hybrids didn't have any control over their element, knowing the whole time you could? What kind of shit is that?" I don't know why I'm angry.

He sighs, running a hand through messy hair. "I don't have the power you do, but I can hold my own."

I look around at the destruction. "You held off earth and fire lessers by yourself for at least thirty minutes. Have you been pretending this whole time? Did that air elemental really knock you out?" A horrible thought enters my mind. "Did you set the fire elemental free to test my skills?" My voice is no louder than a whisper.

"Gods no, Adria. I would never do something like that. Humans died because of her. I would never put people's lives in danger to prove a point." He steps toward me. "The air elemental didn't knock me out. I needed to see if you were the one—if you were Llyr's daughter." Anger forms in my core.

"You put my life in danger to see if I could protect myself? What the hell, Murphy?" I push him back several feet. He holds up his hands in front of his chest. "I could've died, you could've died. For what? So you can get your precious job back with Llyr? Get your glory?"

"That was my plan at first. I needed to get back in Llyr's graces, but that changed when I met you." He steps closer.

"Don't! How am I supposed to believe that? You lied about your reason for being at the compound, you lied about being able to control water, and you lied about being knocked out. What else have you lied about?" Anger forms in the pit of my stomach.

"That's everything. I wouldn't have lied if I had a choice."

My teeth grit in anger. "You always have a choice. That's one thing I learned growing up. We take responsibility for our own thoughts and actions, and you always have a choice."

"Would you have believed me if I told you the truth in the beginning?" His volume matches mine. "The girl who I met that night wouldn't have believed anything I said. She was hurt, sad, and lonely. The last thing she needed was for me to tell her the truth. It was something she had to find out on her own." He moves toward me again. "I had to let you discover your abilities. It had to be you. It's always been you."

I don't say anything else, just jump on the bike and head toward the castle. He's right and it pisses me off. The girl I was then wouldn't have believed him. She'd have kicked his ass right off the compound and continued her miserable, boring existence, waiting on death. I hear his bike behind me, but he doesn't try to catch up to me, he gives me space and I'm grateful.

CHAPTER 17

The sun's still high in the sky as we approach the castle, bringing a sense of calm where chaos reigned hours earlier. Part of me hopes Llyr will be waiting in the courtyard, but with the amount of power that tried to overtake us earlier, if he's alive, he won't be back anytime soon. What's Earwyn's part in all of this? I think through possible scenarios as we enter the abandoned village. If Murphy has the power of water, it's a strong possibility Earwyn has the power of fire.

We park the bikes in front of the door, making for an easy escape if needed. I don't speak as I take off the helmet, set it on the seat, and head inside. Murphy follows me up the stairs toward the landing.

"Adria, I'm truly sorry. If it's any consolation, I made sure you were never in any real danger." I stop walking, fighting tears that threaten to fall.

"You don't get it, do you?" I turn in anger. "I don't trust people. Trusting people will only get you hurt. I let my guard down with you. I broke my own damn rules and look where it got me. I trusted you, Murphy." Tears stream down my cheeks. "You lied to me." I wipe my cheeks with the back of my hand. "What happened between us, was that real or another part of your plan?" He steps toward me and I step back.

"That was more real than anything I've ever experienced." I don't even try to hide the tears. "The connection I felt... I feel, with you is real. It's killing me not to be closer to you right now."

"Good," I say, backing up the stairs.

"I didn't know I could control water until I was a teenager. Like you, the first time was an accident. I was in danger and it just sort of happened. It took me years to be able to control it."

"You said hybrids can't control their element, was that a lie too?"

"*Most* can't. I'm one of the exceptions."

"Does Llyr know?" I ask.

He looks down before answering. "No. You're the only one that knows."

"Why have you kept it a secret?"

"Honestly, I don't know. Maybe because I felt like a freak." He shrugs. "You have every right to be angry at me. I don't blame you, but right now we have to deal with the threat to the island." He follows me up the stairs.

"You don't get off that easy! We're not just going to sweep this under the rug and pretend it never happened. You lied to me, Murphy. I trusted you and you lied!" I walk toward the balcony doors.

He sighs, running a hand through his curls. "I did and

I'm sorry. But, please believe me when I tell you I didn't lie to hurt you. I had to know the truth about your powers."

"So, you pretended to be knocked out while a full-fledged air elemental attacked both of us? What kind of screwed-up logic is that?" I feel the rumble of power forming in my stomach. Murphy senses it too and backs away.

"Adria, I know you're angry..."

"No shit, Sherlock. What gave it away?" Swirls of energy explode from my chest ready to wreak havoc on the man in front of me.

A whirl of pulsations reaches me just as I'm about to release a destructive force into Murphy. It's the same feeling I felt at the compound. "Is that another one of the 'things' you didn't tell me about? What the hell is that?"

"I don't know, but it happens when I'm nervous." The pulsations relax me, releasing the tension I've built up. "From what little research I've done on it, the sensations are similar to that of sonar."

"I'll add that to the list of secrets you've kept." I turn, heading toward my room and my escape. He doesn't try to stop me.

I sit in my room, wrapped in my new favorite fluffy blanket for several hours, contemplating everything that's happened over the past few days. My life is a whirlwind and I'm the vortex.

"That bastard," Hannah says, sitting in the seat beside me, overlooking the crystal-clear water.

"My thoughts exactly," I answer. "I trusted him, Hannah."

"I know you did. You were right to trust him." I turn to her.

"What? Did you miss the entire last few hours? He lied to me. He lied about why he came to the compound to start with, then he pretended to be knocked unconscious while I fought off an air elemental, and to top it all off, he lied about being able to control water." Tears threaten to fall again. "How was I right to trust him? I let him in, and he lied."

"This doesn't sound like the Adria I know. That girl didn't put up with anything. But man, once you got through those thick-ass walls she put around herself, she was remarkable. She would fight for you, even if it meant her life was in danger." Hannah props her feet on the railing.

"I don't want to talk about that," I answer.

She sighs loudly. "Maybe you *need* to talk about it." She turns toward me. "It wasn't your fault."

"Hannah, stop."

"I was dumb," she continues. "I should've listened to you in the first place."

"Stop." My voice is no louder than a whisper.

"I got cocky. Thought I was faster than she was, thought I was stronger." She pauses. "I left the path. I knew better, we all know better. Hell, I trained people to know better, but I did it anyway."

Tears stream down my cheeks. "You should've let her get me."

"What good would that have done?" she asks.

"It was me she was coming after."

"But it was me that veered from the path," she repeats.

The memory of Hannah's scream as the fire elemental ripped her to shreds replays through my mind, causing me to cover my ears. "I tried to get to you. She was too fast."

"I know," Hannah answers.

"Why did she let me live? After you, after you died, she let me live. I wanted to die with you."

"I saw that bitch heading straight toward you and refused to let that happen."

I look up confused. "How could you have seen her? You were already... gone."

"My body was gone, but my soul was there with you."

"It was you?" I ask, remembering a hidden detail from that day. Hannah nods. "You opened the door and pushed me through?"

She doesn't answer for a while. "I didn't want you to end up with the same fate as me." I turn to face her, my best friend, the girl who saved my life not once, but twice.

"I'm sorry I didn't save you." Tears stream down my cheeks.

She turns fully toward me. "We can't change our destiny. What happened that day was supposed to happen. It's what led you on this path of finding who you truly are. Our fates are intertwined, and I'll always be with you. Yes, knowing that Murphy lied hurts, but in the big scheme of this shitstorm you're in the middle of, it's nothing more than a speck of sand."

I reach for her as the blanket falls to the seat of the chair. "Hannah?" She's gone. I stare into the sea, replaying her words over and over. She's right. If my choices are to try and save the world, or pout over lies, the choice is simple.

Murphy's standing with his hand ready to knock as I open my door. I don't give him time to speak. "How do we fix this?"

He lets out a sigh of relief before answering. "I'm so sorry, Adria."

I hold up a hand, stopping him. "I know and I understand why, but we have bigger things to worry about right now."

"Aye, we do," he answers.

"Who else knew about the wards?" I move past him back to the landing.

"There's only one other person."

"Earwyn," I answer, walking toward the balcony.

He moves beside me. "Llyr trusted him too much."

I look up in fear. "Does Earwyn know about the bunkers?" If he knows where the humans are, he'll lead the lessers straight to them.

"I don't think so. Those bunkers were built decades ago. The only reason I know about them is from growing up with Ethan and Bonnie. It's a secret between the villagers and Kyler Smith."

"Let's hope you're right." Stepping out into the night air, the sun has completely set, casting a glow over the sea below. "Before Llyr left, he said you would know what to do if he doesn't return by nightfall. What does that mean?"

He looks down. "I'm supposed to call Shu."

I turn quickly. "That's Llyr's plan? To call Shu, my grandfather? The one who he demanded not know I'm here because he's unstable?"

"Aye. Despite everything that's happened, Shu pledged

his loyalty to Llyr before the great battle." I stand dumb-founded, unsure of what to say. "Brigit has tried to over-take the rest of them before. It's why she's created new lessers after she signed the pact. Dagda is weak and follows her orders. If we take down Brigit, we stop the battle before it happens. Shu's the only one that can help us do that."

"Llyr literally just said if Shu sided with Brigit and Dagda, it would be a fight he would never win, yet you're supposed to call him to come to the rescue?" I cross my arms in front of my chest.

"Aye, he did."

"Then why call him? Am I missing something?"

Murphy sighs. "Because he's our only choice. Despite what's happened, he pledged his loyalty and that over-powers everything else."

"Are you willing to risk our lives, the lives of your family, the lives of every human on this planet on the chance he'll be loyal to a pledge made a millennium ago?" My tone has changed to anger.

Murphy joins me at the railing, lowering his head. "Aye, I am. This castle is more than just a home. Under-neath, buried deep into the seabed, is an arsenal and a prison built to sustain a First." I turn completely toward him.

"Llyr built a First elemental prison underneath the castle?"

"Aye. When you live as long as he has, you prepare for the inevitable."

"Does Earwyn know?" I ask.

"I don't know, possibly. It's a risk we have to take."

I take a deep breath. "Okay, how do we get Shu here?" Murphy pulls out his cell phone and hands it to me. "Is this a joke? You want me to just call him on the phone?"

"Aye, it's listed under 'air arsehole'." I laugh out loud. "What?" he asks, with a serious face. "You should see what Brigit's listed as."

My face changes to serious. "What do I say? Hi Grandpa, I'm in the UK and we need you to come?"

"That works," he answers. He unlocks his phone, pulling up the contact. True to his word, the contact is listed as "air arsehole". I try not to smile, remembering that I'm still pissed at him.

"Yes?" a deep voice on the other end says.

"Shu?" I ask.

"What do you want, Murphy?" His voice is short and clipped with a hint of an accent I can't quite place.

"This is Adria... Adria Kane." Shu pauses. Butterflies take flight in my stomach waiting for his response.

"I don't have time for jokes," he says.

"This isn't a joke. It's Adria, Claire's daughter."

"Adria?" he whispers.

"Yes. I'm on the Isle of Man. We need you." He hangs up without responding.

"What did he say?" Murphy asks.

"Nothing. He just hung up." I hand him back his phone.

"Shit. We don't have time to get to him."

"Where is he?"

"It's hard telling, but his home is a small island off the coast of Southern France. He's been there for almost as long as Llyr's been here." He paces around the balcony. "By the time I get there and back, it'll be too late."

A gust of wind blasts through the room. "I apologize for hanging up on you, but your words came as quite a shock."

I turn toward the voice. Behind me stands a tall, thin man wearing a white linen suit. His dark hair is the perfect contrast against the bright suit. Dark brown eyes, accentuated by high cheekbones and defined eyebrows, the man standing before me is beautiful and looks no older than Llyr.

"Shu," Murphy says, bowing to one knee. Am I supposed to bow? I stand awkwardly, not sure what the protocol is.

"Murphy," the man responds. "Am I to assume this is Adria?" He looks me up and down. I'm filthy dirty and my hair is a tangled mess from the helmet I wore earlier. I wave awkwardly.

"Hi?"

"You look just like her," he says, his voice full of emotion. "I only met her once, but you are exactly how I remember her." He walks toward me. "I sense power in you." I hold my head high, not sure where this is going. He looks between the two of us. "What has happened? Where is Llyr?"

"Gone," I answer. "We need to talk." I lead both men onto the landing. I watch as Shu gracefully sits on the edge of the settee. His movement reminds me of a cat, precise and refined. Murphy and I take seats opposite him. "I don't know where to start," I admit.

"Let's start with why you are here. How did Llyr find you?" he asks.

I look at Murphy for moral support. He nods slightly. "Murphy found me in California. I was a Phoenix, training recruits to fight against the lessers." He raises his eyebrows in surprise. "When he figured out who I was, he brought me here, to Llyr."

He sighs before speaking. "I guess you know I'm the one responsible for hiding you from him?" He doesn't waste a moment before jumping headfirst into turmoil.

"Yes," I whisper. "I was hidden in horrible places, with people who did horrible things to me." He looks down, clearly uncomfortable. "For what? To get revenge on Llyr for a daughter you only met once? You denied me a life where I could learn who and what I am, and where I could've grown into my gifts. Where I could've been loved." The last part is nothing more than a whisper. Murphy looks at me.

"I was wrong, I see that now. I let my anger fuel my judgment and I am sorry." Shu's words are slow and precise. "I'm here. I didn't just come because of the pledge I made to Llyr, I'm here because of you."

His words are sincere and tears flow. Dammit, today has been an emotional roller coaster. Hop on and strap in. "How am I supposed to believe you?"

Long fingers rub across the knees of his white pants. "That, my dear, is something you'll have to decide on your own. I was wrong, I'm sorry. I'm here to make it up to you."

Emotions flood me, I fight to keep them contained. It's clear Shu doesn't mince words, and I like that about him. Looking him in the eyes, I feel a connection, and I think back to Hannah's words. Everything I've gone through in my life has brought me to this crux. "I'm not sure forgiveness is in order just yet but thank you for coming."

He stands. "Fair enough. How much time do we have?" he asks Murphy, who stands in front of him. "Not long. They've destroyed the wards on the east side of the island, and the west is damaged."

"The water lessers are guarding the west. I'm not sure how long they'll be able to hold."

"Come, tell me everything." He leads us down the stairs into Llyr's office. Stephen walks in carrying a tray of tea and cookies.

"Stephen? Why are you here? You should be hiding with the rest of the humans." He sets the tray down, pouring hot tea for us.

"My place is here, serving until I can't serve any longer. I'll go when you tell me, but not a moment earlier." I nod in agreement resisting the urge to hug the small man.

"Thank you," I say, taking the teacup from him.

Shu moves behind Llyr's desk and pushes a button I had no idea existed. A hidden cabinet on the opposite wall pops open. Inside are computers, weapons, maps, and stacks of money.

"How..."

"I've known Llyr for a very long time," he answers, sitting down at the desk. "Tell me what I need to know."

I take a deep breath. "When I was at the compound,

we had a 'resident'," I use air quotation marks, "a fire elemental who liked to eat people." He scrunches his forehead in a move that looks very familiar.

"Lessers don't eat humans," he dismisses.

"If I may?" Murphy asks. I nod and he continues the story. "Several years back I received information that Brigit was working on creating new lessers, ones that would devour humans and anything in their way. Evil, cruel monsters. When Llyr confronted her, of course, she denied it. When no proof could be found, Llyr believed her and life moved on." Shu is beginning to look bored. "Once Adria's true identity was discovered and she came to the island, the thought of Brigit's lessers hadn't crossed anyone's mind."

"Until you mentioned the flesh-eating one in California?" Shu answers, piecing the puzzle together.

"Aye. Llyr knew instantly that Brigit was lying and his assistant who'd sworn loyalty to him had betrayed him."

"Tell me this assistant doesn't know who Adria is to him, to Llyr." Shu looks between the two of us.

"He knows," I answer.

Shu stands behind the desk. "Well, this is quite a conundrum, isn't it?" He walks to the brandy cart and pours himself a glass. "You think this is why the island was breached." He states this as a fact and swallows the contents of his glass in one gulp. "He knows you're Llyr's daughter. Does he know you also carry my bloodline?"

"No." I shake my head. "Only two people know. Murphy and Payne." Shu raises his head at the mention of the last name.

"Payne? Why would he be privy to this information before me?" He pours another glass.

"Llyr brought him in to teach me how to control air." Shu slams his glass on the table.

"Payne deserted air, I haven't seen him in many years."

Shit. "Do you think he's with Brigit?" Shu doesn't answer. "Llyr didn't approve of his training style and sent him away."

"Time will tell," he says, downing the second glass of brandy. "Was he successful in his training?"

"If you're asking whether or not I can use air, no. Payne believed I held the power to control it in my throat chakra." Shu grunts.

"If Llyr trusted Payne enough for him to know about your ability, we're going to hope that he didn't make the same mistake he did with this assistant of his." Shu returns to the desk. "What's your plan?" he asks Murphy.

Murphy looks at me, unsure how much to divulge. "Llyr's built a dungeon of sorts under the castle. We need to get Brigit to the island and trap her inside. We need to stop her before she leaves you all no choice but to destroy the world and all of its inhabitants."

"Agreed," Shu responds. "How do we get her here?"

Murphy and I look at each other. "I think that's a job only a First can do," Murphy answers. Shu nods, standing up.

"First thing tomorrow then. Tonight, I teach Adria how to draw on air." My eyes widen in confusion. "Meet me in the gym in thirty minutes?" I nod, excitedly.

CHAPTER 18

$\mathcal{T}$rue to his word, Shu is waiting for me when I enter the gym which took me ten minutes to find. He's wearing white jogging pants and a white tank top. White must be his signature color. "Ah, Adria, I was beginning to think you weren't coming."

"Sorry about that. I got lost." He smirks at my admission. "Most of my training's been outside." I feel an overwhelming need to explain myself.

I look around the vast room. Training dummies are set up against one wall. Large mirrors line the one opposite making it resemble a dance studio more than a gym. Strength-building equipment takes up the far-left corner, with basketball goals on each end.

"Come, sit with me." He crouches to the floor with the ease of a child, sitting cross-legged facing me. He motions to the floor in front of him. "Please," he says. I sit down, copying his position.

"Controlling air is a simple task. Your energy, the life

force inside you, is strong. That energy is what controls the air, it's not a physical part of you. Think of it as an extension of you." His voice is soft and relaxes me. "Close your eyes." I do as he says. "I want you to visualize the energy field that surrounds everything in this room. The floor you're sitting on to the clothes you're wearing, all are made of energy. The trick to controlling air is learning how to bend that energy to do your bidding." He pauses. "Place your hands flat on the floor. Do you feel anything?"

"Just floor."

"Lift your hands slightly. What do you feel now?"

"Nothing?" I answer, unsure of what I'm supposed to feel.

"That's where you're wrong. The floor is still there, and the energy it produces is all around you. Feel that energy." I relax my entire body. "Listen to the energy, it calls you to it."

Something similar to a buzz is all around me. It reminds me of a refrigerator running in the background. Always there, but you don't notice unless you fully listen. The buzzing isn't just around my hands, but my entire body. "What do you feel?" he asks.

"Buzzing," I whisper.

"Yes, that's energy. Now tell it what you want it to do." I sit in the buzz a while longer, not exactly sure how to do what he's asking.

Payne told me I needed to use my throat chakra, maybe he was right. "Wind," I whisper. The buzz around me vibrates faster. "Wind," I repeat. Wisps of hair blow around my face.

"That's it. Open your eyes." I'm sitting in the middle of the gym floor, twenty feet from Shu.

"How the hell?" I ask.

"You controlled the energy. You rode it over to where you are now." I look down.

"I flew?" He laughs warmly.

"Not exactly. It's more like the air picked you up and carried you to where you are now. Try again." I close my eyes. "No," he interrupts. "This time with your eyes open." I follow the same steps as before, feeling the buzz around me quicker this time.

"Wind," I'm instantly picked up and moved closer to Shu. I can't keep the smile off my face.

"This is only the very tip of what you can do. My blood flows in you. Your power is limitless."

"Llyr said the same." I lift myself to a new part of the gym.

"Did he?" he asks. "Now picture the energy creating a windstorm in front of you. Use energy from everything. Borrow that energy and use it as your own." He watches me float around the room.

I stop floating and focus on the energy coming from the objects in the gym. My body vibrates and speeds up to match the frequency of those vibrations. "Storm," I whisper. A whirlwind of air forms in front of me, instantly turning into a vortex of air.

"That's it. Now control it." Feeling the energy, I focus more attention on the right side of the storm, pushing it with my mind. The storm reacts, moving in the same direction. I do the same for the other side, and again, the storm reacts. "Good. Now let it go." I open my palms, releasing the energy inside, and instantly, the storm is gone.

"That was amazing." I smile. "Are you sure I did that?" I turn my hands over, looking for anything unusual.

"That, my dear, was all you." He returns the smile. "You're a quick learner. Using those same techniques, you can move air in any direction you want."

"So, I'm an Airbender now?" I laugh at my words, remembering the movie I'd watched years ago. Shu doesn't answer, clearly, he's not a movie watcher.

I practice moving air around for the next hour, each time getting a little easier than the time before. The clean gym I walked into is now a disaster and windblown. "You have the skills, you just need practice. From what you've told me, there isn't time." I follow him out of the gym, to the elevator.

"There's an elevator? No wonder it took me so long to get here." Shu laughs.

"You might want to do some exploring of your ancestral home." He has a good point.

"Tell me about her?" I ask as we ride to the first floor. He holds the door open for me, following me out.

"I wish I could. The one time I met her, I didn't know who she was. I sensed she had power but assumed she was a hybrid. It wasn't until after she passed that I found out her true identity." He pauses as we enter the empty study. "What I do remember from our meeting that day was her strength. Not physical, but mental. She was determined, stubborn, and beautiful. Much like what I see in you."

"I wish I could remember her." I sit on a large, over-stuffed couch. Shu sits at the other end.

"There are a lot of things I would change if I could. One would be meeting her, the other would be keeping you out of Llyr's reach when you were young." He looks down at the couch. "I had no idea what was happening to you in those homes. I made sure you never had the chance to be adopted or stay too long in one place. I didn't want him to find you, but I never would have knowingly put you in a bad situation." He pauses. "I can never make that up to you, but I hope one day you'll give me the chance to try."

I look at the god sitting across from me, my grandfather, who just asked for forgiveness, and I'm filled with compassion. "As a child, I was drawn into the world of the unknown. When I discovered elementals and lessers, I knew that's where I belonged. Part of me always knew I was different. This world called me from the beginning. It's always been in my blood. The life I lived as a child, led me to today and gave me the ability to accept this world and my role in it. It prepared me to be strong, not give up, and fight for what I want. I don't think I could've had better training anywhere else."

Shu lays his hand on top of mine. "You're an amazing young lady. Your mother would be proud."

His words stir emotions I'm not expecting. "Thank you. It's all in the genes." I smile back, enjoying his energy forming through our touch.

"Once I get Brigit back here, what's the plan to get her in the prison?"

"We haven't gotten that far," I answer.

"Go get that boy who loves you, and the three of us will figure it out." My forehead wrinkles in confusion.

"Oh, no, we're just having fun together. In fact, I'm rather pissed at him at the moment. But love," I laugh, "he doesn't love me. We're just flirting." Shu has a knowing look on his face.

"Okay. Why don't you go get *him* and we'll figure out what's going to happen?" He smiles, enjoying the turmoil he's caused.

I head up the stairs thinking about his words. Love? Murphy doesn't love me, does he? Lust maybe, but love? I stand in front of his door. Shu's words threw me off kilter. I knock lightly. Murphy doesn't answer. I try again, but still no answer.

Turning the knob, I slowly open the door. "Murphy?" I walk in to find him on a chair in the corner, sound asleep. Lifting the curls from his forehead, "Murphy," I whisper. He breathes in deeply.

"Adria?" He looks around confused.

"It's me."

"Was I asleep?" he asks, stretching his long legs.

"Looks that way."

"I missed you." He tries kissing me on the temple and I back away. He doesn't respond, but his energy feels darker in an instant. "Did Shu help?" I focus on the balcony windows.

"Wind," I whisper, blowing the doors open. Murphy looks proud and surprised.

"Was that you?" He looks at the doors. I smile proudly. "It *was* you." He returns the smile.

"Shu asked us to meet with him to figure out what to do with Brigit once she arrives."

"Yeah, that's probably important." He slides to the

front of the chair, stretching out his long legs. "Can we talk?" he asks.

"Yes, but now's not the time. Maybe later?"

"That's better than nothing." He stretches his arms straight above his head. "Using the water element today wore me out. I'm sorry I fell asleep."

"Don't apologize, I'd be doing the same if I could." We stare at each other in awkward silence. "Shu's pretty great," I say, trying to ease the tension.

"He's different with you. So's Llyr. I like seeing them like this. They almost act..."

"Human?" I finish his sentence.

"Aye. Human." Shu pops into the room, standing right in front of us.

"What's taking so long?" Murphy's eyes are the size of saucers.

"I, I..." Murphy stumbles for words.

Shu smiles at the awkwardness he's created. "Thank you for finding her and bringing her here. I wanted to tell you that. This seemed as good a time as any." Murphy relaxes his stance, turning back to me.

"The pleasure was all mine," he answers, with a smirk.

"However, for now, I would appreciate you staying an acceptable distance from her." He raises an eyebrow.

"Shu, I'm twenty-three, not sixteen." I volunteer.

Shu looks between the two of us. "I'm well aware of your age. Allow me this one chance to be an overprotective grandparent." He smiles warmly.

"Aye," Murphy answers. "I apologize for keeping you waiting." He stands, "Shall we?" he motions out the door.

Shu pops out of existence, leaving us alone. "I don't think I'll get used to that," I tell Murphy as we walk down the stairs. Shu's waiting for us in the study with a drink in hand. He looks like he's sat in that chair all evening, entertaining guests.

"Drink?" he asks, as we enter.

"No, thank you," we answer in unison.

"Once you get Brigit here, how do we get her in the prison, and what's to stop her newly created lessers from destroying the world without her?" I ask both of them.

Shu toasts the air in front of him. "Two very good questions." He downs his brandy. "Don't worry. Firsts can't get drunk, but I love the taste."

"She's not going in without a fight," Murphy says, rubbing his temple.

"What if we make a deal with her?" I ask the duo.

"Yes, because that worked so well last time." Shu turns to me. "Flesh-eating lessers, did you say?" Point taken. She's never held a bargain before, there's no reason for her to do it now. Shu props his feet on Llyr's desk. For some reason, it strikes me funny that a First Elemental would prop his feet.

"There has to be something Brigit won't risk losing." The energy in the room changes in a heartbeat. Shu feels it and jumps to his feet. Llyr pops into the study. His hair is disheveled, and his clothes are dirty. The two Firsts stare at each other and the tension is palpable.

"Shu," Llyr says.

"Llyr," he responds. He moves from behind the desk of the former while Llyr walks to me.

"Adria, are you okay?" He searches me for answers.

I nod. "I'm good." He runs his hand down my arm, squeezing my hand. "Are *you* okay?" I ask my father.

He looks at me with a questioning look. "I don't think I've been asked that since... well for many years. Yes, I'm fine," he answers, looking around the room and making eye contact with us all. "I know how to stop her."

"Please enlighten us with your discovery." Shu's words are laced with venom.

Llyr turns to Murphy. "Are the humans safe?"

"Aye, since right after you left."

"Good. We're going to bring her here," Llyr announces.

The three of us stare at each other. "We planned the same thing." Llyr looks at us questioningly.

"Yes, we were just hashing out the plan of getting her into the *prison* below." Shu raises an eyebrow at Llyr. Apparently, today's the first he's heard of the prison.

"That's easy, we use the only thing she's ever loved," Llyr responds.

"I wouldn't think that bitch has ever loved anything." Shu fills another glass.

"Brigit has a child," I announce, as the epiphany hits.

All eyes in the room turn to Llyr. He nods, accepting a drink from Shu. "Yes. Earwyn is her son."

"Earwyn is Brigit's child?" I sit on the edge of the couch. He's like me, the child of a god?

"When I left earlier, I did a little investigating. Several fire elementals needed some convincing, but they told me what we need to know." I don't want to know what kind of convincing it took. He looks at Murphy. "Earwyn has been playing with fire the entire time." I laugh out loud at the pun. Everyone in the room stares at me, making me feel incredibly awkward.

"Sorry. I love a good pun." No one responds.

Llyr turns to Murphy. "We all thought you and Earwyn were cousins, your birth fathers', brothers. That's not entirely true." I turn to Murphy, knowing what Llyr's about to say. "Murphy, Earwyn is your half-brother. You share the same father."

"What the ever-living hell? How can he be Earwyn's father too?" he asks Llyr.

Shu watches the spectacle of humanity. "Let me get this straight. From what I'm gathering, Earwyn is the former assistant that you trusted and who betrayed you. Brigit, the goddess of fire, is his mother and his father's a human with a strange affinity for elementals?" He sits on the edge of the desk. "And here I thought air lessers had a lot of issues."

"Looks that way," Llyr answers, ignoring the last part. "Earwyn's played us all for a fool. He's told Brigit every secret of our island, our defense systems, and," he turns to me, "you."

"This was her plan all along." I rest my head on my hands. "The two of them have planned this from the start. They were responsible for the leaked information about the new lessers so that Llyr would investigate and would be forced to take Earwyn as a consolation prize for his intrusion. Earwyn faked his oath to Llyr, and gained his trust, all the while pushing Murphy out of the way." I stand facing the three men. "Don't you see this was all part of the plan, and we fell right into the trap?"

"She knows Adria's your daughter," Shu says, rubbing

his temple. "She's wanted power since the beginning of time. She'll come after Adria, to hurt you."

"She wouldn't risk coming after her on her own. Even she's not dumb enough for that." Llyr moves to the window.

"How do you suggest we get her here?" Shu asks.

Llyr sighs, "Earwyn will be here within the hour."

"Willingly?" I ask.

"Depends on your definition of willingly. As far as he knows, I've called him back to train you." He looks at me. "Sorry to use you as bait, but I knew Brigit would jump at the chance for him to get close to you again. Once he's here, we use him to get her here."

"I don't mind being bait, as long as I don't have to get near him." I physically shiver at the thought.

"I'll make sure that doesn't happen," Murphy adds. "He won't get within ten feet of you."

"When word gets back, Brigit will attack sooner than later. The group that attacked earlier was a test of our defenses," I say to Murphy. He nods in agreement.

"What attack?" Llyr asks.

"The western ward is cracked and barely holding, the eastern one is destroyed." Llyr walks in a circle, obviously angry. "Adria hit them with a blast and got rid of them for now." Murphy looks at me with pride while he speaks.

"Unless I'm missing something, that still leaves us with how to get Brigit in the prison." Shu pours himself another glass of brandy, shaking the empty bottle. "You need more liquor," he announces.

"We have to make her think Earwyn will die if she doesn't agree to meet and to your terms." As much as I dislike him, I don't wish him dead. He's the only other person on this planet that's like me, the child of a First. We're connected in a dysfunctional family kind of way.

Shu walks beside me. "We may have to kill him. Are you prepared for that?"

Truth is, no. "Yes," I lie.

"When he gets here, Shu and I will take care of him." I look up in question. "Don't worry, we won't kill him, just lock him up for the night," Llyr reassures.

"Speak for yourself," Shu says to Llyr. "I can't promise not to kill him. Especially if he puts Adria's life in danger."

"Aye," Murphy agrees.

The two gods share a look that tells me Earwyn won't survive either way.

"Why can't we just kill Brigit?" I look between the two of them.

Llyr sits at his desk. "Killing a First elemental isn't impossible, but it's only been done once before."

Shu looks up in surprise. "Are you sure we need to talk about this?"

Llyr ignores Shu's warning. "Only the child of a First can kill a First. When humans were first created, Dagda found them fascinating, especially the women. He had," he pauses for the right words, "he had his way with many of them, producing offspring all over the world. Most of the children died before reaching adolescence, only a few survived to adulthood." He goes to a cabinet behind his desk, pulls out a new bottle of brandy, and pours a large glass for him and Shu both. "Griffin, his only son to survive, was smart, strong, and more powerful than his father. He possessed the ability of earth, much like you do with water, and was very powerful." Llyr looks at me. "Dagda was out of control. He would destroy entire populations of humans, just for the sport. He didn't care who he killed." Llyr pauses.

Shu sighs, continuing the story. "We knew there was no other way to control him."

"You had Griffin kill his father?" I ask.

Both gods look down. "We did," Shu answers. "It was an easy fight. Dagda was arrogant and weak. Griffin easily took control and killed his father."

"Where's Griffin now?" Murphy asks, moving to my side.

Llyr takes another drink. "He's alive and well and is the god of the earth. He's with Brigit, at her side as her lover and her fool. His name was changed to that of his father, to prevent the world from knowing our weakness. If one of the elements falls, the world will fall with them." He pauses a minute before finishing, "Only a child of a god can assume the throne."

"That's why you never had children, until me?" I move toward my father.

"Yes," he whispers.

Shu clears his throat. "The two of you get some sleep. We'll take care of him tonight."

CHAPTER 19

"*I*'m still pissed, but don't want to be alone," I say to Murphy as we climb the stairs.

"Aye, me either." He follows me into my room. "I'm going to go take a shower, meet you back in here?" I nod. I feel particularly sticky too.

I slowly remove the filthy clothes from today's activities. I look in the mirror, trying not to laugh at the reflection staring back at me. My ponytail is gone and replaced by a mass of tangles. Mascara has formed a nice little island below my eyes. "Gods, I look horrible." Stepping into the hot shower, the water pouring off of me is literally brown. It takes three shampoo applications before the water runs clear. I fight to keep thoughts of conversations out of my head and focus on not cutting my leg off with the razor. "Shit," I whisper, as a tiny cut on the back of my heel pours blood. "Why do they bleed worse than losing a leg?" Thoughts of the day invade my brain and I decide, for the safety of my skin, to get out of the shower.

I choose comfort tonight with a pair of fuzzy sleeping pants and a tank top. A soft knock on the door brings me back to reality and I find Murphy standing there, wearing close to the same outfit. Seeing him melts the anger away. He hangs his head low. "Before I come in, I need to say something."

I step back from the door. "Okay."

He sighs, running a hand through wet curls. "Hurting you was my last intention. I'm sorry for the pain that I caused."

"Murphy," I try and stop him.

"No, let me say this, please. I rehearsed in the shower." I hide the smile trying to form. "The reason I hid my ability from you wasn't anything malicious. You're the first one to know, not even Ethan and Bonnie know. Revealing it felt personal, like ripping my robe open for all to see me naked. It was wrong and I'm sorry. I asked you to trust me and you did. I should've done the same for you." He leans against my doorframe. "The air elemental wasn't planned, but I used that to my advantage. I needed to see what you were capable of. My powers showed themselves during a time of danger, I thought maybe yours would too." He looks up. "I never would have let it hurt you." He sighs, deeply. "For what it's worth, I'm sorry. I don't blame you for being angry. I hope one day you'll trust me again."

I don't respond. Instead, I wrap my arms around his waist, pulling him close. His warmth and energy relax me. "I understand and I do trust you, with my life."

He sweeps me into his arms. "We're going to be okay.

I'll make sure of it." He sits on the bed with me still in his arms. I nod into his chest.

"It's not us I'm worried about." I look into his soft blue eyes. "Earwyn's the only one in the world that's like me. When I think of him dying..." I bury my head into his chest again. "I mean, he's an ass, but I don't wish him dead."

"Aye," he sighs. "I had no idea he was my brother. I don't know if that would've changed how I felt toward him or not."

"He should be here before too much longer. What do you think they'll do to him?" He doesn't answer for a while.

"I don't think they'll hurt him. They'll lock him in Brigit's room in the prison tonight." He pauses. "After that, I don't know."

Thinking back on my training with Shu, I focus on feeling vibrations from the room around me. Murphy's energy moves in tandem with mine creating almost a purr of vibration. "I can feel you."

He pulls his head away slightly. "What?" He looks down. "That's not even touching you. Not that I would mind it touching you, but it's not."

I snort a laugh. "Not that. Your energy, it's touching me. I feel it whenever you're near me. I felt it at the compound when we first met, and I felt it earlier when I was angry."

"Aye, my sonar." I nod. "Is that a good thing?" he asks, softly.

"It is," I whisper back. "We flow well together." Drawing on the combination of our energies, I whisper,

"Wind." The two of us are lifted off the bed and float out onto the balcony.

"What the hell?" he says, looking down. "Did we just fly?"

I smile. "It was explained to me as floating on air." We move closer to the railing.

"I think I'd like to only float over the balcony, please. We're up pretty high." He looks below to the terrace and holds on a little tighter.

"I'm not going to drop you." I bring us back into the room and back to the bed.

He sits up excitedly. "It looks like your training with Shu went well."

I shrug, "I guess. That's all I can do so far, but I don't think it's going to be too hard to learn. The hard part was feeling the energy and learning how to manipulate it."

"Aye, the same with water." He fluffs his pillow and scoots under the covers. "We need to get to sleep. Tomorrow's going to be a long day."

I mimic his movements. "That's what I'm afraid of." I turn and scoot close to him, becoming the little spoon.

"Be careful how close you get, or you'll be feeling something besides energy." He laughs, wrapping his arm around my waist.

The rhythmic pulse of our combined energies lulls me to sleep quickly.

"Why haven't you sealed the deal with this one yet?" Hannah's standing by the edge of the bed. "I would've been on him like a bee to a honeycomb."

"Shh," I motion with my finger.

"He can't hear me." She moves to his side of the bed

and screams in his ear. Murphy doesn't budge. "See, I'm here for you only."

I walk to the balcony and pick out the fluffy blanket. Hannah sits in the chair next to me and props her feet on the railing, mimicking my first night here. "I don't think I'll ever get used to this view." She pulls a strawberry Laffy Taffy from her pocket.

I look out over the sea. The water is smooth and calm, with no evidence of what's to come. "Me either."

"Earwyn's here. Llyr and Shu have him in the prison below," she says between chews. "Before you ask, he's fine." Nervous energy fills me thinking of what's to come.

"Is this going to work?" I ask my dead best friend.

She sighs. "Truth is, I don't know. I learn things in order of what you need to know. I'm not shown the future, just truths." She looks back on the bed to a sleeping Murphy. "He'll die for you."

I slide forward on my chair. "What?" Hoping I misunderstood.

She shifts forward and sighs. "Tomorrow, you'll be faced with choices. One will result in his death, the other will result in yours. Choose wisely."

"Hannah, what are you telling me?" I watch as she disappears before my eyes. Simply gone from existence. I stare at the empty chair, trying to wrap my brain around her parting words. Everything she's said in these dreams has come true. Tears stream down my cheek. If I'm forced to choose which one of us will die, there's no choice. I crawl back into bed, curling as close to Murphy as I can. He pulls me tightly to him and gently kisses my neck.

"Are you okay?" he whispers.

"I'm good. Just a bathroom break," I lie. "Go back to sleep." He sleeps the rest of the night, while I float in and out of consciousness until light peeks over the horizon.

Dread fills me. If Hannah's right, this day could be the end of one of our lives. Murphy's arm stretches straight out under my head. "Good morning," he whispers into my neck.

I turn toward him. "Good morning." His curls are a mess of frizz, and up close, I can count the number of freckles he has across the bridge of his nose. "Murphy, no matter what happens today, we're going to be okay, both of us."

"Aye." He kisses my cheek gently.

"He's here," I say, softly.

"Who?"

"Earwyn. Llyr and Shu have him locked in the prison already." He sits up, confused.

"Did you go down there?" I shake my head.

"I just know." Murphy crawls out of bed, heading toward the door.

"I'm going to take a quick shower and get dressed. Meet you on the landing in thirty minutes?" I nod.

"Murphy, wait." I wrap my arms around his neck and place my mouth on his, separating his lips with my tongue. He doesn't hesitate to return the gesture. Instead of the rushed, passionate kisses we've shared before, this one is slow, soft, and perfect.

"Now I don't want to leave," he whispers, placing his forehead against mine.

"There'll be time for more later. We have a mission today." He nods, leaving my room.

I take a quick shower, talking to the water the entire time. With my words, I'm able to direct the stream toward certain areas of the basin. It reminds me of dancing.

I quickly braid my hair into two French braids and slide into the training gear I haven't worn since arriving, but today feels like a day for protection. I slide several weapons into my boots and hidden spots on the vest and head to the landing. Murphy's here already dressed in almost identical gear. "Looks like we're on the same wavelength," he says, kissing me on the forehead. "Oh, I almost forgot." He hands me a coffee that smells like a cup of sunshine.

"This is a little slice of heaven. Thank you." I chug half of it down, despite the heat. "It tastes even better than it smells."

"You're welcome." He laces his fingers through mine as we head downstairs.

Stephen has the breakfast table set as if today's an ordinary day on the island. Shu joins us, wearing house shoes and white silk pajamas. "Good morning," he says, pouring a few drops of brandy into a coffee cup. "Nothing better in the morning than a little Irish coffee." He takes a few sips. "I trust you two slept well." He glares at Murphy, sending a silent warning. I try not to laugh at the gesture.

Llyr comes downstairs minutes later, dressed in similar lounge clothes, his hair disheveled and his eyes looking sleepy. "Good morning," he says as he reaches the bottom step.

Murphy and I glance between the two gods and each other. "Did we miss something?" he asks.

"What do you mean?" Shu takes another sip while Llyr sits at the head of the table.

"He means, you two look like you just stepped out of a nineteen-sixties sitcom, and we're dressed for battle. Aren't we expecting Brigit at any moment? Earwyn is in the prison below?" Llyr and Shu exchange glances.

"That he is, my dear," Shu answers for the both of them. "We sent word this morning that he was indeed being held captive on the island and would be executed by noon. The only way to save his life would be for Brigit to agree to a meeting."

"Then what the hell are you two wearing?" Murphy takes the words out of my mouth.

"We're dressed for the meeting," Llyr answers.

"You wear loungewear to First Elemental meetings?"

Llyr smiles. "I know it's a little out of the ordinary, but if Shu and I appear any other way, Brigit will know something's off before we begin. Dagda will no doubt be at her side and the four of us need to appear as we always do. This is how we've met since before the beginning. We are of no threat to one another, so we need not present ourselves as such."

Murphy nods his head at me in understanding. "Seems really strange, but it makes sense."

"Earwyn is below, locked safely in the prison. Brigit will sign the treaty to protect the life of her son, and the world will go on as it has before." Shu sounds like this is an everyday occurrence.

"What makes you so confident she'll follow the terms of the agreement? She never has before." I look at Llyr. "She wants your power."

"Truth is, we don't know. But we have to appear as ordinary as possible. She won't rest until she succeeds, it's been a battle that transcends time. Whether that battle is now or five hundred years from now will be determined today." Llyr moves closer to me.

"You two need to stay hidden, stay protected. If she finds you, she won't hesitate to kill you." He turns to Murphy. "Don't leave her side, no matter what you hear or see."

"Aye."

"Brigit is notoriously late. Why don't you two join us and have a bite to eat?" Shu motions to the table full of food. Energy fills the room before we have a chance to move.

"Except today." A voice appears out of thin air. A huge rock of a man next to a tall, beautiful red-haired woman stands at the entrance of the castle. Both are wearing loungewear.

"Go," Shu mouths as a huge blast of energy forms a wall in front of us. Without asking, I know he's hidden us from view with some sort of an air invisibility cloak. He walks toward the guests. "Brigit, Dagda... what a pleasure it is to see the both of you."

"Cut the bullshit, Shu. Where's Earwyn?" She's clearly angry. Murphy and I exit the balcony doors and onto the terrace.

We run off the terrace and around the corner of the house. "No way did they come alone," Murphy says what I'm thinking. "We need to find out how many more are here."

"We can't risk being seen."

"Think you could do what Shu did?" I have no idea. I focus the energy around me, pulling from the air, the sea, the grass, everything I can pull from, and envision a clear bubble of cloaking air surrounding the two of us.

"How do we know if it worked?" He steps away from me, looks back, and nods. "Perfect," he says, stepping back inside our cloak. We walk side by side to the front of the driveway. Just as we expected, two men larger than Dagda, and a shorter woman block the bridge leading to the main island. I can sense the power in each of them, most likely hybrids.

"Shit," I say as we work our way back around the castle. "They're powerful."

"Aye, hybrids, and two of them as large as a house. There's nothing we can do right now. We have to wait until the meeting is over."

"I can't just sit here and wait, it's not in my blood."

"I won't see you risk your life. We'll know soon enough." He laces his fingers through mine. "This is all part of the game they've played for eternity. We're doing what we can right now, and that's keeping you safe."

"Hang on to me, I have a bad feeling." I focus my energy and say, "Wind," before we lift off the ground to the top of the third-floor balcony.

"A little warning would've been nice." Murphy laughs, nervously.

"Sorry, I want to see what's going on at the wards." We look over the island. "Can you see anything?"

"There." He points to movement near the eastern ward.

"They're attacking the island while Brigit and Dagda

meet with Llyr and Shu." From our viewpoint, we can see earth lessers climbing up the sides of the cliff, breaching the island. Water lessers are knocking them down but they're definitely outnumbered.

"Aye, and the hybrids are blocking the bridge." He turns to face me. "Adria, the villagers are safe, we can't do anything against that number of lessers. We need to stay here and protect the castle." He's right. As much as it pains me to see the island destroyed, that would be a fight we couldn't win. "You need to reserve your energy."

"Dammit!" I kick the stone railing, knocking a section out with my boot.

"Feel better?" he asks, looking at the dent I made.

"Murphy, I have to do something. I can't just sit here and watch this island be destroyed while the Firsts shoot the breeze in their pajamas."

"I understand, but our hands are tied. We serve them better by keeping you safe." He runs a finger along my cheek. "We can't take the chance of Brigit finding you."

I turn to face him. "Maybe we *can* do something."

"What are you thinking?" He doesn't look convinced.

"Earwyn. Can you take me to him?" I lace my fingers through his.

"Aye, I can, but how will that be doing something?" He faces me.

I look at the newly dented railing. "I don't know, but it's worth a try."

He sighs, leading me off of the terrace to a staircase off of the kitchen. We descend a wide set of stairs taking us to a dirt floor cellar. The stonework is older and looks like it's original to the castle. "This is nothing more than an old cellar. Where's the prison?" I walk the perimeter, running my hands along the rock.

"Over here." Murphy walks to a wall that looks older than the rest. He pulls a stone away revealing a hole leading nowhere. "Help me take these down."

"This is the way? These stones look like they've been here since the castle was built." Lifting the stones takes more effort than I expect.

"Aye. This is it." We pull enough stones away that a human-sized hole appears. "I'll go first and get the light." I watch as he contorts his long body into a hole one-quarter his size, then disappears into the darkness.

"Murphy?" Several minutes pass in silence. "Murphy!" I yell into the hole. A faint light moves in front of me.

"I'm here. Come through." He holds a lighted torch that looks straight out of the middle ages in front of me.

"Did you mug a knight during a renaissance fair for that?" I try to hide my laugh.

"Aye. There's an entire show going on down there. Hurry, we're just in time to see the jousting match."

I laugh loudly while squeezing through the hole. "Sometimes you're an ass."

"That's why you like me," he says, leading us through the darkness. It's one of many reasons, but I don't share them.

"I have a hard time believing Shu and Llyr used this passage to bring Earwyn down here." Cobwebs line the walls, sticking to my skin as I rub my hands along the ancient stones.

"They didn't. This is the back way. The main passage will be blocked by wards and protections that we don't have time to get through." We come to the top of an old, winding staircase. "Not much further. The prison's at the bottom of the stairs." I follow him down to a dirt landing. He places the torch into a holder on the wall and pulls open a thick, wooden door. We're met with modern ceramic tile floors, fluorescent lighting, and a hallway lined with doors. I feel like I just jumped time-lines. "He'll be in number 3, Brigit's room." I walk to the third door.

"Do I just knock?" I question, not sure what to do.

"The doors won't open. Here," he opens a small port-hole on the top of the door. "The hole is protected against all elements."

"I knew you'd come," Earwyn says through the hole. "She's here, isn't she?" Neither of us answer. "I can feel her, mother is here." He sighs loudly. "She came to get me."

"What makes you so sure about that?" Murphy asks.

"Because she loves me." His voice sounds almost child-like as he speaks about his mother. What happened to the warrior?

"If she loved you, why'd she send you to America instead of keeping you with her?" Murphy's trying to get a rise out of him.

"It was for my own good. I needed to be trained." His voice sounds increasingly disjointed.

"Trained for what?" I move closer to the door.

He doesn't answer for a while. "To be stronger," he whispers. Murphy and I share a look. "I was weak. She said it was the human part of me. I needed to be stronger."

"Why America? Why not with other fire elementals

who could help you learn who you were?" Earwyn moves closer to the hole in the door.

"At least my mother didn't abandon me on a doorstep." His words are meant to hurt Murphy.

"No, she abandoned you in an entirely different country," I retort.

Earwyn walks to the back of the white room. "You won't survive the day," he says. "You and your little boy toy will both be dead by sunset." He laughs.

"How do we stop this?" I ask, not expecting an answer.

His laugh turns sinister. "You think *you* can stop her? You couldn't even stop me, could you?"

I ignore his prodding. "We can't let the humans on this island be killed."

"Why should I care?" His voice sounds bored.

"You're half human," Murphy answers. "Did you forget about that?"

Earwyn laughs. "That part of me was weak. Just like the ones on this stupid island."

"We share the same father." Earwyn doesn't respond. "Did you hear me, brother? We share the same human father."

"Is that supposed to change anything? Are we supposed to embrace each other like we've been best friends our entire lives?" He circles the inside of the cell. "It doesn't mean anything more than the same weak human donated his sperm for both of us. You mean nothing to me." He pauses. "She'll save me."

I close the port hole. "What the hell's wrong with

him?" I whisper to Murphy. "He's acting like a psychopath."

He shrugs. "Maybe his mind is weak."

"If he were human, I might believe that. He's half First Elemental, he's either acting like this on purpose or he's been crazy the entire time."

"Either way, it's clear he won't be any help." He opens the port hole again. "You're right, she's here. But she hasn't asked about you."

Earwyn inhales deeply. "I can smell her."

"Okay, that's not normal," I say into the hole. "You might want to let her know they make special cleansers for that." My words anger Earwyn. He turns quickly.

"Don't talk about her like that you filthy whore." He walks toward us as Murphy closes the porthole.

"We're done here," he says. "There's nothing he can do to help, and I won't allow him to speak to you like that."

"I hate seeing him like this."

"Aye. Me too." He wraps an arm around my shoulders. "You can't help someone who doesn't want help. We need to get back before you're missed." I nod, turning back to the wooden door.

CHAPTER 20

e sit on the balcony, watching, as earth and fire lessers destroy the island. I wipe tears as home after home is burned to the ground. Those that aren't burned, are knocked down by small earthquakes. I've never felt so helpless in my life. Energy bubbles around me and Llyr pops onto the balcony, inside our bubble of protective air.

"It took me a while to find you. I had to search for your energy signature." He looks around the bubble. "This is brilliant."

"They're destroying the island." My voice is sad.

He looks over the land. "It's happened before. What's important is that the humans are safe. The island can be rebuilt."

"How's it going down there?" Murphy asks.

"About as well as expected," Llyr answers. "The last treaty we made took many years to complete."

"The island won't survive that long." I wipe more tears.

"That's why I need you to trust me right now." I look up in question. "I would never deliberately put you in harm's way." I nod. "I need you to come to the meeting."

"Absolutely not!" Murphy jumps to his feet. "You told me to protect her, and I will do that with my life. You'll be taking her right where Brigit wants her."

Llyr holds his hands up. "I understand. Shu and I both feel this is the best thing at this point. If not, the island will be destroyed, and the humans eventually discovered, while she purposefully stalls our talks."

"I'll do it," I say without pause.

Murphy turns his head toward me. "Have you both lost your minds?" Anger pours off of him. I take his hand into mine.

"I'll be okay. Llyr and Shu won't let her hurt me." I reassure him.

"Have you forgotten that Firsts can't harm each other? All your father and grandfather would be able to do is watch as she burns you alive or slits your throat." He pulls his hand away from mine.

"Then I'd kill her child," Llyr answers. His voice sounds monotone.

"At that point, does it matter?" Murphy walks to the edge of the balcony.

"Do you think I'd put her at risk if there were any other way? Those bunkers will only hold for so long. With the number of lessers pouring onto the island, it's only a matter of time. I won't risk the lives of every human on this island."

"But you'll risk the life of your daughter?" Murphy's accent is stronger than usual, fueled by anger.

"Murphy, stop. This is the only way. Did you forget Bonnie and Ethan are in those bunkers?" He looks up, tears filling his eyes. "I won't risk their lives over something I can possibly stop."

He pulls me close. "I don't want to lose you."

"You won't," I whisper. "I've got this." I look up at Llyr and nod. He runs his hand along my cheek.

"You are stronger than any of us." He blinks out of existence.

Murphy wraps his arms around me, hugging me so tight I can barely breathe. "You're not going alone. I will be right at your side. If I get any bad juju vibes from any of them..." he doesn't finish his sentence.

I nod, understanding. "Let's go." I release the wall of air hiding us from the world. Murphy takes my hand, and together we enter the castle and head down the stairs. The further we descend, the louder the voices are. "Are they laughing?" I ask, hearing what sounds like cackles coming from below. He squeezes my hand.

We walk into the study, heads held high. I don't dare look weak in front of them. "Ah, this must be your daughter." Her voice is high-pitched and shrill with an accent I don't immediately recognize. "Isn't she lovely? She even has your hair, Llyr."

Brigit approaches me. Her housedress is a beautiful shade of crimson red, of course, with soft, flowing fringe around the bottom. Long auburn hair is pulled back on the sides, accentuating her narrow face. Her eyes are a beautiful shade of copper, the same as Earwyn's. "I can feel her," she says, reaching toward my face. It takes all of my strength not to wince as she tries to touch me. I feel Murphy tense the closer she gets.

"Brigit," Shu stops her. "You've met her, why don't we continue our negotiations?" Brigit ignores his words and circles me like I'm her prey.

"I sense something else." She looks at my father. "Have you been keeping something from me, Llyr?" She continues circling. She doesn't frighten me, but I can tell her being this close frightens Murphy. "I sense another element, maybe?" She turns to Dagda. "Do you sense anything, dear?"

Dagda has dark hair and dark eyes. He's at least a foot taller than Murphy, which is saying a lot. "I don't sense anything." His accent is thick and difficult to understand.

"You wouldn't, would you." She belittles him in front of everyone. He doesn't seem to mind and walks back to his seat. "No, I sense something I can't quite put my finger on." She senses the element of air, Shu's power.

"You sense me," Murphy interrupts. She turns her attention toward him, running her finger along his chest.

"Now, who is this fine specimen?" she smiles seductively at Murphy. I try to hide my reaction to her touching him. She doesn't need to know our connection.

"Murphy McKenzie," he answers. "What you sense is my power." He sends a small stream of water into a glass on the table. Llyr and Shu look surprised at his display.

Brigit claps. "Well, well. Looks like you have a very special little hybrid here." She licks her lips while staring at him. The energy pouring from her is gross and I fight the urge to kick her ass right here.

"Your son is in prison. He's being cared for, but I'm sure he's ready to be out." Llyr uses her weakness to focus her attention. "Why don't we continue these negotiations?" He turns to me. "Adria, why don't you and Murphy return where you were?" He's asking me to hide.

"No," Brigit says. "She and this delicious hybrid stay here." The two large men and the younger woman from the bridge enter the front door. "Perfect timing. Allow me to introduce you to *my* special hybrids." They move to her side. "These two," she points to the earth hybrids, "are Erick and Derrick. They're twins, and no, I didn't name them." She laughs and motions for the girl to come to her side. The girl has striking features. Long auburn hair ends in soft curls. She's beautiful in a familiar way. "This is Astrid. She's the daughter of one of my higher-level lessers. I agreed to bring her along for training purposes."

I sense something in the young girl. More than just being a hybrid. I reach out to her energy and am met with a wall of protection. I try again and meet the same wall. Something's not right.

Shu and Llyr are polite and greet the hybrids. Llyr and I make eye contact, he senses my uneasiness and looks around the room for the source. Brigit sits back in her seat next to Dagda.

"What will it take to get my son back?" she asks.

"It will take you calling off yours and Dagda's lessers from destroying this island, and not creating any new ones," Shu answers.

"What would be the fun in that?" she retorts.

"I think the fun would be your son surviving the day." My words spit anger.

"She speaks." Brigit turns her attention back to me. "And quite a little tongue she has on her."

Llyr laughs. "She has a touch of her mother in her." I know he means that as a compliment, but Brigit doesn't take it that way.

"Looks like you chose the wrong human to mate with." She laughs sarcastically. She's clearly pushing me. I refuse to lower myself to her level. "I do find it hard to concentrate with everyone standing. Please have a seat." She motions to a chair behind her and the young girl sits. Murphy and I move to seats behind Llyr and Shu. I need eyes on Brigit at all times. "That's much better."

Brigit reminds me of the drunk friend that embarrasses the entire friend group. Clearly, the other three are bored with her but held captive at her whim. "So, how do we go about getting Aiden from your prison?"

The gods in front of me look at each other. "Aiden?" Shu asks.

"That is his real name. He couldn't very well infiltrate the high and mighty castle on this island with a fire name, could he?" She asks. The more she speaks, the more her crazy shows.

Llyr stops her one-woman production. "Whatever his name is, he's sitting in my prison and he will die if you don't continue these negotiations. No more games, Brigit."

"I'm getting bored with this," Shu adds, as he leans back in his chair and crosses his legs.

"Oh, all right. I forget how mind-numbingly boring you two are. What was it you wanted in exchange for him?" Llyr sighs and repeats himself.

"You will stop the attack on the island and agree to not produce any new lessers."

"Oh yes, now I remember." She turns to Dagda. "What do you think?"

"I'm not allowed to think," he responds.

"That's only because we both know you can't." Dagda looks offended but does nothing about it. Astrid's still sitting behind Brigit. While the latter wastes everyone's time, I compare the features of the two. Both have strong, distinct noses, high cheekbones, and narrow faces. Their eyes are the same shade of copper, and both have deep auburn colored hair. Oh, my gods. Astrid isn't the daughter of one of her lessers, she's Brigit's daughter. That's why she's stalling.

Astrid makes eye contact with me knowingly. I refuse to look away and the two of us stare each other down for a few minutes. Raising one side of her mouth, she grins right at me. Holy hell, Astrid's a god killer. She's here to kill Llyr or Shu or both. I have to warn them now.

Brigit continues to stall for time as Astrid sends dark waves of energy toward me. I feel them hit me in ripples. Two can play this game. I set up a barrier around me to reflect the waves back to Astrid. Her smirk disappears quickly as the first wave is returned. Her gaze turns to Llyr. Like a cold, calculated killer, she's telling me what she's going to do. She thinks I'm not smart enough to pick up on her body language. I refuse to follow her look, instead sending waves of energy toward her filled with warnings. She looks back at me as we continue our silent conversation.

I have to warn Shu and Llyr. I pull my eyes away from

the vixen, looking around the room for anything of use. I can't risk telling them here. If a battle breaks out, the Firsts can't hurt each other, but the rest of us won't survive.

I listen as Brigit drones on about something that happened between them in the ninth century. The others aren't even pretending to listen. I stand. "Please excuse me. I don't feel well." Murphy stands to go with me. "I'll be right back." I put my hand on my stomach for added effect. "Please continue without me."

"That seems a bit rude." She looks at Llyr. "Bad breeding's what I say."

"I agree, and I apologize. My stomach didn't care for the muffin I ate for breakfast." Murphy knows I didn't eat a muffin and knows I'm trying to leave the room without him. *Trust me*, I say with my eyes, hoping he won't follow. He closes his eyes and relaxes his stance. "Five minutes," I say, holding up five fingers for drama.

I step out of the room and focus all of my energy to form an air bubble shield, hiding me from the world. I step back into the room, praying Brigit and Dagda don't pick up on the amount of energy I'm using, and walk behind Llyr. "Astrid is Brigit's daughter," I whisper.

I return to the room, still holding my stomach. "I apologize. Did I miss anything?" Llyr looks at me knowingly.

"No, we learned that Brigit had a gown made by the same designer that once made a gown for Marie Antionette," Shu says, sarcastically.

"Sounds thrilling," I add, sitting back in my seat. Murphy sighs when I return.

Llyr stands, moving toward Astrid. "Tell me about this lovely specimen," he says, running his hand along her hair. Brigit is visibly anxious as he touches her daughter. I'll give her credit. Astrid doesn't flinch as the most powerful First Elemental in existence touches her.

Brigit doesn't move from her chair. "I told you, she's the daughter of one of my higher-ups. I'm trying to train her to be smarter than her father." Brigit's not the best actress. She's pretending the girl doesn't matter, clearly Llyr being near her brings Brigit stress.

"Her hair reminds me of someone, I can't quite put my finger on it," Llyr says as Shu looks between the two of us, picking up on the energy.

Brigit stands quickly. "We're done here." She turns, taking Astrid's elbow into hers.

"I don't think that's the best idea right now. What about your darling boy, the one you came all the way here to retrieve?" Shu moves toward the girl.

"Stop!" Brigit says.

"Why are you so protective of this girl?" he asks, moving next to Llyr.

Astrid stands tall, despite two very powerful gods within arm's reach. Brigit pulls her closer. "Leave her alone. She's young and inexperienced."

"Then why bring her with you?" Shu asks.

"Oh, for my sake Brigit. Tell them the truth. It's clear they already know." Dagda leans back in his chair, not getting up from the table. "Astrid is Brigit's daughter, yada, yada, yada. I'm ready to leave this boredom. Just agree to whatever, and let's get out of here."

Shu raises an eyebrow. "Daughter, did you say?"

Dagda waves a dismissive hand in their direction. "Whatever, who cares. Brigit, I'm ready to go."

"Not without Aiden," she says through gritted teeth. A loud explosion outside draws our attention away from the scene before us.

Murphy moves to my side. "What was that?" I ask.

"I would imagine lessers are close to the castle," he answers.

"Call them off!" Llyr demands. Brigit pulls her daughter closer.

"Not without Aiden. I will see this castle and island destroyed first."

"If we release him, will you call them off?" Llyr asks. Brigit nods.

"She's lying," Dagda responds. "She won't call them off until you're dead." His tone sounds monotone. "Oh, was that something I wasn't supposed to share? You're right. I shouldn't be told anything since I'm unable to think."

Brigit doesn't respond as an explosion, even closer than the last, rocks the windows of the room we're in. "My children are enjoying themselves," she says with a smile.

Llyr zaps from one spot to another. In an instant, he's an arm's length from Astrid, pulls her away from Brigit, and holds a hand to her throat. "I'll snap her neck," he warns. "Call them off."

Brigit shoots fire across the room, the curtains engulf in flames. Shu sends a wall of air, instantly choking her fire. She tries again, and this time a chair behind me bursts into flames. A wall of water hits the flames, extinguishing them. Brigit stands in the middle of the room, her hands straight out at each side. "I'll bring this whole castle down, killing anything with human blood inside."

"You won't do that," Llyr challenges. "Astrid and Earwyn will die too."

"They're freaks of nature anyway." Fire forms at her feet, slowly working its way up her torso until where the once beautiful First was, a pillar of flames stands.

"Holy shit," Murphy says. "We have to get out of here." He pulls me toward the balcony door.

"No, I won't leave them. They're the only connection I have to who I am. They're my family."

"Go!" Shu shouts toward us. "Murphy, get her out of here. We'll be fine!"

Something takes over me, rushing me from the inside out. Power fills every inch of me, crawling its way through my skin, burrowing its way to the surface. Murphy senses the change and puts space between us. What's left of Brigit sees his movement and shoots a wall of flames straight at him. He deflects the flames with water, but his strength is nothing compared to hers. I watch as the fire pushes his water back until it reaches his hands. Murphy screams in pain as his hands begin to blister.

"Murphy!" I scream and release the tension straight into Brigit. "Storm!" I shout, watching what looks like a mini hurricane form over her, knocking her to the ground. She gets up quickly, still a pillar of flames.

"You can't fight me, girl. I'm a god!" she shoots a wall of flames straight toward my head.

"Wind!" I shout, riding the wind out of the way of her blast.

"That's what I sensed in you!" she screams. "You have the element of air! Shu, you've been a naughty boy!"

"Adria, feel the energy in the room, pull from it," Shu shouts orders. "I can't hurt her, but you can!" I nod in response. Releasing all the air in my body, I feel for every item in the room, reaching for its energy. I pull it to me, forming it into a bomb of pure energy. I envision a circle of light forming in my hands. Brigit senses the energy and throws a streak of fire straight at Murphy. A wall of water blocks it, as Llyr uses one hand to protect Murphy and the other to hold Astrid.

"Her eyes are the source of her strength," Llyr yells. "Take them!"

Llyr has his hands over Astrid's eyes, keeping her power controlled while Shu shoots walls of air at lessers who have breached the courtyard. All the while Dagda has his feet propped on the corner of the table, watching the show in boredom.

My attention comes back to Brigit. Two white circles are in the place where her eyes should be. How do I take her eyes, when they're not there? "Leave him alone," I shout, my voice sounds deadly, even to me.

Where her mouth should be, a wicked smile emerges. "Partial to this one, are we?" She turns fully toward Murphy, hitting him with a blast of fire nothing could withstand.

"Murphy!" I yell.

"Go!" he answers. I watch the flames extend past his hands, to his wrists, as time slows down to an unbearable crawl.

"Llyr, help him!" He's still holding Astrid in one arm

and using his power to fight lessers who have entered the castle. I've never felt so helpless in my life. Time stops and I watch what's going on in the castle through someone else's eyes.

Hannah's words play through my mind. "He'll die for you." She appears in the room, standing next to Brigit, unaffected by the flames. "Choose, Adria. Choose now. He'll die for you."

I'll be damned if I let that happen. Time catches up and Llyr nods at me while fighting. I know without asking, he's giving me permission to kill Brigit, to kill a First. I look at Griffin, who, being the only one to kill a First, was forced to take his place and now sits bored at the fight raging around him. If I kill Brigit, what will happen to me, to Adria? "Two choices... one will result in his death, the other will result in yours," Hannah whispers over the roar of the fight.

Murphy screams in pain as the flames race toward his elbows. Without hesitation, I release the energy straight into Brigit. The world stops.

CHAPTER 21

*B*rief moments of clarity filter through the darkness that encompasses me. Several times, I imagine hearing Murphy's voice, his skin touching mine. It's like I'm on the verge of a great discovery, awaiting the final results. Always on the edge, not quite over the top.

"She's strong," voices whisper above me, just out of reach.

"I'm here!" I shout before the darkness consumes me. I don't know how much time has passed if any. Did I destroy Brigit? Questions plague my mind as disjointed sounds echo through the silence.

"Adria," a familiar voice whispers.

"*Hannah?*" I echo through the dark.

"I'm here," she says louder.

"*Where?*"

"Here, with you."

"*Am I... am I dead?*" Hannah stands in front of me in

the dark. A dim glow gives me enough light to see she's wearing the alien hoodie and a pair of jeans, full of holes.

"No," her voice sounds normal. "The part of you that was is gone but will be reborn."

"*What does that even mean? I'm going to start over, be reincarnated? What about Murphy, what about my life?*"

"You will be reborn as Brigit, the goddess of fire." She steps closer.

"Did I, did I kill her?" I'm able to speak, as she slides a loose hair behind my ear.

"Yes, you did, and rather effectively I might add. When she died, the old Adria died along with her."

"I chose to save him," I remember the fight, remember the flames, remember his screams of pain.

"Yes, you chose to save Murphy." She pauses. "You made the choice I knew you would." Tears run down my cheek.

"Is he okay? Did he survive?" I don't make an effort to wipe them as they flow off my face.

"He did." She smiles. "He's been sitting by your side day and night, waiting for you to awaken." I smile, picturing him asleep in a chair.

"What if I don't want to be reborn as Brigit?" I ask, knowing the answer.

"It's not for us to choose. You made the decision to sacrifice yourself to save the man you love." I look down at the seemingly bottomless blackness beneath me.

"Why does everyone think I love Murphy?"

"Because you do," she answers. I don't argue.

"What is this place?"

"The void. It's a place in our universe that's void of

any outside interference. There are no elements that plague our world, no lessers, no Firsts. There simply is nothing." Hannah takes my hands into hers. "The time has come for you to return. You're ready."

"Hannah," I whisper as she disappears into nothing. "Don't leave me, I don't know if I can do this without you."

"You've done it without me this whole time. You're ready."

"What if I'm not?"

"You are..." her voice whispers from nowhere. "And I'm keeping my hoodie."

I huff a laugh.

......

Something smooth and fibrous rubs gently across my cheek. "Come back to me, mo chridhe." My eyes open slowly. Murphy's sitting next to me, his hands and arms bandaged to his elbows. "Adria!" he says excitedly. "You're awake."

"Hi," I whisper, my voice sounding raspy. I look around the room, nothing looks familiar. "Where am I?"

"My parent's home." A tear streams down his cheek.

"Bonnie and Ethan?"

"Aye." He sniffs.

"Are they..."

"They're fine," he interrupts. My eyes land on a group of people behind Murphy.

"Sophie?" I smile.

"Aye," she says, walking to my side. Bonnie and Ethan follow.

"You gave us quite a scare." Bonnie flashes her warm smile. "Do you need anything, food, water?"

"She just woke up for crying out loud. Give her a minute to breathe." Ethan pulls Bonnie away from my side.

"No, thank you," I whisper. "Thank you for asking." My eyes wander back to Murphy. "The island?"

He looks down at our connected hands. "Most of the island survived the attack. All of the humans are well. You saved them."

I look out the window, squinting at the sun. "The castle?"

He shakes his head. "For the most part, destroyed. But it can be rebuilt." I'd only known the castle for a short time, but it was home and had been Llyr's home for over a thousand years.

Murphy wipes a stray tear from his cheek. "Why are you crying?" I ask.

He sighs. "I thought you left me. After the explosion, I thought you were... dead."

"I'm alive, I think." I try to smile.

"You're alive." He returns the smile, wiping another tear. "I love you, Adria." He snorts loudly.

"I love you too," I whisper. Trying to reach his face. My arms feel like they're made of putty and weigh a million pounds each. "Why do I feel like shit?"

He huffs a laugh. "You fought a First and lived to tell about it. Your body is trying to recover."

"Llyr and Shu?" I ask. "Are they okay?"

"We're here." The two gods walk toward me. Murphy stands, giving them access to my sides. Each takes a hand into theirs. "We're both so incredibly proud of you, Adria."

I look between the two of them, my father and grandfather. "What now?" I ask. They know my meaning without elaboration. Shu walks toward the window.

"Much the same way a Phoenix is reborn, so will you be."

"That sounds painful." I laugh, wincing at the pain it causes.

Llyr touches my cheek. His face is full of love. "Adria, from this moment on, you will be eternal. Never growing old, never dying. You are one of us in every aspect of the term."

Feeling more energized, Llyr helps me sit up. "I don't want to change my name. I don't want to become Brigit. My mother named me Adria, and it will stay that way."

Llyr and Shu nod in agreement. "Adria, goddess of water, air, and fire, has a nice ring to it," Shu says, walking back to my side. My forehead wrinkles in confusion. Shu smiles. "It's true, you will be reborn, but you can't get rid of Llyr and me so easily. Our blood runs through your veins. You now have the power to control three of the four elements, you're the strongest of us all." The gods bow at my feet. Sophie and Murphy do the same.

CHAPTER 22

"Breakfast is ready, dears," Bonnie calls down the hall to the room I've lived in for the past three months. One of those months, I spent mostly unconscious, visiting the void and Hannah often. The last two have been spent recovering my energy. Llyr thinks with the combination of expending every bit of my energy and becoming the goddess of fire, my body was pushed to its limit. I know the truth, I died. The Adria that once was, died that day.

"Coming," I call down the hall. Murphy sticks his head in the door frame.

"Let's go, I'm hungry!" I laugh at his admission.

"That sounds like the Murphy I know." Bandages only cover his hands now, since his arms have healed enough that they don't have to be covered every day. His scarring is minimal, thankfully.

"Aye, I'm starving." He comes to my side, making sure I have enough energy to stand. I motion him away.

"I'm good. I'm stronger every day."

"I know, just in case." He wraps a hand around my elbow. "Llyr's here." He tells me as we walk to the kitchen.

"In the apartment?" I ask, excitedly. I feel his energy before getting halfway down the hall.

"You're a sight for sore eyes," Llyr says, meeting us at the entrance of the kitchen. "You look great. How are you feeling?"

"I'm getting stronger. Before long I'll be kicking Murphy's ass again." Llyr takes my elbow from Murphy.

"I look forward to that," he says, wiggling his eyebrows.

Bonnie pops him with a towel. "Sit down." She laughs.

I sit between the two men. "Why is it taking so long to heal?" I ask my father.

"Your body is being reborn from fire. In the human world, it's a slow process. In our world, it's the blink of an eye. It took Griffin almost a year to transition."

"Well, he's dumb. I'll do it in half the time." Llyr laughs at my words.

"No truer words have been spoken." He puts several slices of bacon on my plate, with a scoop of scrambled eggs. "Bonnie, this looks amazing. Thank you." He offers food to the rest of the table.

"You're welcome. Now eat up."

I move the food around on my plate, trying to make it look eaten. My appetite has been waning since the transition began. I don't get hungry, and when I try to eat, it tastes different.

After a relaxed conversation over a home-cooked meal,

Llyr stands to leave. "Thank you, Bonnie, for such a delicious meal."

"My pleasure, Dr. Smith." She begins cleaning up the plates littering the table.

He turns to Murphy and me. "Can you two come by the castle this afternoon? We need to discuss the next step."

Murphy looks at me. "Aye, we'll be there." Llyr kisses me on the forehead, before turning to leave.

Several hours later, we sit on the one remaining bench beside what used to be the fountain. As far as the villagers are concerned, the town was destroyed by a natural disaster, a wicked storm that parked on top of the island for several days, leaving a path of destruction in its wake. Which isn't far from the truth.

"I'm going with you," Murphy announces.

"Where am I going?" I ask, with a laugh.

"To Brigit's home. I'm going too." He laces his fingers through mine. "I think that's what Llyr wants to meet with us about."

I haven't even thought about the fact that Brigit lived somewhere different. "I don't want to leave."

"Aye, but you may need to." He presses the back of my hand to his lips. "It's time to go to the castle." He helps me to my feet.

Crossing over the bridge, it's the first time I've seen what's left. Workers are everywhere, resembling ants milling about the colony. Scaffolding lines each wall, as masons lay new brick and stone, rebuilding the walls one stone at a time. The tower is laying on the ground in the drive and the top of the castle looks to be open to the elements. "You should've seen it before. Looks much better now," Murphy says as we move up the stairs.

"Is this from me or the lessers?"

"I think it was a combination of all." He opens the front door for me. There are as many workers inside buzzing around, as out. What furniture remains, sits covered in sheets for protection. Several windows are covered in plywood, while others have already been replaced.

"She's seen worse," Llyr says, coming out of the study. "The Norse left her in worse shape than this."

"I'm sorry."

Llyr walks to me. "Don't be sorry. You saved the world. Rebuilding a medieval castle is nothing compared to what could've been." He motions to a dust-covered chair. "Sit, please."

Shu walks around the corner. "Did you get started without me?"

"Shu!" I smile. "It's good to see you."

"It's better to see you," he says. "I'm sorry I've been gone. I had pressing matters to take care of."

Murphy squeezes into the chair beside me. "Shu's been preparing Brigit's home for you," Llyr says.

"Do I even want to know where that is?" I ask.

"Iceland," the gods say together.

I stare at them hoping I misunderstood. "Iceland?" I repeat. "Isn't that made completely of ice?"

"No, that's a myth the Vikings started to keep people away," Shu answers. "Kind of ingenious, at least until word got out about the farce."

"Why would the goddess of fire live in one of the

coldest climates in the world? Why not somewhere in the Pacific Ocean? They're riddled with volcanoes." The few high school geography lessons I attended taught me that.

"Iceland is full of volcanoes. Many underwater and many above ground. It's been the birthplace of fire lessers since before time, and most still call it home. They must have leadership. Without it, they'll lead us into another great battle. You're their leader now." Llyr props against what's left of his desk. "Murphy, I'm hoping you'll go with her. She'll need someone she knows. Someone she can trust. Someone I can trust."

"I'd have it no other way," he answers. "Especially with Astrid."

I look at him quickly. "What about Astrid?" I assumed she was killed in the explosion.

Llyr looks down, hesitant to answer. "She escaped."

Shu continues, "When you hit Brigit with, whatever you hit her with, Astrid was knocked out of Llyr's arms. When we dug out of the rubble, she was gone."

"Earwyn?"

"He didn't make it," Murphy answers. "That part of the castle collapsed on top of the prison and his room was destroyed."

"Did someone actually see his body? I've seen too many movies with this same plot."

"I did," Shu answers. "He was definitely gone."

"So, I killed Astrid's mother and brother in one moment. Am I the only one that thinks she's not going to let that go?" I make eye contact with each of them.

"She's young and inexperienced. She won't come after you. Plus, she's mortal. She won't live forever. You can stay one step ahead of her for eighty years or so." Shu dismisses the threat.

"Are you kidding me?" I stand quickly.

"Told you she wouldn't like it." Murphy moves to my side.

Llyr crosses his arms. "Adria, she can't hurt you."

"She's the child of a god. She's the *only* one who can hurt me. You're the one who taught me that!" Energy buzzes underneath my skin.

Shu intervenes. "Wherever she's gone, I guarantee it won't be to Iceland. She's young, but she's not dumb enough to risk her life by returning."

"What about Dagda? What if he helps her?" The gods share a look.

"Dammit, stop looking at each other and just tell me. I'm the goddess of fire, not a ten-year-old child." Energy flows to me from every corner of the room. I don't fight it.

"We think they're together," Llyr answers. "They're both missing."

I walk around in an attempt to displace the energy building under my skin. "This is great."

Murphy moves to my side. "They'll lay low for a while, long enough for you to take control of Iceland and the lessers who served Brigit."

"He's right," Llyr adds. "Brigit's legions will be at your command. They'll fight to the death to protect you."

I could argue more, but my strength is zapped. "We've made arrangements for you to travel to Iceland next week," Llyr announces.

Murphy looks surprised. "Is that wise? She's not fully completed the transition."

"We're out of time," Shu answers. "The lessers need a leader, now."

I nod. "Okay. I'll be ready. Whether I'm here or in Iceland doesn't make any difference as far as Astrid's concerned. If she's coming after me, my location is the least of her worries."

"Bastards," Murphy mumbles as we exit the castle.

"They're doing what's right for the world."

He sighs, "I only care about you."

I can't hide the smile his words bring. I grab his hand, lacing our fingers together. "I'll be fine. I'm getting stronger by the day and you'll be there to protect me."

"That, I will."

......

I force myself to move more over the next few days, trying to regain my strength. I even jog around what remains of the village without getting too winded. The week passes quickly, and my strength is returning. I packed what little clothes could be salvaged from the castle into a meager suitcase. The irony of what I arrived here with and am leaving here with doesn't escape me. What's left is nothing more than a few pairs of jeans, several pairs of shoes, and a couple of simple t-shirts. Maybe this is the universe's way of telling me to keep it simple.

"We'll get more clothes once we get to Iceland," Murphy says, watching me sift through what remains of my closet. "The plane should be here within the hour."

I zip the bag, moving it to the door. "What if they don't follow me?"

Murphy lifts an eyebrow. "Who?

"The lessers. What if they don't follow me?" He moves in front of me.

"I don't think they have much of a choice. You're the goddess of fire. If they don't pledge their loyalty, they die." Murphy makes it sound simple. Something tells me it won't be.

We arrive at the airport several minutes before our scheduled flight. Murphy leads us to the private jet awaiting us on the tarmac. We climb the stairs and are greeted by Daniel, reminding me of when I arrived at the island. Seems like years ago. This time he bows when I enter the plane. "My lady," he says.

"Please, call me Adria," I remind him. He nods, walking to the front of the plane.

"Adria!" Sophie calls, running down the aisle. "You look wonderful!" She gives me a warm hug.

"I hoped you'd be on the plane with us." I return the hug.

"I traded with someone to make sure I was." She takes my carry-on, stowing it away in the overhead bin. "Iceland, huh?"

"Apparently." I choose a seat by the window. Murphy sits next to me, taking my hand into his. His energy is relaxing, and I rest my head on his shoulder.

"Ladies and gentlemen," Daniel announces over the speaker. "Please make sure your seatbelts are properly secured and all luggage is stowed safely in the overhead bins."

The plane heads straight to the runway and into the sky without having to wait for any other take-offs. The seatbelt light goes off and Sophie jumps to her feet. "I have something for you two." She heads to the back of the plane and returns carrying two large garment bags.

"Shu sent these." She holds the bags out to us. "He said to tell you, a good first impression is a key to your success."

I unzip the bag, finding a gorgeous, full-length, red sequin gown. Murphy whistles when he sees it. "That should do it," he says, unzipping his bag. Inside is a pair of black tuxedo pants, a black dress shirt, and a red patterned jacket. "We're going to look hot." His words make me laugh.

"He sent everything you need for me to do your hair and make-up." Sophie pats a seat in front of a mirror. "Come on, let's have some fun."

Murphy disappears to the back and I hear water running. "Is there a shower on the plane?"

"Aye, Llyr spares no expense."

"I can see that." I close my eyes as Sophie twists, turns, curls, and does anything else she can do to my hair. She turns me away from the mirror so I can't see the final product as she applies layers of primer, concealer, highlighter, bronzer, and a lot of stuff I barely know how to use.

"Almost finished," she says, applying lipstick, the same red color as the dress, and long eyelashes. She steps back, admiring her work. "Beautiful. Are you ready to see?"

I nod as she turns my chair back toward the mirror. I look nothing like Adria and for the first time, I notice my eyes are shaped the same as Shu's. Why haven't I noticed that until now? My hair is pulled high on my head in a grand, explosive bun. Small tendrils of curls hang by my ears, just enough to add class, not trash. I look older, refined, and important. A Phoenix reborn.

I step into the dress and Sophie zips me to the top. It fits perfectly. "Shu's good," she says, handing me sandals the same color as the dress.

"He should be, he's had many millennia to make connections," I answer with a laugh.

Murphy walks out of the back of the plane dressed in the tux Shu sent. I can't stop staring. His soft auburn curls are perfectly styled, and the tux jacket fits like a glove. "Damn," I say with a smile.

He turns around, throwing his hips around, making a weak attempt at modeling. "Like what you see?"

"Maybe," I answer.

"I certainly do," he says, staring at me. "If they don't pledge their allegiance to you based on your element, that dress will definitely convince them."

"Ladies and gentlemen, please secure any loose items and fasten all seat belts as we approach our destination. It's currently six thirty p.m. in Reykjavik, Iceland."

Murphy sits beside me, staring awkwardly. "You look hot."

"Thank you," I smile. "You said that already."

"Not in those exact words." He smiles as the plane touches down and we taxi to our gate.

"You are now safe to depart. Thank you and have a great evening," Daniel says.

"Wait!" Sophie comes out carrying a long black overcoat and long white fake fur. "Shu sent these too. He said you might not be used to the cold." Of course, he did. We slide the coats on and exit the plane. I'm thankful for the coat when a blast of ice-cold wind hits me as soon as I step into the night.

We're ushered straight into a waiting car. It's too dark for me to see what model it is, but I see Mercedes markings on the interior. "Welcome to Iceland, I'm Rhys," an older man says. His accent is short and clipped.

"Thank you," Murphy answers.

"The castle is about thirty minutes away." We sit in silence for the drive, not sure what this man might know of our world. Murphy holds my hand the entire time, giving me comfort and strength through the connection and his pulses.

The lights of the castle are visible before the castle itself can be seen. "What's that?" I ask Rhys.

"There's a party tonight, in honor of you, my queen." We crest a large hill, and in front of us sits a castle that rivals that of the ruling party in London.

"Are we at the correct address?" Murphy asks.

"Yes," Rhys answers. We pull to a stop underneath a covered canopy. The castle looks to be half a mile wide. Rhys opens my door, bowing in front of me. When he stands, his copper eyes flash bright red. He motions to the entrance. "They're waiting."

Murphy takes my hand as we enter. Two men greet us, with deep bows. "My queen," they say in unison. "Your guests await you in the ballroom."

Ballroom? A tall man, with hair the color of soot, motions for us to follow him. The furnishings and décor are the complete opposite of what I expected. Lush, thick fabrics line each window. Ornate antiques accent each wall and fill the rooms with warmth and comfort. Murphy looks as surprised as I do. The tall man stops at a set of doors. "May I take your coats?" His voice is deep and raspy. His eyes flash the same color as Rhys', as we hand him our coats. He steps away. "Welcome," he says, opening the double doors.

Murphy grabs my hand and we step into the room together. The room goes silent as the mass of people below bow in our direction. Whispers of "My queen" rush through the room as fire lessers pledge their allegiance to me. Murphy squeezes my hand, signaling the start of a new world. A world of fire.

ACKNOWLEDGMENTS

Adria Kane's world first took shape in my mind during a dream. Chapter 1 is based on a particularly lucid dream of leading someone out of a building filled with monsters. Within days the first chapter was completed, and the rest of the story quickly fell into place.

I hope you will fall in love with Adria and Murphy as much as I have. Adria's character represents the strength each of us carries inside. No matter what your past holds or what your mind repeats, you are worthy and capable of greatness.

Thank you to my friends and family who have read chapters throughout the writing process, helping me build characters that are not only relatable but lovable.

Thank you to you, the person reading this! Without you, I wouldn't be able to do what I love.

ABOUT THE AUTHOR

Madalyn Rae is an emerging author who loves telling a story. As a teacher of tiny humans during the day and author by night, she hopes she's able to draw you into her world of fantasy, make-believe, and love.

She lives on the beautiful white, sandy beaches of the Gulf Coast, with her husband and two loyal, yet mildly obnoxious dogs, Whiskey and Tippi. She's the mother of two amazing adult children and a brand new son-in-law.

When not teaching or pretending to write, Madalyn is immersed in the world of music. Whether playing an instrument or singing a song, she is privileged to know that music is the true magic of the universe.

Phoenix of the Sea is the first book in the Elementals series. There might be a FREE prequel for newsletter subscribers... *hint, hint.*

madalynrae.com

Printed in Great Britain
by Amazon

35959540R10169